SIGIRIYA

BY THE SAME AUTHOR

Non-fiction
   The Story of Sigiriya
   The Story of Anuradhapura

Children's Books
   Zu-Zu series

SIGIRIYA

A TALE OF LOVE AND TRAGEDY

Senani Ponnamperuma

PANIQUE MEDIA

Senani Ponnamperuma/Panique Media

This is a work of historical fiction. Any references to historical events, real people, or real places are used fictitiously. Other names, characters, places and events are products of the author's imagination, and any resemblance to actual events, places, or persons, living or dead, is entirely coincidental.

SIGIRIYA: A Tale of Love and Tragedy/Senani Ponnamperuma. 3rd ed.

Paperback ISBN 978-0-6484429-1-2

PART ONE

1

Kasyapa remembered little of that day. When they covered his mother with a linen shroud, placed her on a funeral pyre, and set her aflame. He only recalled the sweet, pungent stink of burning sandalwood crackling and hissing in a mournful, golden glow.

When he visited the place early the following morning, there was nothing left. Only a pile of smoldering ash, occasionally picked up by a wayward gust of wind and whiffed away to eternity.

He sat alone on the damp grass, a short distance from where he had seen her last, staring at the place his mother had once been. He didn't know what to do.

He ran his stubby fingers through his long black hair and watched a tiny sliver of greyish smoke emerge from the ash and curl skyward.

He rubbed his large tear-filled brown eyes with his fists.

Where did my mother go?

He was just five years old.

ONCE THE SUN ROSE HIGH and began scorching his bare back, he stood up, adjusted his tiny triangular loincloth, and returned to the village.

Kasyapa sat on the front step of the small thatch-roofed hut that was his home and watched his grandfather. Skinny and hunched, the old man methodically swept their tiny front yard with an ekle broom.

"Where is my mother?" he asked, in-between his grandfather's sweeping strokes.

"She is reborn, Kasyapa," his grandfather said, his eyes firmly fixed on the ground before him.

"When will she return?"

His grandfather did not answer. His face was ashen and drawn. Bent over, he swept more vigorously away from the young boy.

Kasyapa stood and walked to the lean-to that served as his grandmother's kitchen. There, he found her kneading dough.

"Who will make my favorite sweetmeats, Grandma?" he asked.

"I will," she replied, looking over her shoulder with puffy eyes.

"Will you make them as tasty as she did?"

"Of course, and even better," she said with a burdened smile.

Kasyapa doubted anyone could make sweetmeats as well as his mother had.

"Who will take me for walks by the river?"

"We will," she said.

Slowly, it occurred to him. His world had changed.

LATER THAT SAME MORNING, Kasyapa and his grandmother were throwing fistfuls of dried rice to three scraggly chickens in their front yard. Suddenly the hens craned their necks and stood bolt upright. The top hen cackled *kuh-kuh-kuh-kuh-kack,* and they scattered helter-skelter. There was a great commotion in the village. An important-looking man had arrived.

Grandmother gasped and fell to the ground, pulling Kasyapa with her. She prostrated herself in the dust and remained motionless.

"What is it, Grandma?" he called out.

"*Shh,* be silent, Kasyapa. It is the king, Dhatusena," she whispered and held him tightly against her body.

"You are squashing me, Grandma!"

"*Shh* Kasyapa."

Kasyapa peered from under his grandmother's tight embrace.

"He is coming towards us, Grandma."

"*Shh* Kasyapa. *Shh.*"

"Why is he coming towards us, Grandma?"

"I knew him once when he was a young warrior. Now be quiet."

"Rise, woman," the king commanded as his gaze fell upon the young boy clenched tightly against her body. Slowly a deep frown creased his brow. He turned to the old woman and searched her face.

She looked back at him with eyes weathered with grief and murmured, "Your son."

"My son?"

"Yes, he is yours," she replied with a hint of disdain.

"I didn't know." The king's eyes glazed over, and his lower lip quivered as the words escaped his lips.

Kasyapa twisted and turned in his grandmother's grasp, broke free, and ran to Nalu the woodcutter who stood at the periphery of the village square.

Nalu was a short, spindly old man with a leathery face and a bulbous, pockmarked nose. Bent over with age, his chin almost touched his knobby knees. He too had known the king as a young warrior. In fact, it was Nalu who had trekked for three days and nights to bring the sad news to the king—that a grave illness was consuming the woman he knew the king had once loved. Alas, the king arrived too late. She was gone.

The villagers assembled around the distinguished stranger. A hush fell over the crowd. He beckoned to the boy.

"Go, Kasyapa. The king calls you." Nalu nudged with his spindly fingers.

"I don't want to go to that man. I'm hungry. I want my mother."

"No. You must go to the king," Nalu urged, pushing him forward.

The stranger took his hand and declared, "Beautiful Uppalavanna is no more, but she lives on in this young boy. I proclaim here and now for all to hear. This child is borne from my loins. He is a son of the house of Moriya."

The assembled villagers listened with their heads bowed in reverence.

"After due observances, this child shall join me in the resplendent city of Anuradhapura. There, he will reside in my house—the king's house."

The strange man mounted his horse and rode away.

2

Later that day, Kasyapa sneaked out of the village, past the large pana-sa tree laden with jackfruit and to the village stream. There, he sat on his favorite rock. It was a large, black boulder with a flat surface that formed a ledge just above the waterline. It overlooked a picturesque wa-terfall splashing into a pristine pool below. It was a special rock—his and his mother's rock—maybe even his father's favorite rock too.

He sat on the ledge and splashed the water with his foot, releasing a thousand tiny diamond-like sparkles into the air.

Why did Mother go to that 'reborn' place? Why didn't she take me with her? She always took me with her.

She used to laugh as they sat together and paddled their feet in the stream, watching little rivulets of water trickling through their toes. Often, she had spoken about his father.

"Your father was a great warrior, Kasyapa. He fought for a noble cause," she had said, throwing her arm around him and pulling him close against her. "He and I used to sit on this rock, too. This is where we met. His name was Dhatusena. He was so shy. The first time we met, he couldn't speak. He was so smart and funny. Did you know he trained to be a monk, a bhikkhu, before he gave up the robes to become a warrior?"

"Why did he become a warrior, Mother?"

"At the time, a wicked usurper from Jambudvipa, the land of India across the sea, ruled our kingdom. This foreign ruler, whose name was Pandu, tried to kill your father when he was a young boy."

"Why would anyone want to kill a little boy, Mother?"

"Because Pandu's fortuneteller told him that your father, Dhatuse-na, was of royal blood and would fight him and become king one day.

But his uncle, Thera Mahanama, got wind of the assassination plot, and they escaped just in time. For many years, they lived like hermits, hiding in the forests and in temples. Did you know they stayed at our temple too? Yes, the Naindanawa Temple just up the road."

"Did you meet him when he was at our temple?"

"No. I only met him when I was sixteen, after he became a warrior. He was about eighteen."

She had glanced at him with her large brown eyes, arched her eyebrows, and tousled his hair. She had loved to do that. Then she'd stare at him cross-eyed and finger-combed his hair back into shape. He had liked that.

"What happened next, Mother?"

"As I said, I met him here. I just came out of the stream after my bath, and he stood there. I had to talk first. I still remember my first words. 'You, sir, are rude. Disturbing a young lady as she returns from her bath,' I said. He muttered and stammered. He said I was the most beautiful woman he had ever seen." She giggled and shook her head from side to side, tossing her long black hair in the breeze. "Do you think I am beautiful, Kasyapa?" She tickled his ribs.

"Yes. You are more beautiful than the prettiest butterfly."

She'd laughed. "He told me that my name, Uppalavanna, meant one with the hue of the blue lotus blossom. Dhatusena and I were together for just five weeks. They were the happiest days of my life. Once, he brought a garland of forest jasmine he made himself. I love the smell of jasmine. I was so happy."

"But where is my father now?" Kasyapa had asked.

A pained expression fell over her face, and she had looked away. She'd twirled the copper ring she'd worn on her middle finger as tears filled her eyes and cascaded down her cheeks. They had fallen like tiny pearls onto the rock's surface. Kasyapa moved close and pressed his tiny body against hers. From that day onward, he didn't ask questions about his father. He just listened.

As he sat there alone on the rock, things were beginning to make sense. *The man who had come to the village, Grandmother said, was Dhatusena. Grandmother told the man I was his son. So, he must be my father. That was the man Mother often spoke about. He looked so sad.*

Just then, a rustling sound startled him.

"It's only me, Master Kasyapa. How is the strong young man?" Nalu, the woodcutter, shouted out as he emerged from a nearby thicket.

"All right." Kasyapa shrugged. But actually, he wasn't all right at all. He wanted to cry all day and all night.

"So, you are going to stay with your father, I hear?"

"My father?"

"Yes, Kasyapa, your father. Dhatusena—the king."

"What is a king, Nalu?"

"A great man, Kasyapa, a great man. Come, let me take you home."

"I will help you carry some wood."

Nalu's overgrown white eyebrows arched skyward. "No, no, Master. It is not proper. The king's son can't be seen carrying firewood."

Kasyapa shrugged.

"I think you are a great man, Nalu. You killed a leopard with your bare hands and saved a young boy. Are you a king?"

"No, Master Kasyapa. I am just a lowly woodcutter bent over with age."

"My grandfather is a good man, Nalu. All the villagers come to him for advice. Is he a king?"

"No, Master."

"Then who is a king, Nalu?"

"You remember the man who came to our village and held your hand?"

"Yes, he had warm hands."

"He is the king."

"He looked like a king. Strong and powerful and important looking." Kasyapa nodded knowingly, even though he had no idea what a king should look like.

"Yes, Master."

"Will I become a king, Nalu?"

"You may, Master Kasyapa, if you are good, kind, and strong, you may."

KASYAPA PROUDLY SKIPPED into the village, carrying a small bundle of firewood on his back as Nalu did.

Grandfather was not pleased. The village headman's grandson and the son of the king did not carry firewood like a woodcutter. He glared at Nalu, who shrugged and flashed a crooked toothless grin.

Kasyapa did not understand what a king was or what his father was. He only wanted his mother to hold him, to walk with him, to play with him and make him cakes.

KASYAPA MET NALU AGAIN the day before he was to go to the city. As they walked through the forest, they spotted a group of men in the distance.

"Who are those men, Nalu?"

"They are the king's men, Master."

"I don't like you calling me master, Nalu. My name is Kasyapa."

"I know, Master," Nalu said with an open-mouthed grin. "But I must call you Master now."

"Why?"

"Because the king acknowledged you as his son."

"What are the king's men doing here, Nalu?"

"They have come to drain the swamps and build a new reservoir to rid us of those deadly mosquitoes."

"I heard a villager say a mosquito killed my mother."

"It is true."

"How can a little mosquito do that, Nalu?"

"Well, Master Kasyapa, there are some bad mosquitoes. If they bite you, you can become very sick and die. A bad mosquito bit your mother." Teary-eyed, Nalu sniffled and turned his back to the young boy. He squeezed one nostril with a grimy thumb and exhaled sharply, propelling a large blob of snot into the bushes nearby.

"Grandfather said she went to reborn. Where is reborn, Nalu?" Kasyapa continued oblivious to the old man's grief.

"It is another place, Master Kasyapa."

"Can't I go to reborn and be with her?"

"No. It's another place. Reborn means you have a new beginning and are born again someplace else as something else. No one knows for sure."

"Is it the reborn place my pet squirrel went to?"

"Yes, Master, all things are reborn."

"My squirrel never came back from that place. Does that mean Mother will never come back either?"

"Yes, Master Kasyapa. She will never come back to us." He turned away, hid his face from the young boy.

"Things are so confusing to me, Nalu."

"They are, Master Kasyapa. They are, indeed."

3

As the king commanded, Kasyapa and his grandparents left their home in Ma-Eliya and traveled by foot to Anuradhapura, a distance of three days travel by road and jungle tracks. They announced themselves at the palace gates. A short while later, a man emerged.

"Hello, Kasyapa. I am the chamberlain, the minister of the king's household," the man said, peering down over his large, round belly.

Kasyapa didn't understand what the man said. The only word he recognized was "king."

"Hello, sir," Kasyapa replied, staring up at the man. *He looks like a pomegranate—like a roly-poly, bubble man.*

The bubble man turned and addressed his grandparents. Kasyapa couldn't understand what he said to them either. But it didn't matter. He enjoyed staring at the funny man. Then the man stopped talking, took Kasyapa by the hand, and led him through the palace gates.

"Say goodbye to your grandparents, Kasyapa," the bubble man said.

Kasyapa didn't know what that meant, but he did as he was told. He saw his grandfather hunched over his grandmother, who was weeping. He waved them goodbye.

THE AWESTRUCK KASYAPA ACCOMPANIED the chamberlain into the inner palace with many grand buildings set around a formal courtyard. They proceeded to the far end of the grounds, where the bubble man opened another gate into a small compound with a large building and two smaller ones.

"This is your new home," he announced, pushing open a wooden door and entering the large building. It had a single room with bare walls, a bed, a stool, a small table, and a small greyish-brown closet against the wall.

The bubble man flashed a broad smile, spun around, and walked away.

Kasyapa was alone and wanted to cry. So, he sat on the small three-legged stool and cried and cried and cried. He missed his mother. He wanted his grandparents. He yearned for his village with the babbling stream. He missed Nalu, too.

When he couldn't cry anymore, when nothing more came out of him, he paced about his room, pulled the stool to the window, climbed up on top, and peeped outside. All he saw was a dirty wall with a big black crow sitting on it. "*Cawk, cawk, caaaawwwwk,*" it squawked at him. He jumped off the stool and tried out the bedding. It was soft. He reached for the bundle his grandfather had given him earlier, slowly untied the great, big knot holding it together and spread its four corners open. Right on top, he found a small packet wrapped in banana leaves. Inside were three of his favorite sweetmeats, the same sort his mother had often made. But when he took a bite from the first, he realized it wasn't as tasty as his mother's. As he was hungry, he didn't mind. While holding his sweetmeat in one hand, he continued to rummage through the pile. Right at the bottom, he found a small, tightly wrapped parcel. He fished it out and examined it while finishing his cake. He wiped his hand on his clothing and attempted to unravel the tiny package.

Kasyapa had difficulty untying it. He tried to bite through the twine, but it was too tough. Finally, he used his teeth to grab hold of a turn in the knot and tugged on it. Slowly, it came free.

Once he'd removed the string, he opened the cloth and found another small bundle tied with string. This time, the string came undone easily. Kasyapa spread the second cloth open, and there, in the middle, lay his mother's copper ring. He recognized it immediately. She had always worn it on her middle finger on her left hand because that was the only finger on which it fit. She had never removed it. He had often seen her kissing it. Sometimes, as she daydreamed, she'd twirled it around her finger using her thumb. He wondered why it was so special, and why she got such comfort from it.

Kasyapa took the ring and placed it on his middle finger. It was far too big. It slipped off and fell to the floor with a minuscule ting. He picked it up and tried it on his thumb. There also it was too big. After reflecting on it for a moment, he crossed his legs and brought his dirty little foot up onto his thigh. He tried the ring on his big toe. It seemed like a reasonable fit there. He got up and walked with it. No, wearing it on his big toe was certainly not practical.

He removed it from his toe, held it up, and peeped through its center and out the window. He twirled it between his fingers. Afraid that it too would be snatched away from him, he joined the bits of string together and fashioned himself a belt and strung the ring through it. He tied it around his waist and knotting it multiple times so it wouldn't come undone.

As he was bare-bodied, he hid it beneath his loincloth. He became obsessed with its safety, checking and rechecking it often.

Having nothing else to do, he sat on the front step of his new home, rested his chin in his hands, dug his toes into the soft sand, and wondered about nothing.

LATER THAT AFTERNOON, the bubble man reappeared with three people trailing him. From his pint-sized vantage point, Kasyapa crinkled his eyes against the sun and watched.

He walked funny, like a duck. Waddle-waddle from side to side on two twiggy legs with two big dangly earrings, swinging from side to side. Oh, he was a funny-looking man, indeed. The chamberlain stopped in front of him.

"These are your servants. Ayah here will be your nanny. She will look after you. This is Daya, your servant boy. He will play with you and run errands for you. Here is your cook. I am sure you know what a cook does, don't you?" the bubble man asked.

"No, sir."

"She will cook your food."

Kasyapa nodded. He didn't know any better. He had never heard of servants or what they did.

Then the bubble man departed, leaving Kasyapa with three strangers.

Ayah set about tidying their little abode. The cook disappeared into a small outhouse that served as the kitchen. And Daya, with his oval face, large eyes, and flappy ears like an elephant, didn't know what to do, so he sat on the ground, drew his knees to his chest, and watched Kasyapa. Kasyapa sat on the step and stared out at nothing.

At around five, Ayah reemerged. "Time for a bath, young man."

"I don't want to."

She rolled her eyes, grabbed him by the arm, and dragged him to the well at the center of the courtyard.

"Let me go. I don't want to bathe. Besides, there's no stream to take a bath in," he wailed, running in place and going nowhere, as she held fast to his arm and pulled him back.

Ayah wagged her index finger threateningly. "Now look here. You cannot live in this palace unless you are well-scrubbed, young man."

Kasyapa noticed she was missing a front tooth. Air escaped from the gap, making a hissing sound when she spoke. But he had more pressing matters at hand than her missing tooth.

"I don't want to," he screamed.

But she quickly doused him with a bucket of water and scrubbed him from top to bottom with a *polemudde*—a brush made from the husk of a coconut. She pulled off his little loincloth and continued to scrub his front and bottom as he covered his precious ring with his free hand.

"What is this?"

"Nothing," he said, fearing the worst.

"Nothing, huh?" she huffed, but didn't remove his sacred talisman.

The next day, she brought him a small wooden box with a sliding lid. "Why don't you keep your ring in this box? It will be safe there. I will look after it for you."

Kasyapa burst into tears and clung to it for dear life. "No. Not my ring. Not my ring." He quivered.

She knelt, wrapped her arms around him, rocking him back and forth until he stopped crying. She didn't push the issue any further. The ring remained safely tucked beneath his loincloth.

One day while playing, Kasyapa burst out crying and raced to Ayah, seated under a shady tree.

"My ring, it's not here," he wailed, pointing to his waist.

She reached into his loincloth and pulled out the string. "It's missing, indeed." She clapped her hands and summoned everyone. Even the guard came. "A nice, juicy mango for the person who finds a little copper ring," she declared.

They searched late into the evening, but it was of no avail. Like so many other things in his life, it too was gone. Kasyapa sobbed himself to sleep that night. He had lost his mother's ring.

"Wake up, Master. Wake up. Come outside," Daya shouted.

There, standing outside the door, was Ayah with a gardener who grinned and held up the little copper ring between his grubby fingers.

Kasyapa was so happy; he thought he would burst. He beamed as Ayah threaded it and tied it around his tiny waist once more.

ON ONE OCCASION, for no reason at all, the bubble man appeared.

"Hello Kasyapa, I brought you something," the bubble man said, handing him a large pomegranate.

"Thank you, sir," Kasyapa replied.

The bubble man patted him on the head and waddled off.

Kasyapa thought it funny, the bubble man giving him a pomegranate, because he looked like a pomegranate himself.

Kasyapa ran to the kitchen. "Please cut this pomegranate for me."

"Of course," the cook replied with a warm toothless smile, and deftly split open the fruit and dislodged its crimson seeds into a bowl.

"You take some too, Cook."

"Oh, thank you so much, Master Kasyapa."

Soon, Kasyapa was rushing around with a plate of juicy pink pomegranate seeds, sharing his good fortune with his minders—including the guard outside.

"Just five seeds for me?"

"It's all that's left." Kasyapa shrugged and skipped away.

On another occasion, the bubble man brought him a little toy cart made of clay with its own detachable bullocks and driver, and wheels that turned too.

Kasyapa soon concluded the bubble man with his round, jovial face, small nose, and happy eyes, was a kind man. He looked forward to his visits, which became more frequent.

ABOUT A WEEK AFTER HIS ARRIVAL, Kasyapa was playing in the garden with Daya, when a massive man appeared at the gate. Kasyapa stood speechless, looking up and up at him—and almost peed himself. Daya, who was bigger and two years older than Kasyapa, ran away and hid behind a tree. Kasyapa wanted to run too, but his legs refused to budge, so he just stood there. Certain this giant would grab him and gobble him up. He closed his eyes and held his breath and waited for the worst.

The giant grinned, shook himself while flailing his arms and making a strange *brrrbabrbbr* sound, and squatted in front of Kasyapa.

"How are you, sir?" he asked, with a thunderous voice like an elephant's roar.

Kasyapa looked on in terror.

"I brought you something." He handed Kasyapa a small wooden sword. "I will teach you how to be a great warrior." He grinned through his bushy beard and stood up.

Taking another little sword, he hunched over and pretended to fence with Kasyapa. Daya, who had hidden behind a tree earlier, now found the courage to come out and cheer Kasyapa on. The entire household joined Kasyapa's cheer squad.

The giant stayed until late afternoon. "You will make an excellent warrior, Master Kasyapa," he said as he left the compound.

"Do you know who that man was?" Ayah asked as she tucked him into bed that night.

"No, but he was huge and scary with big, bushy eyebrows and wild hair and beard. His legs were like tree trunks. His hands were massive. He had a big belly too." Kasyapa giggled.

"He is Nila the Giant. He is the king's gatekeeper and responsible for the king's safety. He has been with the king since the very beginning."

"Why is the giant coming to see us, Ayah?"

"He must have heard about you."

"Oh?"

"He and the king were guerrilla fighters together."

"What is a guerrilla fighter, Ayah?"

"A secret warrior."

"Nila said he was going to teach me to be a warrior, too."

Ayah continued. "In those days, the king was known as Dhatusena the Brave. Dhatusena, Nila, and their guerrillas fought for over ten years until they defeated the last foreign ruler, and the brave warrior Dhatusena became our king. During that brutal war, the enemy murdered Nila's family."

"I like Nila the Giant." Kasyapa yawned.

"I think he likes you, too."

NILA VISITED ONCE A WEEK. He always announced himself at the gates with an animated roar. "Where is my young warrior?"

One day, Kasyapa yelled, "catch me if you can," as he ran circles around the giant.

Nila pretended to be confused at first, then he grabbed Kasyapa and tossed him high into the air.

"Do it again. Do it again," Kasyapa squealed. "I want to touch the sky."

The giant obliged again and again.

"Now, Master Kasyapa, it is time to train to be a warrior." Nila laughed, placing Kasyapa on the ground.

"More, more," Kasyapa protested and clung on his arm. The giant lifted him into the air.

Daya worked up enough courage to hang on the giant's other arm, and he swung them around and around until they all were dizzy and collapsed on the ground.

"Now, Master Kasyapa, it's time for me to train you to be a man."

Ayah, who stood nearby, protested. "Nila, he is just a little boy. What are you trying to do to him?"

"One is never too young to be strong," he replied and turned his attention to the boys. "Now, run ten laps around the compound. You too, Daya. After that, ten chin-ups from the branch of the tree over there," Nila hollered.

"Why do you make this child work so hard? You are a cruel man, Nila," Ayah said.

"This little child was uprooted from all those he loved and placed in our care. His life will be difficult. He must be strong inside and out. It is up to us to help him. We must build courage, strength, and good character in him. We must prepare him."

Ayah crossed her arms and nodded. "I will certainly do my bit," she said.

When Nila visited next, Ayah called to him. "I meant to ask. Do you know how old this child is?"

Nila scratched his scalp through his thick head of hair, "About five years old, I think."

"Then, it is settled. Master Kasyapa is five years old. And his official birthday is the day he first arrived at the palace." She didn't question how Nila had arrived at that number.

BECAUSE NOBODY SPOKE OF HIS MOTHER or his grandparents or Nalu in this new place, Kasyapa assumed he wasn't supposed to talk about them. So, he never asked about them. But something was missing—like he could thrust his hand down his throat and twiddle his fingers inside his chest and feel nothing there. He missed them very much.

Within this grand palace, he was alone.

4

Ayah often took Kasyapa and Daya to play in the King's Park. While playing there one day, Kasyapa noticed another boy with an ayah of his own. But he didn't have a playmate like Kasyapa did. Kasyapa and Daya hid behind a large shrub and watched him. He was taller and skinnier than them.

"He walks funny with his butt poking out, and his chest is like a pigeon's," Daya whispered.

"*Shhh.*"

"Why is he throwing stones at the lizards and squirrels? It looks like he is trying to harm them."

"I don't know. *Shhh.*"

Kasyapa and Daya remained hidden until the boy and his ayah disappeared, then they ran back home.

"His name is Migara," Ayah informed Kasyapa later. "He is the king's nephew and lives with his mother, the king's sister, in a large mansion over there. He is allowed to use the park, too."

One day, while they were playing near the lake, Migara joined them.

"I am not supposed to play with you," he said with an air of arrogance.

"Why not?" Kasyapa asked.

"Because you are a bastard. My mother told me so."

"A bastard?" Kasyapa glanced at Daya, who shrugged his shoulders. He figured it must mean something bad, so he and Daya ran away.

"I don't like that boy with the funny walk and yellowish skin," Daya panted.

"I don't either. Let's avoid him."

But one day, Migara surprised them while they were playing chase the monkey. He noticed the ring attached to Kasyapa's waist, grabbed him by his wrist, and yanked him forward.

"Show me what you are hiding, sissy."

"Let me go!" Kasyapa yelped, kicking Migara on the shin.

Surprised, Migara released his grip, and Kasyapa ran away.

"You bastard. You half-caste," Migara shouted after him.

Daya, who was supposed to be his protector, stood by gobsmacked, and then dashed behind Kasyapa. They ran as fast as they could, scrambled over a low wall, and hid behind it. Kasyapa sank on his haunches to catch his breath, sweat dribbling down his face and nose.

"Why does that boy pick on us?" Daya asked.

"I don't know. He always calls me bastard. Do you know what it means?"

"No. But it must be something bad," Daya replied while digging his nose.

They shrugged at each other and ran back to the safety of Ayah, who was resting under a shade tree.

That afternoon, in the safety of their compound, Kasyapa and Daya tried to imitate Migara. First, they covered their eyes with their cupped hands. "Bug Eyes," they shouted, running around the compound.

Then Daya stuck his chest and butt out in opposite directions. "Look at me!"

Not to be outdone, Kasyapa walked while dragging a leg behind him like a leaden weight. "I am a monster."

"I am a worser monster." Daya improvised even further by wrapping his arm around his head and sticking his grubby fingers up his nose.

They howled with laughter.

That night, Kasyapa lay in bed and stared at the ceiling.

That yellow-skinned boy called me a bastard. He called me a half-caste. They must be rude names. Children in the village used to call me names, too.

He rolled over and watched Ayah, fast asleep on a mat, in the far corner of the room.

Why do they say things that make me feel miserable? I wish Mother were here. She would make me feel better. Or Nalu, he would have told me what these words mean.

The following morning, Kasyapa handed Ayah the small box with the ring inside. He had wrapped the ring in its original linen cloth and tied it with the remaining thread.

"You can have it back any time you want, Master," she said.

Kasyapa suspected Ayah knew why he had given it to her. She always knew what was going on.

Initially, he asked for it often and sat alone in the garden playing with it, thinking of his mother, and Nalu, and his village. But as time wore on, as his memory of them dimmed, he asked for it less and less.

5

Ayah placed her hands on her hips and chuckled. "Why the horse Nila?"

"*Shh*. Where is Master Kasyapa? It's a surprise for his eighth birthday." Nila winked as he walked through the gate.

Kasyapa ran to Nila. "What's that animal, Nila?"

"It's a pony. Have you not seen a pony before?"

"No."

"Today, I am going to teach you how to ride a pony. When you become a competent pony rider, I will teach you how to ride a horse. And if you are an excellent horseman, I will teach you how to ride an elephant. A fine warrior must know all these things. Are you a fine warrior, Master Kasyapa?"

"Oh, yes. I am very good. I beat Daya every time. When I grow bigger, I am going to challenge you to a duel."

Nila's whole body quaked when he cackled. Actually, it was more like a lion's roar. He heaved Kasyapa onto the pony and walked him around the compound until Kasyapa complained of a sore bottom. Nila took him off the pony, tousled his hair, and sent him to Ayah.

ON ANOTHER OCCASION, Nila was less generous when Kasyapa complained.

"I am tired," Kasyapa whined, dragging his legs with an overstated stoop.

Daya followed a few steps behind, uncertain as to what posture he ought to adopt.

"Tired? I'll show you tired," Nila yelled and jumped to his feet. He opened his eyes wide, exposing the whites of his eyes. Then he pulled at his tousled hair, contorted his face baring his discolored teeth, stuck out his tongue, and danced a devil dancer's jig in front of the young complainants.

Kasyapa and Daya ran away, screaming and flailing their arms. They continued their allocated training with renewed vigor.

Ayah placed her hands on her hips. "You are some character, Nila. That child loves you."

"I used to do that when I was a warrior. It scared the living daylights out of my opponents. Most just ran away. Spared me having to kill them." He scratched his ample belly and chuckled.

IN THAT SAME YEAR, KASYAPA's ayah came to him, holding a long rectangular piece of cloth.

"You need to start wearing a dhoti."

"A dhoti? Why?"

"You are going to the school for aristocrats' children. You must be properly dressed."

Ayah deftly unfurled the cloth, wrapped it around his waist, passed it through his legs, and knotted it at the waist. "There you go. You are ready for school," she said proudly.

At school, the students treated him with respect. Ayah said it was because he was the king's son. Migara, however, was the exception. He hadn't changed. In fact, he had gotten worse. He liked to scrunch up his face to look intimidating.

"You shouldn't be here. You are not noble," he said and sneered.

Kasyapa avoided him.

While Kasyapa spent his spare time reading and studying, Migara surrounded himself with an assortment of hangers-on, playing tricks on other students and intimidating them. Sensing Migara's hostility toward Kasyapa, the other students stayed clear of him—all but one that is.

His name was Abaya, a large, quiet, and imperturbable boy with brooding eyes. The son of the queen's brother, Abaya, was a member of the Lambakanna clan, whose name meant "those with long earlobes."

The Lambakannas had a reputation for being ferocious when provoked. For this reason, Migara may have thought it prudent to leave Abaya alone.

Abaya was studious like Kasyapa, and they often sat together. He had little to say. What Abaya did say, however, was well-considered and honest.

"What does noble mean?" Kasyapa asked, looking up from his studies.

"Why do you ask, Kasyapa?"

"Migara told me I wasn't noble. He called me a half-caste."

"I think noble means both your parents are of the Kshatriya caste."

"I don't know what caste my parents are from."

"I think your father is a Kshatriya."

"Why is that?"

"My mother told me only a Kshatriya could be king," Abaya said.

"I don't know what caste my mother was."

"Well, Kasyapa, if your father is from the highest caste and your mother is not of the same caste, then she must be of a lesser one."

"I guess I am a half-caste then. Like Migara said."

Having discovered these truths, Kasyapa dared not ask Abaya what bastard meant. He no longer wanted to know the answer.

"Where is your mother?" Abaya asked.

"She died."

"Do you miss her?"

"Yes, very much, but I think I am not supposed to miss her."

"Don't worry about whether you are noble or not, Kasyapa. You are the king's son. No one will hurt you. Not even Migara."

Kasyapa was glad Abaya was kind to him. In the village, the children had shunned him too. He had never understood why. It was nice to have someone who didn't.

Kasyapa loved school and excelled at his course work. Migara continued his disruptive behavior. But since Kasyapa and Abaya had developed a close friendship, he restricted his harassment to the occasional snide remark.

WHEN KASYAPA WAS ELEVEN, he noticed another ayah with a very young boy. Kasyapa thought they must be important because a bevy of attendants surrounded them.

"That's Prince Moggallana, the heir and future king," Ayah said. Then she leaned over and whispered. "He is your half-brother."

Kasyapa didn't understand what she meant or why Ayah whispered this in his ear. He didn't think much about it at the time.

The two ayahs soon struck up a friendship and arranged to visit the park at the same time. They synchronized their visits to avoid running into Migara.

As he grew older, Kasyapa frequently played with little Moggallana. In fact, Moggallana ran to him whenever he saw Kasyapa. Their ayahs laughed at their close friendship. Moggallana often sat in front of Kasyapa, spellbound as he read him stories from the *Jataka Tales*. Kasyapa playfully embellished the stories just for him. Having heard of Kasyapa's recitals, the Queen and the princess Sakula often attended as well. They were polite and friendly.

"You recite well, Kasyapa," the queen commented one day.

"Thank you, Your Highness."

"Do you like to read?"

"Yes, very much."

Consequently, she often brought him books to read. He wasn't sure whether she purchased them for him, or if they were her own.

FOR KASYAPA'S FOURTEENTH BIRTHDAY, Nila brought an elephant. It was too large to fit through the compound gates, so Nila obtained permission to use the royal stables adjacent to the palace.

"Since you are now an expert horseman and swordsman, it's time we trained you on an elephant." Nila grinned. "Now climb on its knee, grab onto the animal's ear, and pull yourself up."

Kasyapa followed Nila's instructions.

"Oh, be careful," the chamberlain jittered with a muffled squeak.

The elephant lifted its leg.

"Now hoist yourself onto his neck," Nila yelled out.

"Oh, my," the chamberlain cried, grasping his cheeks.

"Now, straddle its neck, Master Kasyapa. Hold onto it gently with your legs to get a better balance."

"It's prickly up here. Its hair is pricking my bum," Kasyapa yelled.

Nila scratched his hairy belly and roared with laughter. The chamberlain clapped with glee as Ayah giggled with hysterical pride.

As in all previous years, only Kasyapa's minders, the chamberlain, and Nila attended his birthday party. No one else attended, not Abaya, Moggallana, the Queen, or Sakula. And certainly not the king.

THE DAY AFTER HIS BIRTHDAY, Kasyapa visited the park as usual. He brought Moggallana some leftover sweetmeats from his party. They sat by the pond and gobbled them all. Kasyapa remembered a game Nila had played with him when he was much younger. Since they finished the sweets, and he didn't have anything handy, he took out his little copper ring, which he hadn't yet returned for safekeeping with Ayah.

"Guess which fist it's in, Moggallana," he said, switching the ring from hand to hand.

Moggallana didn't have much luck guessing. Sensing his growing frustration, Kasyapa wriggled his little finger in the fist containing the ring.

"I found the ring!" Moggallana cried out and embraced his older brother.

Kasyapa laughed and let little Moggallana play with it for a while.

"Who knows, Moggallana, one day you may gain it from your older brother," he said.

6

As Kasyapa grew older, Nila's drills grew more rigorous. While sword fighting, he shouted, "Always make your opponent underestimate your capabilities. In this way, you have the advantage. You, in turn, must observe him closely and note his every weakness."

Then his tone changed, and he was no longer teasing. He taunted instead. "You fight like a sissy," he said, using the diminutive in a way intended to enrage. "Look, I can fight you with only one hand. Look, I can even close my eyes. How can you be a warrior? You would be better off as a poet."

"Don't you dare call me a sissy!" Kasyapa snapped.

Nila danced around Kasyapa, swishing his sword over his head. A cruel sneer grew on his rumpled face as he leaned forward, eyes bearing down into Kasyapa's. Fierce, fiery eyes they were.

"What are you going to do?" he taunted.

Kasyapa rushed at him, intent on inflicting a redeeming blow.

Nila glared back, grabbed him by the neck, and flung him to the ground. He kicked Kasyapa's sword out of his hand and stomped his foot on his chest with such force, Kasyapa was certain he would suffocate. Nila removed his foot, laughed, and stretched out his hand.

Kasyapa hesitated, wondering if it was a ruse, but extended his hand, nevertheless. The giant yanked him up.

Kasyapa's eyes welled with tears. "What was that about, Nila?"

The giant snorted. "It's a lesson, Master Kasyapa. Only a lesson. Never let anyone provoke you. See what happened? You lost control. I tell you this. Always stay in control."

ABOUT TWO MONTHS LATER, while practicing angampora martial arts, Nila said, "Now, here is the most important lesson of all. Remember, Master Kasyapa, I have trained you to use force, but it must be used only as a last resort. Violence is morally wrong. It shows a weakness of temperament. It takes more courage to follow the path of peace than the much easier route of aggression."

Nila then retired under the shade tree. "Daya, get this aging warrior and his sidekick a drink," he bellowed, resting his back against the tree. "You tired me out, Master Kasyapa." He panted.

Kasyapa sat beside him, beads of sweat dripping from his face and chin.

"Ayah tells me you knew my mother," Kasyapa began cautiously.

"Yes, Master Kasyapa, I knew her. I met her at Ma-Eliya when the king and I were young warriors."

"I remember so little, Nila. And I still miss her. Tell me about her."

Nila stared into the distance. His face softened, and he started in a low and mellowed voice.

"If the gods excelled, she was their masterpiece. She was the most beautiful woman I have ever met." He scratched his greying bread thoughtfully and continued.

"When her face lit up with that dimpled smile, what man would not fall in love with her? She spoke with a soft sing-song voice."

"Yes, I remember."

"She used to roll her head from side to side and tease the king. She called him 'Dhut-tu-se-na' because he had stuttered his name like that when they first met. No one else dared tease him except for her. He has a terrible temper, your father. She wasn't scared of him. She was outright feisty."

Daya returned with some fresh coconut water.

"Now, go and bring us something to eat," Nila ordered.

"Why didn't you tell me that before?"

"Because, you fool, you should know those things for yourself. How can you be your master's manservant, if you can't anticipate what your master's needs are? Now go."

Daya grumbled and stormed off.

"I will tell you this, Master Kasyapa, and you may not understand these things yet. She made him human. She made him want to love and be loved. He loved her very much. I was there. I was with him as he agonized over it. He wanted to be with her. He didn't want to leave her."

"Why did he discard my mother then? Why didn't he come for her?"

"He was fighting for a cause more important than himself. He was fighting to rid the land of the infidels, for the people, and the restoration of our religion," Nila said with a trembling voice.

"As he returned from the south, at the head of a victorious army, his advisers convinced him he would have to marry a noblewoman if he wanted to be king. At first, he refused, but eventually, they convinced him. A village girl could never be queen."

Kasyapa exhaled a long, tortured sigh, trying to grasp the significance of Nila's revelation.

Just then, Daya returned with a bowl of freshly cut sugarcane.

"Now leave that tray here and go. Your Master and I have important private matters to discuss," Nila thundered.

Daya put on a sulky face and withdrew.

Kasyapa shouted after him, "Daya, come and take some pieces of sugarcane for yourself."

Taking a handful, Daya grinned at Kasyapa, sniggered at Nila, and ran off.

Having already chewed a piece of sugarcane, Nila spat it out with such force it bounced off the ground three times before coming to a stop. Kasyapa followed suit and merely spat his past his foot.

Nila was about to pop a second piece into his mouth when Kasyapa asked, "So, the warrior Dhatusena abandoned my mother to become king?"

"He had little choice. He loved your mother. They forced him to discard her. To forget her." Nila chomped on his sugarcane with the corner of his mouth.

"Your father is a troubled man, Master Kasyapa. Two things changed him forever: giving up your mother and her death."

"Why does he ignore me, Nila?"

"I don't know. I have known him for many years, but I cannot fathom him. I feel he carries a deep emptiness within him. You know they sent him to become a monk when he was just six years old. I don't think he saw his parents again. He never spoke of them. He never tried to visit them. Maybe, in his mind, they had abandoned him. He was bullied at the monasteries as a young boy too, you know. I think he had an unpleasant childhood. He only spoke of the great Thera Mahanama, and of course, he couldn't stop talking about your mother, Uppalavanna. Your father is a good man. Even a great man. But he is a very troubled man."

Nila stretched himself and placed his hands behind his head. They sat in silence, neither knowing what to say next. After a while, Nila grabbed a handful of sugarcane, got up, and left without a word.

7

When Kasyapa was about seventeen, Migara walked into the schoolyard in the foulest mood. He now walked with a swagger and glared at any students who dared cross his path. He had also taken to brandishing a flogging whip, which he carried in a linen pouch, tucked into his dhoti, so only its hilt poked out. It had an ivory handle with a makara—a grotesque dragon-like mythical creature—with two ruby-red eyes embedded into the head of the handle.

On this particular day, he stopped in front of Moggallana and kicked dust at him and tousled his hair.

"Get out of my way pee-pee head pissant," he sneered.

It was bold indeed of Migara to behave this way toward the royal heir. In normal circumstances, it was an act punishable by death. Migara, however, believed he could do many things with impunity. After all, his mother was the king's sister. His audacity impressed his goon squad of bully boys, who always hung around him.

Disturbed by the shouting, Kasyapa, who had been reading inside, came to investigate. When Moggallana spotted him, he ran as fast as his little legs could carry him and cowered behind his half-brother.

"What Kasyapa? You defending a sissy?" Migara snarled, his bug eyes bulging with contempt.

"Leave him alone." Kasyapa's heart galloped so fast it almost leaped out of his chest.

"So, what are you going to do?" A disdainful smirk grew across Migara's face. He advanced a step closer, pulled out his flogging whip, and poked Kasyapa in the stomach with its makara-head handle. Then he pushed it harder into Kasyapa's stomach.

"You don't deserve to be here, you lower-caste idiot."

Kasyapa didn't know what overcame him. He pulled his arm back as far as it would go and punched Migara in the face. It was as if all those years of bearing up to Migara's insults, ridicule, and scorn finally burst out from his clenched fist.

He watched in amazement as the world around him stirred in slow motion. Abaya rushed in and stood behind him. Migara recoiled from the impact and tumbled backward, his entourage stepped aside, and Migara hit the ground hard. He looked up in astonishment as he wiped his mouth with the back of his hand.

His bug-eyes almost popped out of his head at the sight of his blood.

"You'll be in big trouble now, you bastard. You will regret this one day," Migara snarled through bloodstained teeth and ran home in tears.

Kasyapa stood in the middle of the courtyard uncertain what to do next. Abaya stood silently behind him with his fists still clenched. The teachers, guards, and attendants flew into a tizzy and huddled together.

Kasyapa overheard one say, "This is serious. If the chamberlain hears about this, or god forbid, the king, we will be harshly punished. Possibly have our hands chopped off, if not our heads."

"Worse still, it won't be long before the old fire-dragon comes here." A guard added.

"We have no choice. We must summon the chamberlain," the principal declared in a quavering falsetto.

The minutes passed as though they were hours. The students milled about in the schoolyard aimlessly. Migara's goon squad had long since disappeared into thin air. The principal cowered in a corner, comforted by his apprehensive staff.

"What's going on here?" the chamberlain barked as he hurried into the schoolyard. He had hardly finished his sentence, when sure enough, she turned up—the fire-dragon herself.

A short, thin wisp of a woman, she hurled herself at breakneck speed and screeched to a halt in front of Kasyapa. Pointing a knobby finger, she wagged it up at him. Her lips curled, exposing her discolored yellow teeth. She coiled her body like a vicious snake and spat out her words.

"You won't get away with this, you lowly half-caste rampallian. The king will hear of this. You will be sent back to the village to plow fields and dig shit holes."

Kasyapa noticed Migara standing behind her, morosely wriggling a wobbly front tooth with his tongue.

Then she turned on the chamberlain.

"What are you going to do about this, you overstuffed dimwit? You spineless turd. How dare you allow this bastard to attack my son?" Noticing Moggallana hiding behind the bhikkhu who gave religious instructions, she called, "Move out of the way, you orange-robed fairy. Let me get at my brother's pissant son." The bhikkhu stood his ground. Kasyapa wasn't sure if he did so out of bravery or sheer terror.

Finally spent, she narrowed her eyes into terrifying slits and spun around, glaring at each of those assembled as they passed her line of sight. She grabbed her son by the arm and stormed off.

The chamberlain stared out after them with a glum expression. Once they had disappeared, he listened as the principal explained the circumstances of the incident, then hurried away.

"THE KING IS RESTING, YOU BETTER WAIT HERE," Nila declared, halting the chamberlain in his stride as he rushed to the king's quarters.

Not wishing to miss an opportunity to share some tittle-tattle with Nila, the chamberlain drew in a deep breath and described at length what had happened.

"So Master Kasyapa's actions were justified?"

"Of course, my good man. They were justified. It is high time someone put that wicked boy Migara in his place. He's been provoking our Kasyapa for years." The chamberlain wagged his index finger emphatically at the giant.

"Good. I see he fought well."

Breaking off his florid narrative when the king emerged, the chamberlain hurried to him.

"What's the urgency, Chamberlain?"

"It is your sister, my king."

"My sister again? What has she done now?"

The chamberlain recounted the story of the fight. He told the king how Kasyapa punched Migara in the face and almost knocked out a tooth. He paused, expecting the king to be furious, but much to his astonishment, the king burst out laughing.

"Good. That's good." The king clasped his hands behind his back and walked away.

The chamberlain did not get an opportunity to tell him of the events that followed, but he was certain the king would hear about those, too. If not from the fire-dragon herself, then from others who were in attendance. He chuckled and went about his work. This was the first time the king had acknowledged his first-born son, even if it was in the most oblique way.

WHEN AYAH HEARD THE STORY from the chamberlain, she was strangely sympathetic toward Migara and his mother.

"This is an odd stand you take, Ayah."

"Yes, I know. I feel sorry for them. I hear their lives are joyless. Did you know her husband ran away?"

"Yes, many years ago."

"Left them destitute."

"Yes. The king supports his sister."

"The father ran off with the servant girl."

"Yes."

"Soon after, he was bitten by a snake in his sleep and died. Some say the wife had a hand in it."

"Do you think so?"

"I don't know. Anyway, the mother is very protective of her son. They are inseparable."

"I know."

MIGARA STAYED IN THE COMPOUND a few days longer. At first, he avoided Kasyapa. Then he pretended to be civil. He treated Kasyapa with far more caution and didn't bully Moggallana again. Not long afterward, he disappeared from school. Kasyapa learned later that he had transferred to an army barracks for military training. The compound was a different place once Migara left, and Kasyapa was happy to see the back of him.

ǀ

*****

THERA MAHANAMA, the king's uncle and hence Kasyapa and Moggallana's granduncle, visited the school often. On one such occasion, he sat alone with Moggallana.

"Now, Moggallana, repeat to me the ten royal virtues of a Dharmaraja, a righteous Buddhist monarch."

Moggallana stuttered, "B-be mild of speech."

"Yes, that's good."

"Injure no one to benefit another," he continued, stopped, stomped his foot, and crossed his arms.

Then, a voice from the shadows quietly recited:

Let your conduct be for the good of your people.

Let the love of your people exceed the love of yourself.

Favor no one to the injury of another.

Injure no one to benefit another.

Be upright and let no fear prevent you from doing justice.

Heed good counsel and avoid doing evil through ignorance.

Be charitable.

Be patient and mild of speech.

Be merciful and without malice.

Inflict no torture.

Mahanama twisted around and smiled at Kasyapa. Turning back to Moggallana, he continued, "Now Moggallana, let's try this again." His voice trailed off as Kasyapa walked away.

MAHANAMA RECOGNIZED Kasyapa's talent. In him were many of the same laudable traits he had noticed in Dhatusena years earlier. While he could not publicly acknowledge this as he was not the heir, Mahanama frequently took Kasyapa aside and carried on a discourse with him. He often arrived with a manuscript or two tucked under his robe for Kasyapa.

Moggallana, on the other hand, paid little attention to his uncle and preferred running around the schoolyard, his arms spread out as though he were soaring like an eagle.

8

By now, Mahanama was a highly respected scholar-monk. Even the king did not sit above him in his presence. Instead, he sat at the thera's feet as he had always done, the teacher and pupil, mentor and student.

"You will be pleased, oh King," Mahanama began.

"Why is that?"

"I have brought you a present. The draft of the first installment, as you requested," he said with an inscrutable smile.

The king waited for the Thera to continue. Mahanama took out a bundle from his satchel and proceeded to unwrap it, revealing a freshly made manuscript.

"What shall we call it, learned Thera?"

"I didn't give that any consideration. I assumed it would be called the Dipavamsa as before."

"I see you are modest as always. Let us call it the Great Chronicle— The *Mahavamsa*."

"It is an excellent title, my king, for a chronicle of our great religion and the history of our people."

"Now, Thera, will it be ready for the festival?"

"Yes, the story of our first illustrious Buddhist king will be ready."

"Good. Let's make it a memorable ceremony then."

Mahanama nodded.

"Now who will recite it? How about you, learned Thera?"

"No, not I. My voice doesn't carry, and it lacks eloquence also." The thera was a modest man.

"Then, who?" The king rattled off some names. Mahanama remained noncommittal. The king looked at the thera, "I see you have someone in mind."

"Yes."

"Who is it?"

"Since the crown prince is still of a tender age, may I respectfully recommend your son, Kasyapa?"

The king almost jumped out of his skin. "Kasyapa?" the king muttered in disbelief. He had never mentioned the boy's name in the nearly twelve years that Kasyapa had lived in the royal household.

"Yes, he is of age," Mahanama continued. "He is your son. He will be a great asset to you."

"A great asset?" The king never questioned the wisdom of his mentor. In fact, he often wondered why Mahanama had not spoken to him about Kasyapa before. Sometimes, he wished the great Thera had. But he understood his mentor well. Mahanama had never mixed temporal and spiritual matters since Dhatusena became king. But the thera was speaking now and he, Dhatusena, would indeed listen.

THE CHAMBERLAIN HURRIED into the courtyard, his ample tummy bouncing merrily in front of him, and his splayed feet kicked up small puffs of dust as he approached.

"Where is Kasyapa?" he asked, looking about impatiently.

"I am here, Chamberlain," Kasyapa said, stepping into the courtyard.

"Kasyapa, I have great news. The king wants you to orate at the Great Festival," the chamberlain said, wringing his hands.

"Me?"

The chamberlain nodded, his dangly earring flapping about his head.

"The king wants me to orate?"

"Yes, he does."

"But Chamberlain, I fear I will let the king down. I have never spoken in public before."

"What nonsense, young man," the chamberlain said firmly and leaned into Kasyapa's ear. "This is your great opportunity to prove yourself."

"You are right. It is my opportunity, indeed. I will do my father proud."

"I know you will, Young Kasyapa."

KASYAPA DID NOT SIT WITH THE ROYAL FAMILY ON THAT DAY. At the appointed time, he walked to a podium below the royal dais. Kasyapa wore a plain white linen dhoti, wrapped around his hips worn full-length like a skirt, and held in place by a modest handwoven sash. As was the custom, he was bare-chested and wore a simple beaded chain around his neck. His luxuriant black hair was oiled and combed back and glistened in the sunlight.

Kasyapa nervously twirled his little copper ring, which he wore on his little finger, with the tip of his thumb. Ayah had given the ring to him earlier that morning, saying, "It will bring you strength and comfort." He took a deep breath, and in a well-modulated baritone voice, he began:

> In the second year of Tissa's rule, while the king was hunting
> alone in the mountains of Cetiyagiri, he came upon a hermit
> who addressed him thusly: "Come hither, Tissa." The king was
> taken aback. "Who addresses me thus?" he asked. The hermit
> declared, "Recluses we are, oh great King, disciples of the King
> of Dharma." King Tissa realized that this might be a messen-
> ger and engaged in several lengthy discourses, one of which is
> recorded here thusly.

The king observed Kasyapa in silence. He hadn't laid eyes on him for nearly twelve years, having left the child's upbringing to the chamberlain. His son was handsome, indeed. His shoulders were broad, his frame lean and muscular, and his complexion was honey brown. He had a perfectly symmetrical face, with smooth beardless skin and well-defined features.

On the whole, like his mother had been, he was beautiful to behold. A sense of pride swelled in his chest. He noticed the copper ring. He remembered it well. As a young warrior, he had walked over fifteen miles in search of a blacksmith to have it made. He had given it to the woman he loved, the woman he had forsaken for this kingdom. He recalled the joy in her eyes when he'd given her the ring, seated on that rock by the babbling stream near Ma-Eliya. A teardrop surfaced in the corner of his eye. He quickly scrubbed it away with his hand.

What name does this tree bear, oh King?

This tree is called a mango.

Is there yet another mango besides this?

There are many mango trees.

And are there yet other trees besides this mango and the other mangoes?

There are many trees, but those trees are not mangoes.

And are there, besides the other mangoes and those trees, which are not mangoes, yet other trees?

There is this mango tree, sir.

Thou hast a shrewd wit, oh ruler of men!

Hast thou kinsfolk, oh King?

There are many, sir.

And are there also some, oh King, who are not kinsfolk of thine?

There are yet more of those than of my kin.

Is there yet anyone besides the kinsfolk and the others?

There is yet myself, sir.

Good! Thou hast a shrewd wit, oh ruler of men!

Kasyapa paused. There was a deafening silence—a lump formed in his throat—a quiver raced down his spine. He feared he had failed his father.

Then he heard a single person clap. It was loud, slow, and purposeful. Kasyapa's eyes darted through the crowd, searching for its source. It was his school friend, the aristocrat's son, Abaya. More and more people joined in until the whole multitude rose to applaud him. Kasyapa turned apprehensively to his father, who nodded. The queen smiled her usual warm, reassuring smile.

After the ceremony, while on his way out, the king chanced on Thera Mahanama.

"Well written, learned Thera."

"Brilliantly orated, my king," the Thera replied.

"Yes, yes, well orated indeed," the king mumbled and returned to his palace.

The chamberlain came barging through the crowd. "Well done, Young Kasyapa. You were most brilliant."

"Was I, Chamberlain?"

"Absolutely, young man. I am proud of you."

"Do you think my father liked it?"

"Of course, I heard him say so himself."

"Then, I am happy." Kasyapa beamed.

While leaving the event, Migara, dressed in his new army uniform, drew Kasyapa aside.

"Well done. The people loved it," he said in a disingenuous babble, dripping with contempt.

"Your compliment is appreciated, Migara."

But Migara couldn't help himself. He immediately followed with words intended to inflict hurt. "Remember, you are still a half-caste. You will never be king."

Before Kasyapa could open his mouth to respond, to say he had no desire to be king, Migara disappeared into the crowd.

KASYAPA RETURNED TO HIS QUARTERS a happy man. That night, he relived every moment and every nuance of the day: his father's nod, the queen's encouraging smile, and the applause from the crowd. The elation of finally doing something noteworthy, of being recognized, was exhilarating. But as the night wore on, he remembered his mother. He tried to recollect her face, her smile, her presence. The harder he tried to remember her, the more her memory slipped away from him. He missed her, and his grandparents, and Nalu. They too were a dimming memory now. He wondered if they would be proud of him.

Toward the morning, he awoke unsettled. What Migara had said rankled him. Knowing Migara as he did, Kasyapa knew his barbs were intended to provoke. And they did. The sting of it was painful. For the first time in his life, Kasyapa contemplated his future and the line of succession to the throne.

9

A week after the festival, the chamberlain dashed into the compound, skidded to a halt, and patted his forehead with his ever-present silk handkerchief.

"You should have been an actor," Kasyapa said and chuckled.

"Good news," the chamberlain wheezed. "The vizier wishes to speak with you."

"What about?"

"I don't know," the chamberlain feigned and looked away.

"Oh, Chamberlain, of course you know. You know everything."

"Yes—yes, I know, but I can't tell you. It's good news, Young Kasyapa. Come quick," he sputtered and waddled away.

THE VIZIER WAS THE KING'S CHIEF MINISTER. A tall aristocrat of about fifty, he was of fair complexion, with a long thin face and large ears with tufts of white hair sprouting from them. His expression was stern.

"Sit, Young Kasyapa." His voice was soft and measured.

The vizier made a triangle with his hands and studied Kasyapa in silence. The chamberlain, in the meantime, hovered in the background, pretending to be invisible.

"Oh, come here, Chamberlain. I know you want to be in on this," the vizier called out.

The chamberlain scurried over and sat with them.

The vizier spoke. "The king wishes me to advise you that you will work with the sthapati—the king's architect. This position will expose you to many exciting things—many things that will interest you. You will also move out of your present accommodations and into a compound outside the palace. You may take whatever staff you presently have with you."

"Yes, Vizier," Kasyapa replied.

This man spoke with such dignified eloquence. His grammar, diction, and syntax were flawless. To Kasyapa, every word he uttered resonated with importance and authority. He made a mental note to emulate this man, to project himself as the older man did.

THE CHAMBERLAIN WAS UNCHARACTERISTICALLY QUIET when they left the vizier's pavilion.

"I will miss you, Young Kasyapa," he mumbled, coming to a stop in the middle of the courtyard. His eyes flooded with tears.

"Why, Chamberlain? I will still be here."

"Yes, but it will be different from now on. This is your rite of passage, Young Kasyapa. You will move out of the palace. You are moving out of my protection." He pulled out his silk handkerchief, dabbed his eyes, folded it, and carefully tucked it behind his elegant breast piece. "You must forge your own destiny now."

Kasyapa turned to face the chamberlain and placed his hands on his shoulders. It was then he realized, for the first time, he was looking down on his roly-poly bubble man. The man he had looked up to all these years was now just a short, round, balding old man. He, Kasyapa, had grown into an adult.

"Chamberlain, you have been like a father to me. I will always love you dearly and visit you often."

The chamberlain sniffled.

Kasyapa made an effort to sound reassuring. He picked his words carefully. "You talk of my destiny. I must be truthful. I haven't given it much consideration, as my rightful place was to await the king's command. He has conveyed his wishes now. No doubt my dear, dear Chamberlain, you had a large part in his deliberations. I'm eternally grateful to you. I won't let you down."

The chamberlain scuffled his feet. Kasyapa wrapped his arm around his shoulders to comfort him.

"Let me show you your new home outside the palace, Kasyapa."

10

The sthapati was an aristocrat who traveled in a carriage, a hackery of sorts, if one could call it that.

It was a flimsy contraption with two large wooden wheels drawn by a single pony with a spare in tow; the latest model, he would boast. He was a nobleman with an air of arrogance far in excess of his position. What Kasyapa noticed most was his small, fine-fingered hands. Kasyapa was to be the sthapati's underling—his apprentice—but he had no official title or role.

Kasyapa joined the sthapati on his rounds, visiting the prolific construction projects undertaken by his father, the king.

The sthapati waved out of his carriage window. "It's raining. Join me in my carriage, Young Kasyapa."

Kasyapa clambered aboard.

"I hear many promising things about you from the chamberlain."

"The chamberlain is kind."

The sthapati nodded.

As they trundled along at a lazy pace, Kasyapa grew to like the sthapati. He had a keen mind and dropped in and out of topics with consummate ease. Like Kasyapa, he had a passion for the arts. He was also astute in avoiding conversations dealing with politics.

MUCH AS HE ENJOYED THE STHAPATI'S COMPANY, Kasyapa preferred riding or walking outside. He wanted to see his country and meet its people. He hadn't experienced much of either since he was a young boy. He wanted to see, feel, smell, and taste it all.

The sthapati shook his head in bemusement. "Why do you persist being in the stifling heat rather than in the comfort of a carriage?"

Being an aristocrat, he did not fraternize with the common folk. To him, Kasyapa's behavior was unbecoming.

Kasyapa laughed. "Let me get some fresh air."

Some days later, the sthapati parted the curtains of his carriage and craned his head out the window. "What do you find so interesting in the common riffraff?"

"You know, Sthapati, the common riffraff also has a voice. Sometimes it is the meek and humble who possess the most profound wisdom. If only we listen."

The sthapati's eyes glinted. An amused smile played on his lips. "Well said, Young Kasyapa. You have put this pretentious old fool firmly in his place." He closed his curtains and retired to the juddering solace of his carriage.

ABOUT TWO MONTHS LATER, after a meal of sweet-smelling rice prepared with milk and the flesh of a deer cooked in condiments and vegetables, they sat under the shade of a Babula tree, enjoying some freshly peeled mangosteens.

"My dear Kasyapa, you spend an excessive amount of time with the common folk. I still fail to understand what you find so interesting about them. I personally find them tiresome."

"We must keep in mind, Sthapati, it is these people and their inescapable drudgery who are the wellspring of the country's prosperity."

"True."

"We of privilege assume it's our inalienable right to enjoy the luxuries of life, while these people toil. It is they who make our decadence possible."

"Decadence indeed. Thank goodness they haven't wisened up to this, or we would all be properly dead," the sthapati muttered in jest.

AS THEY TRAVELED THROUGH THE COUNTRY, the sthapati and Kasyapa often detoured along their route to visit some temple or cave reputed to contain interesting works of art. For the first time, Kasyapa experienced first-hand the rich cultural heritage of his people, which he had only read and heard of before.

After one such visit to Denawaka Vihara, the sthapati was deep in thought. His ladylike fingers fidgeted with his delicate golden chain. "What did you think of the decorations on the temple walls?"

"You mean the artwork?"

The sthapati pursed his lips, gazed out of the carriage for a few moments before returning to the conversation. "Yes."

"It is well executed. Obviously done by a competent artist."

"Artist or a painter?"

"Huh?"

"Was it done by an artist or painter?"

"What do you mean, Sthapati?"

"We have just seen a decoration on a wall. Do you think it was the work of an artist or a painter?"

"I don't know."

"An artist can also be a painter. But a painter can never be an artist."

Kasyapa waited for the sthapati to elucidate.

"An artist is creative. He is capable of producing something unique and beautiful to admire. A painter is a copier, a follower. He will generate the ordinary."

"I understand now."

"The art depicted in this kingdom of ours is lifeless. It is two dimensional and familiar. Where is the creativity in that?"

The sthapati went silent once more. It was humid inside the carriage. After a while, he shouted out to his page for a drink while tapping his fingers on his knee.

Then he returned his attention to Kasyapa.

"You have been with me some six months or so. From now on, whenever we visit a site, I want you to observe, study, and report. I want you to provide me with a critique."

"As you wish, Sthapati."

"Let us call this the education of Young Kasyapa."

11

On Kasyapa's third tour with the sthapati, they headed south through low-lying, undulating hills and lush green valleys studded with picturesque villages set amid verdant rice fields, each with a ubiquitous temple nearby.

"We will be visiting the Naindanawa Temple near the Ma-Eliya Wewa," the sthapati announced.

Kasyapa pretended he did not hear. He gazed into the distance.

"Did you know the king built the Ma-Eliya Wewa? He ordered the eradication of mosquitoes around the village of Ma-Eliya, and the construction of the Ma-Eliya Wewa reservoir close by."

Kasyapa feigned disinterest.

On reaching the temple, the sthapati excused himself and disappeared. It was quiet, except for the distant swish-swish sound of a bhikkhu, stooped and bent, sweeping the far corner of the temple grounds.

Spotting Kasyapa standing alone, the bhikkhu rested his broom against a tree and strolled over to him. "What is your name, young man?"

Kasyapa dropped his gaze. He didn't want to reveal his identity, but to rebuff a bhikkhu was highly impolite. Etiquette demanded his reply.

"Kasyapa. My name is Kasyapa," he said in a low voice, his eyes downcast.

"Kasyapa, Kasyapa." The bhikkhu toyed with the name, enunciated each syllable with great care, and clicked his tongue. "Ahhhh. Kasyapa—Uppalavanna. Uppalavanna—Kasyapa. She had a little boy named Kasyapa." He bobbed his head enthusiastically.

"Yes, bhikkhu, Uppalavanna was my mother."

The old man's eyes lit up, and his age-worn index finger shot into the air. "Uppalavanna! Her father brought her to me for training. I didn't want to teach her at first—we taught only boys. But she had the most intelligent eyes. I realized I had to make an exception for her. Come. I will show you where she sat." They walked to the rear of the temple and came to a stop under a large Bo tree.

"She sat here. The boys used to tease her. She was the smartest of them all. Such a shame. So sad."

Kasyapa acknowledged his empathy with a lukewarm smile.

"I knew young Dhatusena too. You know, he is king now. He lived with us here as a young novice bhikkhu. He came with his uncle, Thera Mahanama. Do you know the thera?"

"Yes, I know him."

"The young Dhatusena revisited us when he became a warrior also. Is he not your father?"

"Yes, he is." Kasyapa blanched. He was growing more uncomfortable with each of the monk's assertions.

"Yes. Yes. Uppalavanna, Dhatusena, Kasyapa." He ambled to a small stone bench, dusted it with his hand, and dropped himself onto it. He adjusted his faded robe, slightly frayed in places, across his knees.

"You know, I am old now. But I was there. I witnessed it all. Do you remember much of those days?"

"No, Bhikkhu, I don't remember." Kasyapa slouched his head and studied his feet.

"She was the most beautiful woman you could ever set eyes on— both inside and out—radiant like a goddess. A bhikkhu is not supposed to say such things, but it is the truth. She suffered because of her love for the warrior. Her parents did so, too. I think they loved each other— the warrior Dhatusena and the beautiful Uppalavanna. But it was not meant to be."

Kasyapa gazed uneasily into the distance. A sharp pain gnawed at his stomach. He wished the monk would stop. He wished he was some-place else. A dull throb started at his temples. He rubbed them with his fingers, but the bhikkhu persisted.

"The villagers stopped their sneers and innuendoes when Dhatusena became king. But she was never happy again, except for you, her son. Your grandfather and grandmother, they were very proud of you. Did you know they visited resplendent Anuradhapura every year for the Great Festival in the hope of catching a glimpse of you?"

Kasyapa shook his head, feeling more and more despondent. It was so long ago. Memories of his family were so distant now. He remembered his grandmother crying and his grandfather comforting her, the last time he had seen them. But they had always remained with him, deep in the recesses of his mind.

The bhikkhu continued, "Only last year, they were overjoyed when they came to see me. They said they saw you. Your grandmother told me you looked like a true prince, and your grandfather agreed. They said you gave an oration. What was the oration?"

"It was the story of the mango tree. Thera Mahanama rewrote it."

"Then it must have been splendid indeed." He shifted in his seat and rearranged the fold of his robe. "Your grandfather fell ill that year and died, and your grandmother departed this life soon after. They were both cremated in the clearing near their daughter."

Tears clouded Kasyapa's eyes. He brushed them aside with the back of his hand. "What then of Nalu?"

"Ahhh, the old woodcutter. He breathed his last just a few months ago," the bhikkhu replied with a heavy sigh, eyeing Kasyapa as he shifted his seat on the bench.

"The new village headman refused to cremate him in the clearing reserved for the villagers as he was of lowly birth, an outcast. The boy he saved from the leopard spoke in his defense. The villagers then agreed that Nalu could be cremated, but only at the edge of the clearing. It is sad, the threads of life."

The bhikkhu looked down at his faded orange robe and arranged its folds between his knees.

"Even in death, the woodcutter—a good and honorable man—could not overcome the accident of his lowly birth. Do you understand these things, Kasyapa?"

Kasyapa stood with his head hung low. It was as though the bhikkhu was in possession of some long-forgotten manuscript, slowly turning its crumbling pages, each with its haunting revelations of the past. Things Kasyapa had suppressed, things he never known, things kept secret from him—for all these years. He spotted the sthapati pacing impatiently in the distance.

"I must beg your leave, Bhikkhu. I must go."

The monk lifted himself from his seat with a low groan and stood hunched and withered before him. Kasyapa averted his gaze.

"Look at me, young man," the bhikkhu admonished, pointing a crooked finger at Kasyapa's nose. "Let me see your eyes."

Kasyapa did as he was told.

The monk squinted. His clouded eyes scrutinized Kasyapa's face. "You have eyes like your mother's," he affirmed with a nod. "I see great promise in those eyes. Use your gift wisely, Young Kasyapa. You will overcome your adversities. There is greatness in you."

The bhikku's words unnerved Kasyapa and left him feeling naked. With just a few carefully chosen words, the bhikkhu had exposed him for who he was—the illegitimate son of a village girl. Kasyapa rushed back to the sthapati, his mind burning with a hundred disparate thoughts. Not only about what the bhikkhu had told him but also about his position in the royal hierarchy. Why had the bhikkhu been so insistent in resurrecting his past, his roots, his pedigree?

Is there a lesson, a grain of truth, a gem of wisdom to be gleaned from this encounter? What did he mean—to use my gift wisely? What did he mean—you will overcome your adversities? Why did he say there is greatness in me? The bhikkhu, too, addressed me as "Young Kasyapa." The chamberlain and vizier also attached this prefix when they address me. Others refer to me as master, sir, sire, and young—never prince. Am I too sensitive, seeing slights that do not exist and imagining snubs unintended? Expecting more than what is rightfully mine?

"Who was that?" the sthapati asked as Kasyapa rejoined him.

"An old bhikkhu. He said he knew my mother."

"I see."

"We lived in the village of Ma-Eliya. Not far from here."

"I know."

"You know?"

"Of course, I know. Would you like to visit the place?"

"I don't know," Kasyapa said in a subdued and tentative voice.

"A part of me wants to rediscover my roots, but another resists. There is no one there now. Maybe it's best I leave my memories as they are."

"Yes. We have much to cover on this tour. Let's go." The sthapati ushered Kasyapa away.

THEY TRAVELED AWAY FROM THE TEMPLE, along an unpaved road skirting the hamlet of Ma-Eliya. Kasyapa gazed out of the carriage window.

"Stop!" Kasyapa shouted out to the coachman, banging on the side of the carriage.

The sthapati, who had been dozing off, jumped up with a jolt. "What's going on?"

"Give me a moment, Sthapati. I recognize this place from my childhood." Kasyapa sprinted to the panasa tree, the one by the footpath he and his mother had once taken down to the local stream. It was now by the waterline of the Ma-Eliya Wewa reservoir.

Kasyapa rested his hand against its coarse, uneven trunk to steady himself, and locked his gaze to where the little rock by the stream had once been. The rising waters of the Ma-Eliya Wewa, the reservoir his father Dhatusena had built, had submerged the rock by the stream, which had tumbled over a waterfall and into a pool below.

Tears swamped his eyes as long dulled memories flooded in—of his mother, the rock, the waterfall, Nalu, butterflies, and the sweet scent of jasmine. They were all gone.

12

It soon became apparent to Kasyapa that the sthapati not only cherished the arts, he also had an insatiable appetite for women.

"The perks of the job, Young Kasyapa," he said with a wink when Kasyapa had teased him about his dalliances.

"I will readily admit. I love my food, but I love women even more. They are both delectable." He laughed. "See that reed-stalk of a man over there, at the back of my entourage? The one seated in the most ungainly manner on that donkey? That's my pimp—the procurer of women." The sthapati clapped his hands, and the man materialized instantly. "Procurer, this is Young Kasyapa."

"Yes, sir, I know of the king's son." His prominent Adam's apple gyrated up and down as he spoke in a reedy voice.

"Now Procurer, tell this young man what your duties are."

The procurer stood straighter and cleared a phlegmy throat. "My duties are to find suitable bedmates for my master, the sthapati. I visit outlying villages and announce the availability of a night's services for an aristocrat. This opportunity is highly sought-after by local women. I choose only the most desirable ones, of course," he added, puffing up his chest like a cockerel.

"Now, tell Young Kasyapa what I like."

"The sthapati likes his women wholesome, with large breasts and wide hips." Sizing Kasyapa up with an appraising glance and wringing his hands. "What about you, sir?"

"Oh, I like my women lithesome," Kasyapa replied in jest, even though he hadn't been with a woman yet.

SOME DAYS LATER, after Kasyapa had retired for the night, the flaps of his tent drew open. A shapely silhouette of a woman stood against the light. She slunk in and lay beside him—warm and soft and smelling luscious. He lay there motionless, not sure of what he ought to do. Her hands glided over his arms. Her soft breasts compressed against his chest, then her nipples lightly grazed his skin as she worked her way down his body. He nearly fainted when she took him. Kasyapa was certain he was in heaven. He wanted to stay there forever. When he awoke the following morning, she was gone.

As they started their journey the next morning, the sthapati cast his eyes over Kasyapa and winked. Now he understood the reason for the sthapati's appetite for women.

*****

ON HIS RETURN TO THE CAPITAL some months later, the vizier called Kasyapa in for an audience. The chamberlain insisted on accompanying him. When they arrived, the vizier arched his brow and gestured for his guests to be seated.

"I understand you are popular with the people, Young Kasyapa; working with your hands, planting rice, making bricks, casting bronze, painting, plastering, blacksmithing—much to the amusement of the masses."

"Is that a fault, Vizier?"

"No, not at all. I commend you for experiencing life. My guidance to you, however, is this. Be mindful of the mystique of prestige and power. They are potent tools at your command when used wisely."

"Yes, Vizier."

"Be with the masses, but never become one of them. Do you understand, Young Kasyapa?"

"I think so, Vizier. I will remember."

"Also be wary of harvesting adulation. It will lead to jealousy and ill will."

"Yes, Vizier."

The vizier nodded, indicating the interview was over. Kasyapa and the chamberlain walked outside.

"What was that about, Chamberlain?"

"The vizier is well informed. He is merely advising you. You know, unlike me, he is an expert on such things."

"You have a kind heart, Chamberlain. That's more important."

The chamberlain brushed off Kasyapa's comment with a flip of his wrist in a show of false modesty. Kasyapa laughed. He knew all too well that his guardian loved compliments.

"What did he mean about harvesting adulation, Chamberlain?"

"He was warning you to remain unnoticed."

"Is this something I ought to be concerned about?"

"No, not at all, if you are mindful."

"Our vizier is an extraordinary man. I have tried to model myself after him."

"Very sound indeed, Kasyapa."

13

Nearly two years had passed since Kasyapa had cast off the shackles of his childhood. While taking shelter from a torrential shower in the sthapati's hackery, Kasyapa began, "I sense a disquiet among our people, Sthapati."

"How so, Kasyapa?"

"On the surface, the signs of prosperity are everywhere. No doubt a consequence of our king's extensive construction projects. But the people seem malcontent and malnourished."

"What sort of building projects have you noticed? What most catches your eye?"

Kasyapa studied the sthapati with bewilderment. He had spoken of disquiet and hunger, and the sthapati responded with a reference to buildings. Kasyapa chose to answer the sthapati's question, nevertheless. "Temples and monasteries come to mind, and reservoirs to a lesser extent."

"Who benefits most from these temples and monasteries?"

"The clergy, I presume."

"Do the people benefit from these monks in their monasteries?"

"Not directly, but spiritually they must?"

"Would you say, then that spiritual contentment will fill a hungry belly and bring happiness?"

"No. What are you saying, Sthapati?"

"You told me the people are malnourished. I am trying to understand why." The sthapati retrieved a small pouch. He opened the bag and picked out a cardamom pod, which he tossed into his mouth.

"My thinking is that the king's largesse isn't filtering down to the people," Kasyapa said.

"Again, my question to you is why? Let me guide you."

Kasyapa waited while the sthapati pulled the skin of the cardamom pod he had been chewing out of his mouth and tossed it outside the carriage window.

The sthapati chewed on the astringent cardamom seeds. "Once a monastery is built, what resources are required to maintain it and to feed, house, and clothe its monks?"

"I don't know."

"In your travels, how often have you seen temple properties?"

"Very often," Kasyapa replied.

"Have you seen monks working?"

"No."

"Then who works on these properties?"

"Serfs?"

"Where do these serfs come from?"

"They are gifts from the king, indentured farmers, and slaves."

"What do you conclude from that?"

"Many serfs are being retained by the religious establishments for the upkeep of the monasteries and their estates?"

"Interesting conclusion," the sthapati replied, spitting the pulp from his cardamom seeds out the window.

"Much of the nation's wealth is being spent on one vast enterprise."

"Is that your supposition, Kasyapa?"

"Yes."

"Now, to your next assertion—The people are unhappy?" The sthapati shifted himself on the narrow carriage seat. "Do the temples pay taxes?"

"No."

"Do the people pay taxes?"

"Yes."

"Do the people pay for the upkeep of the temples?"

"Yes, directly and indirectly."

"How?"

"By the supply of labor and by the offerings and gifts they make at the temples."

"Are they recompensed for their labor and offerings?"

"I don't know."

"You are being defensive, Kasyapa. Respond to the question directly." The sthapati broke off his conversation, stuck his hand out the window, and banged against the side of his carriage. "What are you fools doing?"

His man-servant appeared, drenched from the monsoonal deluge outside. "We are trying to dislodge your carriage, sir. It is stuck in the mud."

"Then don't just stand there. Get to it and bring us something to eat." Turning to Kasyapa, he continued. "Now tell me about this free labor—this *rajakariya*?"

"Since the foundation of our kingdom, it has been customary for every able-bodied male to provide forty days of free labor annually to the king."

"Do the men of the temples and monasteries also provide this free labor to the king?"

"No. The temples and monasteries are exempt. But..."

"But what, Kasyapa?"

"Whereas temple lands are exempt from this requirement, these institutions also demand an equivalent free service from their tenant farmers."

"Why then do the people gripe? The rajakariya is nothing new?"

"Because our king increased it from the traditional forty days of labor to fifty days, and the temples followed suit."

"I see," the sthapati replied, accepting a dish of food handed to him by his man-servant. "Have some."

Kasyapa wasn't hungry, but he accepted the sthapati's hospitality, nevertheless. He selected a small morsel and popped into his mouth.

"If the people are already impoverished, then these things would only make them more so."

"Is this your inference, Kasyapa?"

"Now I see what you were alluding to some months ago."

"I do not recall."

"The influence of religious establishments with tens of thousands of monks are becoming omnipresent. The generosity of the king toward these religious fraternities is fueling discontent. The people are not benefiting from the king's largesse. The increase in the rajakariya is, in fact, an increase in taxes. Albeit by sleight of hand."

"Now that was a mouthful, Young Kasyapa. Be cautious. Do not venture these opinions to others," the sthapati added, flicking crumbs off his clothes.

The carriage juddered and started moving once more.

Perhaps the common man's blood careening through his veins gave him unique insights. It freed him to arrive at conclusions unencumbered by class or position. Maybe he, the onlooker, was witness to the bigger picture. The king's well-intended single-minded religious zeal was counterproductive.

As the carriage lumbered along through the monsoonal deluge along a muddy, rutted track, Kasyapa recalled a conversation he had with Nila the Giant many years earlier.

"The king is a troubled man, Master Kasyapa," Nila had said. "He lives with deep remorse, tormented by inner demons. Nothing he does seems to expunge his guilt. The temples, the monasteries, the reservoirs...they are all an attempt to redeem himself. Still, no matter what he does, redemption never comes."

14

One day, much to Kasyapa's surprise, the sthapati confided in him. "I am overcome by boredom. My work is filled with such drudgery. How I wish I were given a commission that stimulates me."

"What do you mean, Sthapati?"

"The monotony of it all. These never-ending constructions are driving me mad. The orthodoxy of it all. Mounds of brick painted white, a courtyard, some buildings, paintings of pious kings and clergy, and numerous deities, over and over again."

"Yes, I have noticed. Everything looks as if it comes from the same mold."

"Do you know why that is, Kasyapa? I will tell you. The depiction of anything other than religious themes according to a rigid formula is frowned upon."

"By whom?"

"Think about it, Young Kasyapa," the sthapati replied, breaking off the conversation.

*****

A FEW MONTHS LATER, at the Ambatthala Vihara in Cetiyagiri at Mihintale, Kasyapa observed a young man at work. He was a short, lean man with a long face, lopsided ears, close-set eyes, and a pronounced Adam's apple.

"What is your name?" he asked the man.

"Agbo, sire, the son of the scribe Kabojha."

"What are you working on?"

"A mural of the story of the coming of the sacred Bodhi tree to this land, sire."

"Interesting."

The resident monks, on learning they had a distinguished guest visiting the temple, hurried to Kasyapa and crowded around him.

"We are honored by your visit," a senior monk, possibly the abbot, said in a subdued tone.

Kasyapa nodded.

Ignoring the presence of the artist, the abbot continued. "We have been concerned about the work of this artist."

"Why so, Abbot?"

"His work is unorthodox and heretical."

"I see. And why do you think it so?"

"It does not follow conventions."

"Dear Abbot, I fail to see why this art offends you. To my eyes, it shows an excellent appreciation of color, movement, and form."

"But sire, this is not how things are done. There are rules. There are standards. Conventions must be followed. We have done so for generations. We don't want fanciful drawings."

"Don't you think, dear Abbot, we should improve on the works of our forefathers?" Kasyapa's voice hardened as he spoke.

The abbot's face flushed, and a flat smirk slid across his lips.

It was clear to Kasyapa these monks of the orthodox Thera School were unmoved. They murmured among themselves.

Indulging in adroit doublespeak, the abbot continued. "We suggest he be replaced. We can recommend other more compliant artists."

Kasyapa fixed his eyes on the abbot and spoke in a low, steady voice.

"No. This artist is to remain. He is to complete his project. Dear Abbot, I hold you personally responsible. You are to make certain no person hinders his work. Now, I must continue my visit."

Agbo, who was seated on the ground, looked up with sheepish bewilderment. Kasyapa walked away, concerned he may have overstepped his authority.

LATER IN THE DAY, Kasyapa met up with the sthapati.

"I had an unpleasant altercation with some bhikkhus today," Kasyapa said.

"Yes. A delegation of them came to see me."

"Did they?"

"Things didn't go smoothly by the sound of it."

"What did you tell them?"

"I said they would get no succor from me. I will abide by the wishes of the king's son."

"Do you agree with my stance, Sthapati?"

"Which stance, Kasyapa? From what I hear, you took many."

"Oh, I didn't realize I had."

"Well done, Kasyapa."

"Was I arrogant?"

"No, not at all. Stand up for your beliefs, young man. Project what authority you are perceived to have. And then a bit more."

"I mean the style of the paintings. What do you think of them?"

"Who am I to comment? Was it not I who recently lamented about the stultification of our art and architecture?"

"Yes, you did. I have taken inspiration from your comments."

"Look here, Kasyapa. You are the king's son. They all know it. Your authority, however, is nebulous—undefined. Exercise it with prudence."

A FEW DAYS LATER, at the chamberlain's residence, while dining on a meal of yellow rice prepared in ghee seasoned with cardamoms, the chamberlain asked, "You had some difficulties at the Cetiyagiri?"

"You heard?"

"Yes. It was reported to the vizier."

"What did he say?"

"Nothing."

"What did you say?"

"Nothing."

"Nothing?"

"Yes. I said nothing. I trust your judgment."

"Does the king know?"

"Yes."

"What did he say?"

"Nothing."

"Nothing? The king, too, said nothing?"

"Yes."

"Chamberlain, I think we have a brilliant artist among us. His work at the Cetiyagiri is outstanding. Alas, those monks will not appreciate it, and will no doubt resent its presence. If I had my way, I would hand the temple over to the more progressive Dhammaruci monks. They would be more appreciative of the refurbished vihara and its paintings."

The chamberlain said nothing.

A few months later, much to Kasyapa's surprise, the king handed over the vihara to the Dhammaruci monks. This caused much consternation among the monks of the Thera School, who were in fierce doctrinal competition with the Dhammaruci monks. They huffed and were greatly displeased.

On hearing the news, Kasyapa chuckled. *I seem to have more influence than I give myself credit for.*

15

Having befriended Kasyapa, the sthapati often invited him to his residence; a large rambling affair located off a nondescript street in the city. His parties were extravagant and included emissaries and traders from foreign countries, poets, writers, and philosophers—but no bureaucrats or clergy.

"Come here, young man," the sthapati called at one such party. "I want you to meet someone." Putting his arm around Kasyapa's shoulders affectionately, he continued. "This is Varahadeva, the chief minister of King Harishena of the Vakataka Empire in central Jambudvipa. He is on a pilgrimage to Anuradhapura."

"I understand from the sthapati that you have an interest in contemporary art," Varahadeva said.

"Yes, I am of the view that our art and culture is somewhat dull. While the sthapati attributes this controversial opinion to me, I think he secretly harbors the same assessment."

"You might be interested to know my illustrious king, Harishena, is a great patron of Buddhist architecture, art, and culture. He is currently refurbishing the Ajanta Caves."

"I have heard of the place. An itinerant monk recently described the paintings and sculptures there as the finest he had ever seen He professed they were the work of the gods themselves."

"Yes, they are spectacular. I, myself, am refurbishing one cave. You should visit them. Come as my guest, Kasyapa."

"Thank you, Varahadeva, for your gracious offer. You may see me in your country, indeed."

The very next day, Kasyapa pleaded with the chamberlain and sthapati to intercede on his behalf for permission to visit the Ajanta

Caves. A meeting was arranged with the vizier, who listened in stony silence and dismissed Kasyapa without comment.

A week later, the chamberlain rushed into Kasyapa's quarters. "It is done, Kasyapa. Believe me, it's done. You can go to Ajanta. The king has granted permission for the visit," the chamberlain said, jigging with excitement.

After further pleading, Kasyapa gained permission for Agbo to join him. Kasyapa, Agbo, and his manservant Daya accompanied Varahadeva back to Jambudvipa three weeks later.

*****

THEY TRAVELED TO NANDIVARDHAHANA, the capital of the Vakataka Kingdom. While there, Varahadeva arranged an audience with King Harishena himself, who Kasyapa found to be most gracious. A friendship soon developed. They spent many hours together discussing Buddhist philosophy and the arts.

Returning to his lodging that night, Kasyapa was reflective. His melancholy grew profound. He stayed awake most of the night. *Here I am in a foreign land, whose ruler greets me as though I were a prince. In my own country, I live on the fringe. Not once has my father spoken to me. I am an outcast. Inside, I feel empty and small.*

With a letter of free passage from King Harishena, Kasyapa's party headed on to Ajanta. The man-made caves with elaborate pillared entrances were located in a sandstone cliff of a semicircular canyon. A large waterfall, and a few minor ones, cascaded over the cliff face, creating a rainbow mist in the valley below.

Kasyapa and his companions resided with the local monks who were eager to show their guests their prized artworks.

"Done by our own Buddhist monks," his hosts boasted with pride as they ventured through the labyrinth of caves and tunnels, each with its unique architecture, sculpture, and stunning paintings.

Agbo was beside himself. "Look at the beauty, Sire," he said repeatedly, smacking his forehead in disbelief.

From sunrise to sunset, Agbo sketched the paintings, the sculptures, and motifs. "There is nothing comparable in Lanka. These are masterpieces," Agbo ranted.

"Yes. They are indeed works of art. I have never seen anything like this before," Kasyapa agreed. Their hosts beamed with modest pride.

Their two-month stay was over in a trice, and it was time to return home. Agbo had amassed an extensive collection of sketches and drawings. He wasn't willing to part with any of them.

"You are a copy-thief, Agbo. You have reproduced all their work."

"Oh, Master Kasyapa, if I were to leave any of my drawings behind, I would surely die," he protested with great sincerity.

Kasyapa laughed and arranged for an additional cart and driver to transport Agbo's collection.

On the final day of their stay, the monks escorted Kasyapa and his companions to a recently completed inner sanctum. There, against the far wall, lay a most beautiful sculpture of the Buddha reposed in the ultimate state of Nirvana—the state of everlasting, highest peace and happiness.

"It is exquisite," Kasyapa said, and Agbo clapped his hands with gusto.

Sadly, it was time to go. King Harishena, provided a large agramandira, a ship with a high keel and stern and three masts, to return his distinguished visitors home.

16

The chamberlain visited the very same day Kasyapa returned home.

"My dear Kasyapa, I kept your abode tidy and your servants active while you were away," he said as he rushed over, with outstretched arms.

"After six months away, I am glad to be back, Chamberlain. I brought you something," Kasyapa replied.

"A turban of turquoise. And made of the finest silk too." The chamberlain stroked his gift as if it were a kitten. "And a yak-hair cummerbund," he added, clapping his hands. His eyes twinkled as he dressed himself up in both.

They spent the best part of the day nibbling on freshly prepared sweetmeats and hot, fragrant toddy as Kasyapa recounted his adventures overseas.

"You seem to have had a splendid time. I am envious," the older man said lightheartedly. "Now, for my news. I must tell you about the marriage."

"Marriage?"

"Yes, Migara's marriage to Princess Sakula." The chamberlain cast his eyes this way and that and leaned into Kasyapa's ear, "I don't like it one bit, such a lovely girl married off to that monster," he huffed.

"Surely, there would have been better suitors?"

"Of course. She is a sweet girl with a happy disposition." The chamberlain replied, letting off a weighty sigh. "You know the king adores her. Her pranks, lightheartedness, and laughter make him happy." The chamberlain's mood darkened. "His attitude toward Moggallana, however, is one of apathy."

Kasyapa dared not ask the chamberlain what the king's views were of him. He was fearful of what he might hear. He suspected it was one of indifference.

"Now, I am rambling. Let me get back to the story," the chamberlain broke in, again lowering his voice to a near whisper. "It's that dreadful woman, the fire-dragon." The chamberlain adjusted himself on his cushion, realigned his new turban, and continued. "While you were away, the previous senapati, the chief of the army, dropped dead. Can you imagine that? Just dropped dead, choking on a chicken bone. Even before his body had grown cold, she was in the king's ear. I don't know why he listens to her. Let me tell you. He doesn't like his sister. Anyway, she got Migara appointed as the senapati even though he was young and inexperienced. The vizier advised him against it. The king was furious and threatened to have the vizier's head chopped off and mounted on a stake. It was awful."

Kasyapa's mind drifted to the fifth royal virtue he had memorized as a boy. *Always heed good counsel.*

"I didn't have any say in it. I don't think the queen did either." The chamberlain made a somber face and leaned into Kasyapa's ear once more. "They all possess volatile temperaments, the king, the fire-dragon, and Migara. Thank goodness you don't have that awful trait."

"So what drove the king to this decision? Surely he knows Migara's temperament?"

"Well, it is customary for a close relative of the king to be appointed senapati. What better way to secure your position than to have your own kin in important positions? Also, by marrying off Sakula to Migara, the king was no doubt convinced he could make the alliance even stronger. I suspect this was his reasoning."

Kasyapa said nothing. He kept his thoughts to himself.

IT WASN'T LONG BEFORE KASYAPA ran into Migara. He had put on a bit of weight and was impeccably dressed, as usual.

"Ah, Kasyapa, I hear you learned a lot in Jambudvipa," he said with an air of jauntiness, cocking his head to one side and rolling his eyes here and there. "You have no doubt heard the good news," he continued, not waiting for Kasyapa's reply.

"Yes, congratulations."

Then Migara, who was taller than Kasyapa, leaned over and placed his hand on Kasyapa's shoulder. "I am the senapati now, the commander of the army, the second most powerful man in the land." Straightening up, his civility dropped away like a discarded cloak. "I have the power to make or break a king. It will pay for you, Kasyapa, to remember that," he said, in a voice laced with malice.

Kasyapa watched him as he walked away.

Why does this man bring out the vilest demons in me? He metes out his taunts with such spite, reminding me of my lowly birth and tenuous position in society. He seeks out and exploits my vulnerabilities. I was raised to show love, grace, and forgiveness, but when my mind turns to this man, there are none of these.

The feeling of exclusion taking hold of his mind was raw and profound. It seemed he was an outsider on the inside. When Kasyapa next met the chamberlain, he raised the matter with him.

"I am the king's eldest son and have proven my competence. Nevertheless, my father does not appoint me vice-regent or sub-king. He holds that place for Moggallana. Nor does he assign me any position of authority," Kasyapa's voice betrayed his bitterness and misgiving.

The chamberlain's face flushed, his cheeks puffed and quivered. He fidgeted with his elaborate breastplate and sucked in his breath. Kasyapa immediately regretted uttering those words. He sensed a speech was coming. And indeed, it was.

"Now listen here, Young Kasyapa. This line of thinking is downright dangerous and borders on treason. The law is the law. Even the king must obey the law. For over a thousand years, the properly anointed king has always been from the ruling Kshatriya caste. The heir to the throne must be of pure, noble blood—both parents of the Kshatriya caste. No one else has the right to rule. There have been usurpers and charlatans in the past, but this is the rule of royal succession. Why, just fifty years ago, Sotthi-Sena, born of a king and a harem woman, lasted on the throne for just twelve hours. He was assassinated. Why? Because he didn't have the right to rule."

The chamberlain paused and took a deep breath as he gathered up his thoughts. "Other offspring of the king have no rights whatsoever, other than those bestowed on them by the grace of the king. You have been lucky. The king brought you into his household. Only children from women of the royal harem are allowed to remain in the royal household." Wheezing, the chamberlain stopped, inhaled deeply, puffed out his ample chest, and wagged his finger at Kasyapa.

"Trust me, Kasyapa. You are most fortunate. My advice to you is to do the king's bidding, and refrain from imaginings of grandeur."

The chamberlain's sharp rebuke was unexpected, but Kasyapa's mind was ill at ease. It was though the misery and hurt dwelling within sucked the light, the warmth, the life out of him.

KASYAPA VISITED THE sthapati the following day. For him, Kasyapa had brought a translation of the *Silappatikaram* (The Tale of an Anklet), a second-century classic from southern Jambudvipa.

"It is gracious of you to remember me. I will enjoy reading this," the sthapati said, wrapping his arm around his guest. "I am delighted your trip to Ajanta was so productive. We must incorporate your discoveries in our future projects. Without raising the ire of those coconut-heads, of course." He joked.

"Sthapati, I am troubled," Kasyapa began. "In Jambudvipa, I was treated like a prince. Here, in my own land, I am inconsequential—a nobody."

"*Shh*, Kasyapa. Let's walk outside."

The sthapati's residence encircled a large central garden dotted with priceless ancient sculptures he had acquired over the years.

"You know I do not indulge in politics. However, I sense my friend is troubled. Talk to me."

"Since I returned, I have come to realize my position in society is tenuous and irrelevant. While Migara, who is no doubt a psychopath, is now the second most powerful man in the kingdom."

"Yes, this is true. However, you are aware of the reasons for Migara's rise to power."

"But it doesn't make it less painful for me. It doesn't seem fair."

"Kasyapa, be patient. Your time will come. When I am impatient, I remember a simple truism my mother taught me as a young boy. 'Slowly, slowly catch the monkey.' Be patient. There are those who champion your cause. Your time will come."

"Who? I can only think of one, the chamberlain."

"Most certainly. He finds no fault with you."

"Who else?"

The sthapati raised his shoulders and dropped them in an exaggerated resignation. "All right, I will tell you. The vizier holds you in some regard. And so do I."

"Thank you. Thank you, Sthapati. Knowing this makes me feel so much better." Kasyapa then added, "What about my father?"

"Kasyapa, I will not discuss the king with you."

"I understand. Forgive me, my indiscretion, Sthapati. My exuberance got the better of me."

17

It happened just two weeks after Kasyapa returned from Jambudvipa. The chamberlain was there, when Sakula came to her father weeping, her face swollen, her makeup smudged, and her beautiful dhoti stained with blood.

"What happened?" the king asked.

She stood in front of her father, trembling, her head bowed in silence.

"Sakula?"

She burst into tears, rushed to her father, and sobbed against his chest. "He beat me, father."

"What! Who beat you? Migara beat you?"

She said nothing.

"How dare he raise his hand at the daughter of the king?" he seethed, his chest heaving with fury.

The chamberlain shuddered. His king was a mild-mannered man, but a volatile one, prone to losing his temper. The signs were ominous. He sent urgent word for the vizier.

"Guards, return my daughter to the care of her mother." The king paced up and down, shaking his head from side to side like an enraged elephant—wild, unpredictable, and extremely dangerous.

The vizier, having received the news, slipped in unnoticed and remained in the shadows. The chamberlain edged closer to him. Neither man wanted to be near their king while he raged.

"Where is that scoundrel? Bring him to me at once," the king snarled.

Messengers hurried out to fetch Migara.

The first returned breathlessly and prostrated himself before the king. "He is nowhere to be found, my king."

Another messenger arrived shortly afterward. He gulped and blurted, "He has fled." Then this foolish man went on in a faulting voice to complain, "I encountered the Senapati Migara's mother. She abused me with the vilest profanities. She said the most despicable things about our princess."

"What did she say?"

The chamberlain heard the vizier hold his breath. The messenger remained prostrate before his king.

The king was livid. He walked around the unfortunate man and kicked him. "What did she say? Tell me, or I will have your head."

"She said..." The frightened messenger trembled. "Tell the king his daughter is a diseased woman of the night—a whore—a lowly charwoman, a latrine cleaner, not worthy of my son," he blurted.

"A whore! She called my daughter a whore!" Like a wild elephant unhinged, the king swayed from side to side, unforgiving and vengeful.

The terrified messenger lifted his eyes to the vizier for guidance, who motioned for him to leave. Still prostrate, the terrified man backed out of the hall and disappeared, thankful his life hadn't come to an end there and then.

"Guards, find Migara. Kill him! Bring me his head. As for that wicked woman—she has tormented me all my life. She is the cause of this. Rid me of her. Take her! Burn her!"

The chamberlain turned to the vizier, who stood stone-faced. This was not a time to trifle with the king.

A detachment of the palace guard, led by Nila, set out in haste. Nila, the king's most trusted lieutenant and a fearless warrior, abhorred violence. But he was the king's loyal servant. He did his duty even though it made him sick to his stomach.

When they arrived at Migara's house, his mother refused to let them in.

"Piss off, you turds," she shouted from the upstairs balcony.

"We have orders from the king," they shouted back.

"Tell your king, his sister is not frightened by him. Wait until my son, the senapati, finds out about how you have come to arrest his mother like a common criminal. He will have you hung up by your testicles."

The soldiers turned to Nila for guidance. "Break down the door. Arrest that woman," he ordered.

They broke down the door, but she barricaded herself in an anteroom. Finding a wooden pounding mortar in the kitchen, the soldiers heaved it at the door, shattering it into smithereens.

Still defiant, she charged at them, cursing, spitting, and clawing. "You sons of whores. You guttersnipes. How dare you touch a woman of the Kshatriya caste?" she shrieked and spat into a soldier's eye.

"This woman is a devil. Let's put an end to her right here," the soldier said as he scrapped the gob off his face in disgust.

"No," Nila roared. "We must carry out the king's orders."

The troops bound her and half-carried, half-dragged her outside before throwing her into the back of a cart. She continued her profanities unabated until they stuffed an old rag into her mouth.

On the outskirts of the city, in a place set aside for common executions, they stripped her naked and tied her to a stake. Then they set her alight.

She writhed in agony as the fire crackled around her. There was no telling how long it took her to die—the flames were too intense to see. In four hours, her body had turned to ash. No one but her executioners attended her demise. She died naked and forsaken.

18

Migara had found refuge in a house on the outskirts of the city. It was a small villa owned by his friend, Palikada. They had known each other since childhood and shared a common predilection for ganja and young boys. This was their shared bond.

In his dingy hideout, Migara sat alone and cursed himself for his recklessness and short temper.

This time I went too far. She has gone to the king. There is no way to reverse the harm I caused. I could flee to Jambudvipa, beg for forgiveness, or commit suicide. None of these are palatable to me—especially not the last.

There was a knock on the door. Palikada slipped in and bolted the door behind him. "I have just returned from the city. The king has demanded your head."

Migara slumped in his seat. "It was reckless of me, wasn't it?"

"It was most unwise of you, my friend. Downright stupid if you ask me. What got over you?"

"This isn't the first time I beat her, you know. In the past, she bore her punishment in silence. This time, she went to the king."

"Punishment? What crime did she commit?"

"Her impertinence toward my mother. Always arguing. Not knowing her place. You know my mother comes first with me."

"What did you expect? She is the princess. Is it not her house you live in? Aren't those servants in their fine livery hers? I tell you, Migara my friend, you are an idiot. An ill-tempered fool. "

"Watch your words, Palikada. You may be a friend, but even a friend must limit his impertinence," Migara snapped, his eyes on fire. Modulating his tone, Migara continued. "I was content as a bachelor. Getting married was my mother's idea. She arranged the whole thing. A desirable match and a plum position as the senapati. How could I refuse? You remember?"

"Yes, I remember."

"It's my mother, you know. Sakula was an obedient wife. She rarely quarreled. Living in our household, Mother always found fault with her. Every day, when Sakula wasn't around, my mother grumbled in my ear. She watched and reported the most trivial of infractions. Sakula overfeeds the servants. She laughs a lot. She invites friends over and spends lavishly. Do you know what the fight was about, Palikada? A piece of cake. Can you believe it, a piece of cake? I had just got home, and the accusations started. I thrashed her with my riding-whip. Now I am in this mess."

"You whipped the princess? With a riding whip?" Palikada gulped. "You fool, what came over you?"

"I don't know. I snapped."

"*Shh*, someone's at the front door." Palikada cautioned and slipped outside.

Migara sat alone in this musty darkened room with mildew-covered walls, waiting for his friend to return.

Maybe I should overthrow the king? Who will oppose me? I am of the right caste. There is no reason I can't be king. After all, apart from Moggallana, aren't I the next in line to the throne? Who is going to stop me? Moggallana is just a boy. And as for Kasyapa, he is just a low-caste wimp.

"We have more bad news," Palikada announced, reentering the room with a soldier in tow.

"What is it, Soldier?" Migara inquired.

"Sire, your mother has been executed. Burned at the stake."

Migara's jaw sagged. "Nooooo. Why punish my dearest, dearest mother?" he shuddered, a cascade of tears streaming down his face.

Then, slowly, his eyes narrowed into squinting slits; mean, smoldering gashes in his face. "I will exact my revenge," he snarled, slammed his fists on the table, and stormed out of the room.

*****

THAT VERY SAME DAY, just before midnight, Migara led a small band of men in a surprise attack on the palace. They quickly overpowered its weak defenses and headed straight to the king's bedchambers.

Nila always slept in a small anteroom near the king's chambers. Awoken by the commotion outside, he jumped out of bed and rushed out semi-naked.

"What's going on," he roared.

"We want the king." A henchman of Migara's stepped forward and threatening the giant with his spear.

"Over my dead body," Nila growled, picked him up and tossed him aside.

"Attack him!" Migara called out.

Though a giant of a man, there were too many of them. Like a swarm of gnats, they attacked him, striking blow upon blow. Soon the giant staggered, blood spurting from the punctures and gashes on his body. Flailing his arms, he refused to succumb. Then, Migara strode forward.

"Move out of the way," he shouted and thrust the curved blade of his sword deep into the giant's belly and twisted it up into his heart.

Nila grabbed the embedded blade and watched in disbelief while it sliced through his fingers as he slid to the floor.

A warped grin washed over Migara's face as he withdrew his sword, wiped it on the dying man's body, and led his mob into the king's bedchamber.

"What is this?" Dhatusena shouted. "How dare you barge into my chambers? Guards, arrest these men!"

They grabbed him and hoisting him upright. "You are king no longer," said one.

Migara approached with a wicked swagger. He brought his face close to the king's. His upper lip curled. His eyeballs bulged. The engorged jugular in his neck throbbed.

"You killed my mother, you son of a whore." His words flew out in a spray of spittle, like barbs from a demon's gob. Tiny bubbles of froth foamed at the corners of his mouth. "Take him to the dungeon and lock him up. I will secure the palace and be there shortly."

*****

A SMALL OIL LAMP FLICKERED IN THE CORNER OF THE DINGY CELL, throwing a ghoulish light across its captive's face as Migara entered the dungeon. With his hands clasped behind his back and his chest puffed out like a peacock, he paced back and forth. Then he stopped in front of the king.

"Where is the royal treasure?"

The king pursed his lips and said nothing.

"I said, where is the royal treasure?" Migara stooped and stood nose to nose with his prisoner and shrieked, "Where is the treasure?"

The king said nothing. Migara straightened himself up, adjusted his belt, and slammed the flat of his hand across the monarch's face, sending the old man's head wobbling backward.

The sentry standing guard gasped, and his mouth dropped open in horror. For who would dare strike a king?

"I will get it out of you sooner or later," Migara scoffed, gathered some sputum in his mouth and spat it at the king, and walked out.

Migara exited the dungeon muttering to himself. *I must have the royal treasure. I need the Senachatra—the white parasol and the Ekavali—the pearl chain of one string. I must have these to legitimize my rule—to be king. Damn it! I really don't want to be king. Where is the fun in being royal? I like my life as it is. But it's too late. I have no choice now. I must stick to my course.*

The moon hung in the clammy night sky like a luminous pearl, casting deep shadows across the courtyard. Migara paced back and forth. *Why am I fretting? I hold all the trump cards. All I need is the treasure. And then... there is another small matter I must attend to.*

He swallowed a string of profanities and rushed into the night.

19

As luck would have it, Migara had stationed his guards outside the palace walls. This may have been to safeguard its contents, the royal treasure in particular, which he believed was stored there. For the chamberlain and his lieutenant, who were still inside, it was fortunate. Using the cover of darkness, they sneaked out of their quarters.

"How unseemly of me. How crass." the chamberlain mumbled as he slide his large frame from shadow to shadow through the darkened palace compound. "Oh, this tension is killing me."

"*Shh.*"

They headed for a large bungalow wedged between the king's quarters and the harem walls. Pandu and his heirs had used this house for trysts with women of the harem. Since Dhatusena's reign, it was boarded-up and used as a storeroom. At the back was a tiny anteroom piled high with disused furniture. Only the chamberlain and his trusted lieutenant knew of its secret: a trapdoor to an underground tunnel out of the palace to a derelict house nearby, where Pandu had once kept a local mistress. The chamberlain had kept the passage operational, even though he had never been in it himself. Besides being claustrophobic, he could hardly squeeze his ample frame into its narrow entrance. Using this passage, the chamberlain's lieutenant carried an urgent message to the vizier, who was in a safe house outside the palace.

When the always dapper and distinguished vizier clambered out of the trapdoor, his white hair disheveled and covered in cobwebs and grime, the chamberlain bit his tongue to suppress a giggle.

They hurriedly discussed the situation and arranged a meeting with the queen. To add insult to injury, the stately vizier disguised himself as an old woman and slipped into the harem. Under normal circumstances, a man caught in the harem faced immediate execution. But these were extraordinary times.

"My apologies, my queen, for disturbing you at this late hour in these most awkward and unusual circumstances. But the news I bring is most urgent," the vizier began and outlined the situation. The queen listened without comment.

"Then I will await your advice. I know you will do everything in your power to..." With a sad polite smile, she let her voice drift into the darkness.

AT THIS TIME, NO ONE, not the vizier nor the chamberlain, nor anyone else deemed it necessary to contact Kasyapa. It hadn't even crossed their minds to keep him abreast of developments. He was not in the line of command or succession. On matters such as these, he was an outsider—a nobody.

20

The loud banging awoke the doorman. Sleepy-eyed, he peered through a crack in the gate.

"Who is it?"

"Open up!"

"Who is it, I ask?"

"The senapati of the king, you imbecile," came a sharp retort.

"The senapati," the gateman mumbled and pushed open the gate, with a slow shuffling gait.

Migara rushed in, posted guards around the premises, and headed straight for Kasyapa's quarters. "Kasyapa, wake up. I have captured the king. You are under house arrest."

"What?" Kasyapa asked, sitting up in bed.

"I've arrested the old bastard. He will pay for his crime."

"What old bastard? What crime?" Kasyapa said, rubbing the sleep away from his eyes.

Migara squatted in front of Kasyapa and glared.

"For killing my mother, you dimwit. Don't you know the old fool killed my mother?" He spat his words like a cobra's venom.

Yes, Kasyapa had heard the news. In his view, the punishment was cruel and foolish, but he had kept his opinions to himself.

"Burning my mother! Burning her like a common criminal." Tears flooded Migara's eyes and flowed down his cheeks like a torrent. "How would you feel if they burned your dearest mother? Oh yes, you never had one, so you wouldn't know, would you?"

The light of a small oil lamp cast a sinister pallor over their faces. Migara leaned towards Kasyapa and squinted his eyes into wicked slivers, the veins of his neck bulged and pulsated erratically.

"The king will die. And you will die if you oppose me. The whole damn family will die. Anyone who opposes me will die. Now listen to me very carefully. Your life depends on it," he said, wagging a bony finger in Kasyapa's face. "Your choice is clear, *Prince* Kasyapa." He dragged the words mockingly. "Work with me, or I will exterminate you—quash you like an ant. I will be king soon. Think what I can do for you," he added with melodramatic flair, stood up, and vanished from the room as quickly as he had entered.

KASYAPA CLIMBED OUT OF BED, threw open the windows, and sat on a stool next to one of them. Holding his head in his hands, he gazed out of the window as moonbeams cast threatening shadows on the floor in front of him. A flurry of half-thoughts swirled in his head. *Why did Migara confide these things to me? Migara is dangerous. No one will dare challenge him.* Kasyapa sat alone and wished for some inspiration, a plan of action, to spring to mind. But nothing of the sort was forthcoming. His mind remained numbly empty.

HARDLY TWO HOURS HAD PASSED when Migara burst in once again. He found Kasyapa stooped over on his stool, his head in his hands.

He kicked the stool's leg hard. "Wake up."

Kasyapa straightened up.

"Do you know where the royal treasure is hidden?"

"No."

"You know he is keeping it for Moggallana."

"Well, Moggallana is the legitimate heir."

"That pissant. You and I both know Moggallana is an idiot. He is a dimwit with buck teeth like a devil. He is not fit to rule. I am more fit to rule than him." Migara paused as if contemplating his last utterance and lent towards Kasyapa. "Did your fat-assed friend tell you where the treasure is hidden?"

"Why would he tell me? As you often point out, I am only an irrelevant lowly half-caste outsider."

"True. True. Why would he tell you?"

"So why haven't you killed me yet?"

"Because you aren't a threat to me. I can dispense of you any time I choose. Besides, I may have use for you."

"What use?"

"I might need a vizier when I make myself the king. You will make a fine vizier. I mean, who else could I turn to?" Migara fashioned his proposition with consummate finesse, making it seem as though his offer was perfectly natural and credible. "You have some excellent traits, even-tempered, intelligent, and well-educated."

"You are presumptuous," Kasyapa replied, his face growing hot. But sensing an advantage, he willed the anger out of his voice. "You assume I will accept."

"Dear, dear Kasyapa. You have no choice. Besides, for a person of your position in society, it would be a plum job indeed. Surely, you wouldn't refuse," he added with a taut honey-coated smile.

"So, what of the king?" Kasyapa asked, uncomfortable with where the conversion was going.

"That old bastard will die," Migara spat out his words.

Kasyapa cringed. It was pointless antagonizing this psychopath. He weighed his options. *I could grab Migara by the throat and kill him. Surely, even if I were to succeed, the guards posted outside would immediately lop off my head. What good would that do me? Regardless of whether I go along with Migara's scheme or not, the king would undeniably die. There was no doubt about that. Migara is hellbent on revenge and would settle for nothing less. However, maybe with my cooperation, Migara could be managed. I could save myself, Moggallana, and possibly countless others. Damn Migara! Curse him! What am I to do?*

Migara butted in. "The choice is yours. You are powerless. I offer you power and authority. Let's face it Kasyapa, in all honesty, I think you will make an exceptional vizier."

Playing on Kasyapa's insecurities and grievances, he continued. "You know, many people think you have been wrongly treated," he said. Seeing little reaction from Kasyapa, he added, "Damn it, Kasyapa. I am making an offer you can't refuse."

"What about my father?"

"He is a dead man."

Kasyapa continued to wrestle with his thoughts.

Can I save my father? Do I want to save my father, a man who ignored me all my life? Morally yes, but a part of me isn't so sure. Can I save my father if I became vizier? No. Migara would not allow this. Can I save my father if I murdered Migara? Maybe but Migara's guards would kill me. The sad truth is my father is doomed.

Kasyapa looked up, his emotions raw in his voice and eyes. "When do you intend to...slay my father?" The words just tumbled out of his mouth, unrehearsed, and unsolicited.

"After he has revealed the hiding place of the royal treasure." Migara snorted, spun around, and marched out, confident he had Kasyapa in the palm of his hand.

At that very moment, in that very instance, as Kasyapa eyed Migara leave, a strange warming sensation overwhelmed him. It was as though he was voiding himself of the years of abuse he had endured from this man. He no longer feared Migara. Migara had lost his sting.

DRESSED IN HIS FULL MILITARY REGALIA, MIGARA SLIPPED INTO THE DUNGEON. He paced back and forth in front of his captive, stomping his feet and whirling around on reaching each end of the small corridor.

"Kasyapa demands the treasure," Migara's voice dripped with contempt. Yes, this was his plan. He would use the hapless Kasyapa as his pawn.

"Kasyapa?" the king mouthed wordlessly.

"Yes, your bastard son, you fool. He is behind this."

The king reflected on his predicament. This situation was of his own making. Not only had he recklessly executed Migara's mother, he had not foreseen Migara's response. This had indeed been a fatal mistake. But he didn't believe Migara. True, he had been unfair and distant from his first-born. But he did not think his son, Kasyapa, openly coveted his throne.

"You keep your treasure for Moggallana, do you? That little pissant can't even pee straight," Migara mocked, cupping his hands over his genitals, pretending to shower urine on the king.

Slowly, Dhatusena realized there was no one to challenge the senapati, and there was no one to blame for this but himself. He had appointed Migara. He had alienated the nobles. He had sidelined Kasyapa. Now, there was no one to save him. This was indeed the end. He resolved to leave this life with dignity.

"If you let me go to the Kala Wewa, and meet the great Thera Mahanama there, you shall learn of my treasure," Dhatusena replied.

"Now we are getting somewhere," Migara snapped, rubbing his hands with satisfaction, and rushed out to make the necessary arrangements.

*****

AT DAWN, A DILAPIDATED CART harnessed to two emaciated bullocks drew up at the dungeon gates. In the driver's seat was a scrawny one-eyed man with clump of unkempt grey hair—the public undertaker. Migara's choice had been deliberate. He had every intention of amplifying the king's humiliation and projecting his power.

Dhatusena was bundled aboard. Then, the dead man's cart trundled through the city, hobbling from side to side on account of a broken axle. The once-mighty monarch stood tethered to the side of the cart. Stripped of his regalia, he appeared before his subjects—a bedraggled old man—a mere mortal. They watched in sullen silence as he passed them by. Their silence was palpable. Dhatusena had accomplished much, but it had been at a great cost to them, his people. He had lost their love.

A bystander whispered to another, "Thus, one's good fortune is as fleeting as lightning, is it not?"

"Yes. How then can a sensible man be intoxicated by it?" the other replied.

The cart exited the city and lumbered westward toward Kala Wewa, some twenty-five miles away.

Migara was so confident of his position and so greedy for the royal treasure, he hadn't thought it necessary to round up and incarcerate the king's ministers and associates. He had left a contingent of troops with secret instructions and accompanied the deposed monarch himself on the pretext of protecting him. But actually, he wanted to make sure no one else laid hands on the treasure.

*****

AT ABOUT THE SAME TIME the dead man's cart pulled up outside the dungeon gates, Kasyapa stood at his bedroom window. He rubbed his stubbled chin and slowly twirled the little copper ring on his finger. He stepped outside his bedchamber and shook Daya awake.

"There are guards at the front and back doors. Sneak out through a window and fetch Ayah. Be discreet. This is important. Are my instructions clear?"

"Yes, Master."

Ayah appeared at a widow soon after, still in her nightwear and with her stringy white hair hanging in limp disarray.

"Ayah, have you heard the news?"

"Yes, Master Kasyapa."

"I need you to talk to the cook. No one will suspect her. Tell her to pretend she is going to the market. Ask her to contact the chamberlain or Nila and find out what is going on."

Ayah nodded and disappeared into the night.

Kasyapa wandered around his room,aimlessly and peered out of the window once more. It was almost daybreak. A listless mist drifted over the slumbering city. Somewhere, a cock crowed, a dog yipped. He observed the cook hobbling across the paved courtyard to the front gate. The guards stopped her and searched her wicker shopping basket. They waved her through.

Standing away from the window, hidden from the guards, he continued to peer out as the sun slowly rose behind the Great Dagoba. At first,
the giant building loomed like an enormous bubble silhouetted against
the sun. Then glowered pink and orange as the sun continued its journey skyward. Finally, it revealed its true color of gleaming white. It was
his father, Dhatusena, who had recently renovated the ancient dagoba
to its previous glory.

Kasyapa took in a deep breath and exhaled a long slow sigh.

21

There was bedlam that morning after the king had been taken away. The royal advisors, those who hadn't already fled, milled about the Great Audience Hall.

"What is the latest news?" a man asked.

"They have bolted the city gates. We are all prisoners here."

"That's not news. They did so late last night."

"Is the king alive?" another asked in a high-pitched whine.

"Yes, they are taking him to Kala Wewa in the dead man's cart."

"Oh, what humiliation."

Someone cleared his throat and interjected, "I heard from reliable sources that Kasyapa had a hand in it."

"Why would Kasyapa do that? He has no quarrel with the king."

"Ah, yes. But secretly, he harbored notions of royal grandeur despite his lowly birth."

"Kasyapa, that scoundrel, ordered the king's execution. His exact words were 'slay the king'," another slobbered.

"The senapati has gone to carry it out," a voice from the back added.

No one dared mention the real culprit. They were certain his spies were among them.

THE VIZIER AND CHAMBERLAIN HUDDLED in the shadows, out of earshot of the milling throng.

"Listen to their rampant speculation," the vizier said in a low voice.

"Oh, this is terrible. Just terrible," the chamberlain squealed while jiggling in place.

The vizier cocked a brow and observed his hapless companion. He wasn't sure if the chamberlain was fidgeting or trembling—perhaps both. They had worked together for a long time. The vizier found the chamberlain's idiosyncrasies amusing but trusted the man. He was competent and loyal to his king.

"Surely these men will rise up and support our king?" the chamberlain continued, edging closer to the vizier.

"See for yourself, Chamberlain. I see only a frightened blabbering multitude, I am afraid."

"But he is the king."

"Yes, but he has little backing among the nobility and people. He has alienated them even further with that terrible act against his sister."

"Such a regrettable incident." The chamberlain grimaced, cast his eyes about, and drew closer to the vizier. "Much as I despised that dreadful woman, I did not condone her cruel punishment. And while I loathe Migara even more, I understand his reaction to her murder."

"Yes. Unfortunate indeed."

"But the land is prosperous."

"True, Chamberlain, true. But who remembers the twenty-four years of plundering and neglect that preceded this monarch's rule?"

"But our king is upright. His personal life is virtually monastic. He eats the simplest foods and sleeps on a hard mattress. He even has little interest in his harem."

"Yes, that's true. But do the people know that? Do they care?"

"Are you telling me our king is unpopular?" The chamberlain's eyes widening in alarm.

"See for yourself, Chamberlain. Do you hear voices raised in support of our king? Do you see forces mustering for his rescue?"

"No. But what about his good works? The eradication of the dreaded mosquito disease, the irrigation projects, the viharas, the temples?" the chamberlain protested.

The vizier mulled over the chamberlain's question, for he wasn't a man who spoke in haste. "The fraternities support him."

"Of course, they do, because of his generosity toward them. They have done well by him," the chamberlain replied, flushing with indignation.

The vizier raised an arched eyebrow once more, noting the chamberlain was indeed more perceptive and outspoken than he may have given him credit for.

"How about the people?" the chamberlain continued, even though he knew the answer. His question was a rhetorical one, not necessarily requiring a response.

"They are indifferent."

"What a sad state of affairs."

"Yes, indeed."

"But Vizier, you were part of the king's council?"

"I do the king's bidding, my dear Chamberlain. I may advise. I may warn. But my duty is to carry out the king's wishes."

"Is there any hope?"

"I fear there is none."

"Can't you muster support among the nobles and the people?"

"I have made inquiries. There is no one willing to support him."

"So, the king is lost?"

The vizier didn't respond.

"Such a sad state of affairs." The chamberlain's eyes swam in tears.

"Migara's men are searching for the royal treasure." The vizier continued in a subdued tone.

"Yes, I heard."

"Moggallana is the appointed heir."

"Yes."

"Poor boy, that Moggallana."

"Yes, and young too."

"And lacking in experience."

"You know he is dimwitted," the chamberlain whispered under his breath, his gaze darting about for fear his brutal frankness could fall on eavesdropping ears.

"A great disappointment to his father."

"Nothing like his brother, Kasyapa."

"Keep your voice down, dear Chamberlain. Be careful with your words."

"But, it is true."

"Kasyapa is a bastard of humble birth. He is not of royal blood."

"Yes, yes. Not all royal blood. But half so."

"Yes."

"Poor Kasyapa. Such a capable man. And likable too."

The vizier weighed the chamberlain's statement before replying. "It is true. By all accounts, Kasyapa is competent and well-liked."

"Migara is of lesser blood than Kasyapa."

"Yes, but his forefathers on both sides were of a royal line. Besides, it would seem he has the upper hand."

They both fell silent, each considering the implications of Migara's as their king.

The vizier spoke first. "If the royal treasure falls into Migara's hands, he will, no doubt, declare himself king."

The chamberlain cast an anxious glance, got closer to the vizier, and lowered his voice to a barely audible whisper, "God forbid that."

"Yes, the evil man."

"What can we do?" The chamberlain sniffled.

"Migara lacks support among the populace, and the nobles fear him even more than our king. He will have difficulty gathering support."

"Only his goons follow him without question."

"Yes. And he commands the army," the vizier added dryly.

"Kasyapa is popular with the people?"

"Yes."

There was a long pause. Neither man spoke nor looked at each other, fearful one may betray the other. Beads of sweat glistened on the chamberlain's forehead. He pulled out his embroidered silk handkerchief and dabbed his forehead.

"What will become of us?" The chamberlain rolled his eyes and curled his handkerchief around his index finger.

"I don't know. I fear we may be put to death—killed at the stake. I am ready. I have already sent my family away to safety in the south."

"Smart move," the chamberlain said, bobbing his head. A shiver ran down his spine as he pictured his plump frame impaled on the stake.

"Maybe they will burn us alive."

The chamberlain shuddered, profusely dabbing his brow with his damp handkerchief.

"I am surprised they haven't come for you yet."

The chamberlain hesitated for a long time. "I know."

"According to tradition, whoever is in possession of the royal treasure, notably the white parasol and the chain with one string of pearls, is king."

The chamberlain fell silent. He knotted and unknotted his beautiful silk handkerchief. Realizing what he was doing and hoping the vizier hadn't noticed, he quickly unknotted it and folded it with great care and held it in his hand. It was his favorite, the one Kasyapa had given him.

"I know where the royal treasure is hidden," he said, in a conspiratorial whisper.

"I assumed you might."

"I can't take much more of this tension. It will surely kill me."

"I know."

"What do you think, Vizier?" The chamberlain's eyes implored the vizier's for guidance as he pulled out his handkerchief and knotted it around his finger once again.

"My loyalty is to the king, my dear Chamberlain. Whosoever possesses the royal treasure is king. I will serve my king," vizier said in a muted undertone and disappeared into the throng. The chamberlain looked around anxiously and hurried away.

*****

LATER THAT AFTERNOON, MIGARA'S MEN RANSACKED the king's quarters in search of the royal treasure. They took the chamberlain away. They stripped him naked and stuffed the ends of his beautiful silk handkerchief, the one that Kasyapa had given him, into his nostrils; making the big man gasp for breath. They kicked his ample belly and prodded him with their spears. With each indignation, his resolve grew stronger. He had nothing to lose. He had no family. He had served his king faithfully.

Convinced he had nothing to reveal, his captors laughed and joked as they heaved him up to the top of the stake they had built for him and impaled him through his rectum. They didn't need to push hard. His weight assisted them in their dastardly deed. Pinned like a fly, he wriggled as the skewer slipped through his body. A bloodcurdling scream escaped his lips as the spike pierced his intestines. He breathed his last before it exited through his mouth. They left him there, his eyes staring emptily at the heavens, his ample belly, now collapsed, drooping grotesquely over his genitals.

22

Mahanama stood by the banks of the mighty Kala Wewa, near the beautiful temple Dhatusena had built for him. His heart ached as he watched his nephew—his protégé—his king, tethered like an animal and dragged before him in chains. The Thera raised his hand high into the air. The soldiers stopped, bowed to the holy man, and withdrew ten paces or so away.

"Beautiful, isn't it, this Kala Wewa?"

"Yes, indeed, my king, the largest reservoir ever built."

A measured smile crossed the king's lips. "I am most proud of it, for it supplies water to thousands of fields and hundreds of villages around here."

"True. The people benefit."

The king studied his mentor's face and looked away.

It was a hot, cloudless day. The desiccated landscape drooped from the prolonged drought afflicting the nation. A cooling breeze wafted from the waters of the reservoir, as the monk and the king sat under a shady acacia tree. As he had always done, the king sat at the thera's feet.

"What misfortune is this that has befallen me?"

The Thera's eyes fell upon Dhatusena. No longer did he see the fire and passion that had once driven this man. Instead, here was a mere shell of a man with life snuffed from his eyes. Mahanama reached out and touched the king. First on his right shoulder and then on his left.

"Everything goes away; does it not? Eventually, everything ends?"

"Yes, my king. What is born will die. What is gathered will be dispersed. What is accumulated will be exhausted. What is built up will collapse. And what is high will be brought low. These are the conditions impermanence."

"Yes. This is so."

"Yet some crave for life's permanence."

"I know. But this is folly."

"Everything that has a beginning has an ending, my king. Make your peace with that, and all will be well."

Dhatusena nodded and walked down the embankment into the waters of the Kala Wewa. There, he immersed himself three times.

Emerging from the water, he pointed to his mentor, and then with a grand sweeping gesture to the shimmering expanse of water before him.

"This here, my friends, is all the treasure I possess."

His guards looked at each other in dismay. They grabbed him and hauled him away.

On hearing the news, Migara was livid.

"I have been duped! This wily bastard, the murderer of my mother, he takes me for a fool. So, he believes this water is his treasure, does he? Then let that son of a bitch live with it in the afterlife. Build him a tomb there, on the bund of his beloved Kala Wewa. Bury him facing east so he can awake each morning to the sight of his treasure. Bury him at a depth where its waters touch his chest, since it is so dear to his heart. Let him rot from his feet up."

Migara had chosen his method with cunning. He would not murder the king. Instead, he would resort to the ancient stratagem of consequential death. He would entomb Dhatusena alive—unslain. The fact that he would eventually expire was inconsequential, for he died of his own accord. He was not murdered. A finer point, no doubt, but a legalistic one of plausible denial.

They chose a location some distance from where the king and his mentor had meditated earlier, as this would position the tomb facing east as Migara had demanded. The soldiers dug a niche into the side of the embankment. It was only a yard wide and about two yards high, and on Migara's insistence, it was about one yard below the waterline.

"Let him rot slowly," he had said.

Dhatusena was dragged down the embankment, stripped naked and affixed to the rear wall. As his earthen mausoleum rose around him, the king remained serene. It was as though he was happy to depart his life and enter the afterworld. He blocked out the jeers and insults hurled at him and reflected on his past as it slowly unfurled before him.

His uncaring mother, his overbearing father, being abandoned by his family, life as a young monk in the wilderness—the campaign. He recollected his great works, the gleaming dagobas and their monasteries, the glistening lakes throughout the land. Peace. Prosperity. Then, he remembered his happiest time. The rock by a babbling stream. The crystal blue sky. The scent of forest jasmine. A little copper ring. A soft, gentle voice. The radiant smile of the woman he loved.

He returned the smile.

"Uppalavanna."

SUDDENLY, A SQUALLING WIND picked up and raced across the waters of the Kala Wewa and over its parched embankments, whipping up a whirlwind of dust and debris into the air. Menacing clouds sped across the sun, turning day into night. Raindrops fell intermittently at first, large as marbles, pitting the parched earth where they fell. The sky rumbled. Shafts of lightning cleaved the heavens, and the earth shuddered. Migara's men ran for cover as a howling wind tore through their camp, uprooting trees and dislodging tents and huts. It wasn't long before the rains arrived, pelleting down like millions of arrowheads.

Migara intended to return to the capital that same night, but his troops were unnerved. They feared it was a bad omen. They refused to depart until the thunderstorm cleared. In his leaky tent, Migara ranted and raved through the night.

It rained all night. Rivulets of water rushed into the dried-up stream beds and the channels Dhatusena had built and into the waters of the mighty Kala Wewa. Overnight, its waters rose, churning, heaving, and thrashing up against its embankments. By morning, the water level had risen above Dhatusena's tomb. The land had eroded too, washing away all traces of the king's last resting place. The monsoon rains had arrived with a vengeance. The drought had broken.

*****

A LONE RIDER GALLOPED THROUGH THE NIGHT. He had escaped the deluge and arrived at the city before midnight. Reaching the palace, he banged on the gates and announced himself. He was Silakala, the senapati's aid, and known to the sentinels. After an animated squabble, he gained entry and headed straight for the harem. A burly harem guard blocked his way, thrusting his halberd menacingly, and threatening death if he did not leave. A bystander suggested he speak to one of the remaining palace officials, who interrogated him, blindfolded him, and took him away.

The vizier and the chamberlain's lieutenant listened glumly to Silakala's story. He was of the Lambakanna clan, a kinsman of the queen. The news was grim. The king was dead.

The vizier sneaked back into the harem. "My queen, I bring you bad tidings," he began, in a faltering voice. "Our king is dead."

The queen lifted her eyes brim full of tears. "Who did it, Vizier?"

"The senapati carried it out, my queen."

She stood up, walked to an open window, and gazed into the emptiness of the night. "Who will rule, Vizier?"

"I do not know, my queen. I have not been able to galvanize support for our cause."

"I will," Moggallana shouted, springing out of nowhere.

Startled by the interruption, the queen turned and returned to her seat.

"What do you suggest, Vizier?" She blinked, and her pooled-up tears slowly slid down her cheeks and fell on her lap.

"At this moment, my primary concern is for the safety of the royal family. In this place, we are under the control of the senapati. I hear from reliable sources that he intends to usurp the throne."

"That man." The queen's voice quivered.

"Yes, my queen... We must hurry. We must spirit you away to safety at once."

"Why can't I be king? I am the crown prince. We can fight the senapati."

"With what, my prince?"

"An army, of course."

"Where is your army, my prince?"

"I will assemble one and fight the senapati."

The vizier drew a long breath and glanced at the queen.

"What support do we have, Vizier?"

"Very little, my queen. Very little indeed." The vizier's usually calm upper-class voice sounded hollow, like an echo in a canyon.

By the flicker of the faint lamplight, the queen searched the vizier's face and looked down at her hands.

"Was our king so despised?" she asked, raising her eyes once more.

The vizier shuffled uneasily on his feet. He did not drop his gaze as he would normally have done.

"As your humble servant, it is not my place, my queen, to comment on such matters."

The queen's eyes filled with tears once more. She nodded.

"I have the right to be king," Moggallana howled.

The queen raised her hand to silence him. "Your day will come, Moggallana. In time, in time, your day will come. For now, we must heed the vizier's advice."

"This is my kingdom," Moggallana wailed and stormed out.

"Do what you must, my trusted vizier," the queen said.

The vizier bowed and retreated from his audience with the queen.

THE QUEEN, MOGGALLANA AND SAKULA, escaped through the tunnel, to the safety of the Lambakanna clan stronghold in the hinterland.

Having spirited the royal family away, the chamberlain's lieutenant turned to the vizier. "Now what?"

"I do not know. I am sad to say good news is scarce these days. I fear the worst."

PART TWO

23

The killing began on the night Dhatusena died. Migara's men searched out the king's supporters, murdered them, pillaged their homes, and raped their women.

The residents of Kasyapa's compound huddled together in the courtyard. They heard the mayhem outside. They saw the flames licking the night sky, and the heat of this murderous night burned their nostrils with the sickening stench of death. Protected by their guards, they were safe.

Kasyapa watched for a while before retiring to his quarters. The cook had returned earlier with distressing news. Nila and the chamberlain were dead. The whereabouts of the vizier was unknown. There was no resistance whatsoever to Migara.

Soon after he had slipped into bed, there was a tap on the door. Bodur, the soldier who stood guard outside his quarters, slid into his room and shut the door behind him. He spoke in a whisper.

"Sir, you must save us," he said. At his trembling voice, Kasyapa glanced up to see the man's face, tears rolling down his cheeks. "It is only you who can save us."

"But, I am your prisoner. How can I do anything? There are guards everywhere. There is no one on the outside to support me," Kasyapa replied.

"I was given this note by my friend at the palace. It is for you."

Kasyapa took the note, held it close to the flickering light of a small oil lamp, and read it.

> *Rise up, Kasyapa. Redeem our kingdom. Govern as a righteous monarch. To you I entrust the sacred talismans of kingship. Your most loyal friend—The Chamberlain.*

Kasyapa sucked in his breath. His hand trembled as he held the note against the flame until it burned to a cinder. He exhaled slowly.

"You have friends, sir. You can arouse the masses. You are more popular with the people than you realize. I will help you escape. Please, sir, save your people from the tyranny befalling them."

Kasyapa walked to the window and watched the sky ablaze. He pursed his lips and tapped them with his index finger. *I will be the redeemer of the people—their protector from tyranny. The blame is Migara's. I must act.*

Kasyapa and Bodur set fire to the kitchen as a diversion. While the guards busied themselves with dousing the flames, they scaled the walls and escaped into the milling crowd outside.

As they scurried through the unruly, streets a teaching of the Great Master flashed through Kasyapa's mind. He wasn't sure why.

> *By oneself, evil is done; by oneself, one suffers; by oneself, evil*
> *is left undone; by oneself, one is purified. Purity and impurity*
> *belong to oneself; no one can purify another.*

KASYAPA TAPPED ON THE DOOR of a rundown building near the outer palace wall. It creaked open. It was pitch black inside. For a moment, he feared it was a trap to murder him. Then a voice in the darkness spoke.

"I have been waiting for you, sir," the man said.

"Who are you?"

"A friend, sir."

"A friend? Identify yourself."

"I am a messenger from the chamberlain. He is now dead. He entrusted me with a sacred duty. Trust me, sir."

Tears welled up in Kasyapa's eyes as he remembered the chamberlain to whom he owed so much. But he was running out of tears. He had to follow his destiny, at whatever cost.

"All right," he said. "What do you have in mind?"

"Come with me, sir. We must return to the palace," the stranger said in a hurried whisper.

"The palace? Who is going to let me into the palace? They will kill me first."

"Trust me, sir. Give me your hand."

Kasyapa stretched out his hand. The hand that took his was soft, no doubt the hands of an aristocrat. He, in turn, took hold of Bodur's hand. They followed each other in the dark. Their escort stopped. Kasyapa heard the sound of furniture dragged across the floor.

"We are going to the palace through a tunnel. Please climb down the ladder and wait for me while I reseal the trap door."

Kasyapa and Bodur groped their way down the dark, dank stairs. A tiny lamp illuminated a corridor that disappeared into the darkness. When the man appeared, Kasyapa scrutinized his face. "I know you."

"Yes, sir, I am the chamberlain's lieutenant. Let us proceed. This tunnel leads straight into the palace."

When they exited, Kasyapa had no idea where he was. They sat in the dark and the lieutenant started in a flat, faltering voice. "Will you be our king, sir?"

Kasyapa's eyes widened as a rush of adrenaline exploded through his veins. The answer sprung instantly from his lips. "Yes."

"The king is dead. Long live the king," the chamberlain's lieutenant declared.

"Long live our king," Bodur added.

A cold shiver ran down Kasyapa's spine. The emotions inside him were so tumultuous he wanted to vomit. Fortunately, he hadn't eaten that night.

Leaving him to his thoughts, the lieutenant disappeared and returned with a small box. Kasyapa didn't think to ask him what it contained.

"We must act quickly, sir. There is no time to lose," the lieutenant urged, dragging Kasyapa away from his self-indulgence.

"Yes, yes," Kasyapa mumbled, dazed by the events unfolding around him. He needed to take control, but he didn't know where to start. He was ill-prepared for such a monumental task.

There was a muffled knock on the door. The lieutenant opened it.

An old woman, shabbily dressed, entered and stood just inside the doorway. Kasyapa couldn't make out her face.

Then the lieutenant fetched his little box, reached into it, and retrieved something. Kasyapa couldn't see what it was. The lieutenant walked behind Kasyapa and placed it around his neck. It was the *Ekavali*, the pearl chain of one string.

Immediately, the old woman's demeanor changed. She shuffled about and prostrated herself before him.

"My king." The voice was familiar and decidedly masculine.

"Who are you?" Kasyapa asked.

The "woman" raised her chin and dropped her shawl.

"Vizier! Am I glad to see you."

But the vizier's response was humorless. He didn't speak at all.

"Come, Vizier, this place is too small for formalities. Sit with me. We must save our kingdom. We have much work to do."

The vizier nodded and sat in front of Kasyapa's feet.

"Gentleman, we are in a vulnerable position and must consolidate our grip on power before the senapati returns. For the moment, he has every advantage, but I am confident we can thwart him. To do so, I need your help and guidance."

As the vizier was the most senior person there, the others remained close-mouthed in deference to him.

"Vizier, what shall we do?" Kasyapa asked.

"We must muster support around you and secure the treasury, my king." His voice was calm and steady.

"Why the treasury?"

"Without the treasury, Migara cannot pay his troops," the vizier replied with a wry smirk.

Bodur spoke up, "Sir, the commander of the city barracks is my uncle. The troops will serve their king."

"Yes, you are right, Bodur. I remember the line of command. The army takes their orders from the senapati and in his absence, they take their orders from the king. Good thinking. Yes, let's do that."

"We must send messages to the nobles soliciting their support, even those who didn't support your father," the vizier said.

"Will they support me?"

"We must convince them."

"Very well then, Vizier, I will leave that to you."

"Sir, what about the masses? The guilds will support you," Bodur said.

"Yes. Let's get as many people as possible out onto the streets."

"I will arrange the proclamation ceremony."

"Good idea, Chamberlain," Kasyapa replied with a grin.

"Chamberlain?"

"Yes, I wish for you to serve me as my chamberlain." Turning back to the pressing affairs at hand, Kasyapa continued, "And gentlemen, what of the royal family?"

"They are safe, my king," the vizier replied.

"No doubt they have been kept advised of developments?"

"Yes, my king."

"What does the queen wish?"

"She has asked for nothing, my king."

"And my little brother, Moggallana?"

The vizier hesitated, then remembered his duty was to his king. "He is young, inexperienced, and easily swayed, my king. He wishes to raise an army."

"What are his chances of doing so, Vizier?"

"Not much chance, my king."

"But the Lambakanna are a powerful clan, are they not?"

"Yes, my king, but they are not fools. They do not put their trust in young Moggallana."

"Poor Moggallana."

"Yes, my king."

"The royal family must come to no harm."

The vizier and chamberlain nodded.

AN UNEASY SILENCE HAD DESCENDED over the city after the night's killing. Just before daybreak, a contingent of troops burst out of city barracks and surrounded the palace. The guards placed there by Migara looked at each other in bewilderment. They guarded the palace, and now the troops guarded them. It was a stalemate.

Soon the city awoke to the sound of heralding drummers, and a proclamation was read out aloud.

"Assemble ye all at the king's palace at noon."

At the appointed time, the palace gates swung open. The gathered multitude hushed. A minute passed, then two, then five. The throng murmured and grew restless. Suddenly a contingent of guards in the livery of the royal household appeared, led by Bodur. The crowd hushed.

Kasyapa strode forward, dressed in a simple white full-length dhoti and a white blouse, the Senachatra—the white parasol of dominion—held above his head. He wore the pearl chain of one string around his neck. He spotted Abaya among the nobles. He glimpsed Agbo with the artisans and temple builders. He noted the troops and the multitude before him.

The people had rallied around him, the son of a village girl and a brave warrior who had forsaken the woman he loved to become a king.

The shout went out, "Long live our king."

THE REJOICING WAS SHORT-LIVED. Kasyapa grew apprehensive as the crowd drew apart before him.

Migara approached, sitting tall on his steed, his bodyguards quick-marched beside him. As he drew closer, Kasyapa's stomach churned. His guards became restive. The senapati continued down the boulevard. There was a disturbance at the rear. A large body of troops loyal to Kasyapa materialized and surrounded Migara's contingent. The crowd held its breath. Migara rode forward, unflustered. Ten yards from Kasyapa, he dismounted and strode toward him, stopping a few feet away.

Kasyapa looked at him steely-eyed. "See the multitude, Senapati. Behold my people."

"My king. My lord," Migara declared and prostrated himself before Kasyapa.

The crowd roared and fell to their knees once more.

Tears welled up in Kasyapa's eyes, and he cast them skyward. He thanked the chamberlain for his deliverance. Then he thanked Nila, whose advice he had followed. He had underplayed his hand and trounced his adversary.

24

That same day, Kasyapa convened a meeting with the vizier and the new chamberlain.

"There is no time to waste. What about bringing those responsible for the recent violence to justice?"

There was a short pause, then the vizier spoke, "Unfortunately, this is not the first time this has happened. In the past, incoming monarchs often eliminated his rivals."

"Yes. Our late king carried out such an extermination. He also confiscated property and punished many nobles for their support of the usurper Pandu and his descendants."

The vizier glared at the chamberlain. After all, he had served the previous king and implemented his policies.

"Chamberlain, it is wise to hold your tongue. It is often most sensible to remain silent. A loose-tongued fool cannot give informed counsel. I will attribute your careless oversight to the exuberance of youthful inexperience."

The chamberlain, stung by the vizier's rebuke, pulled his head into his shoulders and lowered his eyes. He had been imprudent.

The vizier cleared his throat and turned to Kasyapa.

"In this instance, you, my king, did not instigate any pogrom. The men responsible for the bloodbath are the senapati's. However, there is widespread speculation you were responsible for the purges, and I am afraid to say, even for the death of the former king himself."

"But I didn't order it. I had nothing to do with any of it."

"It is my duty to bring to light what is perceived, my king."

"Yes, Vizier, I understand."

"If we prosecute them, we need to bring their commander to justice too. This commander is Senapati Migara. Are we to say these looters—these ruffians—these murderers acted without orders? What about the death of the king? We know the senapati carried it out. But he claims it was on your instructions."

"But I didn't. How could I? I was a prisoner."

"Unfortunately, it would seem to many you had the most to gain from the death of the former king. They say, 'Is it not obvious? He sits on the throne of our dead monarch.'"

Kasyapa hunched in his seat and grasped his head in his hands. The chamberlain glanced at him sympathetically. "Chamberlain, your thoughts?" Kasyapa said, without raising his head.

Given his previous misstep, the chamberlain was wary of causing further offense and remained silent.

Kasyapa sat up and scowled. "Chamberlain, I rely on my advisors for their assessments to make decisions for the wellbeing of this kingdom. Never be frightened, when asked, to advise your king."

"My king, you know the truth in your heart. However, the truth is not what is in question here. Try as we may, no amount of telling and retelling this truth will erase the perception."

Kasyapa winced. "Then am I tarred for life with a tawdry brush, one of patricide—*Anantarika-karma,* the murderer of my father?"

"I guess, from a political standpoint, the senapati did you a favor. He eliminated opposition to your rule. Hence, Prince Moggallana's inability to muster support," the chamberlain added as a well-intended consolation.

"Then, our first order of business must be to deal with Senapati Migara."

The vizier and chamberlain exchanged anxious glances.

Kasyapa continued, "Migara controls the army and will not relinquish it readily. Nor do I believe we have the clout to oust him. We don't know who will support us if we move against him."

"We mustn't be rash." The vizier agreed.

"There is good reason to believe any attempt to relieve him of his position could result in a bloodbath. Am I correct?"

His advisors concurred.

"Then we have little choice but to work with him. Vizier, what do you think?"

"We are compelled to work with him, my king."

"Let's call him in, then. And Vizier, make sure he comes alone and unarmed."

The vizier exited the chamber, gave instructions to the guards, and returned.

"Now, what other pressing matters do we have to attend to?"

"There is the question of your marriage, my King."

"Marriage?"

"Yes, my king, marriage."

"Why so?"

"Because we need to have a consecration ceremony as soon as possible to eliminate any questions of legitimacy. To do so, you must have a queen-wife."

Kasyapa frowned. He was now king, but this question of legitimacy still dogged him.

"Are there any nobles willing to give their daughter to this wretched king?" Kasyapa asked, half in jest.

*****

MIGARA PACED NERVOUSLY OUTSIDE. His palms grew clammy. A nagging voice in the back of his head screamed of his impending doom. *Why had Kasyapa sent armed guards to fetch me when a messenger would have sufficed? I am unarmed and unguarded here. They could murder me. Was I a fool to have come?* His eyes darted about, surveying his surroundings. The day had become uncomfortably hot and balmy.

When he was finally ushered in, Kasyapa greeted him from the bejeweled throne, flanked by the vizier and the chamberlain.

"Greetings Senapati." Kasyapa fixed his eyes on Migara.

"Ah... Are you well, my king?" Migara bowed respectfully.

"Yes." And with an abrupt change in tone and subject, Kasyapa got straight to the point.

"No doubt, Senapati, you are wondering why I have called you here." Kasyapa paused and eyed him. "I have given the present situation much consideration. It is my conclusion the decision I have taken is in the best interests of our kingdom."

Migara's heart thudded in his chest. Would he be executed? He was defenseless here, and he had little influence with the guards around Kasyapa. After all, they defected from his army. But he was confident the rest of the military would stick with him. He had made sure of that. He waited.

Kasyapa secretly twirled the little ring on his finger. "Your terms are these. You will remain my senapati with the same rights and privileges you enjoyed before." Kasyapa paused and waited for his words to sink in. "You are to divorce my sister, and by the grace of this king, as a token of goodwill, you may retain her dowry as settlement. You will swear allegiance to me, your king, and carry out my commands diligently." Kasyapa stared at Migara steely-eyed. "Are you agreeable to this, Senapati?"

"Yes. You have my allegiance, my king."

Kasyapa made a pact with the devil, and he knew it. Having declared his edict, Kasyapa dismissed Migara with a sweep of his hand. He found himself staring at Migara's ass as he departed. His walk always made Kasyapa chuckle. Maybe it was his way of compensating for the inner turmoil Migara had stirred in him for all those years.

Migara walked away from the meeting pleased. *What do I care? As long as I enjoy my powers and privileges, good riddance to her. I am a wealthy man on account of the dowry settlement. It is an outcome I can live with. As for Kasyapa, he outmaneuvered me. I will bide my time.*

The chamberlain let out a soft whistle. "Phew, that was easier than I expected. I don't understand the man. From all accounts, he still has the loyalty of the army. He could have challenged us. He could have become king."

"The man has no desire to reign. He only wishes to command," the vizier replied dryly.

"Yes, and to exact revenge," the chamberlain added.

*****

THE VIZIER CLEARED HIS THROAT as though he was sweeping aside residue from the previous meeting.

"In response to your previous question, my king."

"Which question?"

"On the subject of marriage."

"Yes, Vizier. What now?"

"With incentives, applied with discretion, I am certain we can arrange a most suitable marriage." The vizier waited for Kasyapa to instruct him to continue.

"How?"

"Many nobles are alienated, and also ambivalent towards you."

"Yes, I know."

"However, the prospect of wealth and privilege has a way of facilitating things," the vizier continued in his world-weary manner.

"Yes. Let us bring them back into the fold."

The vizier nodded.

"While on the subject of prospects," the chamberlain piped in, "may I suggest a fair lady from the house of Lambakanna?"

"Why so, Chamberlain?"

"They would be an excellent alliance. The Lambakannas are powerful and claim the noblest of blood. Their women are well educated, civil, and of course, attractive also."

"Are they not ambitious?"

"Yes, but what better way to keep their ambitions in check than to have one of theirs bear forth the future heir. May I add, the former queen and your friend Abaya are both of that clan."

"Well, Chamberlain, I am glad you are looking after all my interests," Kasyapa said with a chuckle. "What do you think, Vizier?"

"Yes. It is an excellent prospect. Let me make some inquiries."

The conversation moved on to matters of governance.

"Vizier, I am aware it is customary to allocate positions in government to members of the nobility. I have little empathy with them, present company excluded, of course. Many of them treated me with contempt. I would like, as much as is practicable, to appoint men according to their merit."

The vizier nodded. He would do as his king commanded. While he was a proud nobleman, he was a servant of the king.

THERE WAS ONE LAST ITEM of business he had to attend to. As the sun set, Kasyapa, the vizier, the chamberlain, and on Kasyapa's specific orders Migara, attended the cremations of the old chamberlain and Nila the Giant.

It was a sad and painful moment for Kasyapa as he lit their funeral pyres and watched the flames licking the night sky, ushering his dearest friends and protectors into the afterlife.

25

It was late. Kasyapa was tired. He hadn't eaten in almost two days.

"Now to return home and get some sleep." Kasyapa yawned.

"Where are you going, my king?"

"To my home."

The chamberlain looked at the vizier dumbfounded. The vizier remained noncommittal.

"But my king, I have the royal quarters ready for you."

"I do not wish to reside in my father's house."

"Vizier, say something," the chamberlain pleaded.

The vizier nodded and intervened. "My king, it is unwise."

"What do you mean, Vizier?"

"Are you not the king?"

"I am."

"The king must reside in the palace."

"Why?"

"Firstly, it is a convention. The king resides in the palace. Secondly, it's for your safety. There are still dangerous elements roaming the streets. The palace is the safest place in the city."

"It didn't protect my father."

"It was your father's choice not to take precautions," the vizier shot back with noticeable annoyance. "It is different now. We have over a hundred guards inside and out, with five hundred more on call from the city garrison."

"What about my old dwelling here in the palace, then?"

The chamberlain's eyebrows rose into a high arch. "But my king, it is so small...unworthy of a king."

"But it is suitable for me."

The chamberlain was incredulous. He rolled his eyes at the vizier, who shrugged.

"If you insist, I can have it ready in a few hours," the chamberlain bowed obediently.

"Good. Then that is where I will stay."

That evening, Kasyapa took a bath at the same bathing well he had used as a little boy. It left him feeling refreshed and purified. He slipped into the fresh clothes laid out for him and climbed into his old bed. He slept soundly until late into the following morning.

ON THE THIRD DAY OF KASYAPA'S RULE, the vizier approached him sullen faced.

"What's the matter, Vizier?"

"I haven't slept well, my king."

"Are you in ill health?"

"No, my king. May I speak with you in private?"

"Of course, let us walk in the garden."

Once they reached the gardens, the vizier spoke. "My king, my mind is not at rest."

Kasyapa stopped and searched the man's face. What he saw was the haggard man. The gleam had vanished from his eyes.

"It is time I retire. I am old now. It is best for me to go."

Kasyapa understood the vizier's predicament. He had been his father's chief minister, his trusted servant, and felt he had in some way been complicit in the former king's death—this lay heavy on his conscience.

"I humbly beg you, my king, to let me leave."

"I am aggrieved to see you go, my most trusted vizier."

"It is time, my king."

"But who could replace a brilliant statesman such as yourself, with so many years of experience?

The vizier remained silent, his head bowed, as they continued down the path.

"I understand your replacement will have to be an aristocrat, for I doubt there would be a commoner with the requisite skills?"

"Yes, my king."

Kasyapa kicked a stray pebble on the gravel path. "What about my school friend Abaya?"

"Excellent choice, my king. Well connected, sound temperament, and well educated."

"Let us ask him. Will you stay on and train him, my dear Vizier?"

The vizier nodded as they continued past carefully manicured gardens toward the lake. "Also, my king, I had word back from the Lambakannas on another matter."

"And what is that?"

"They are willing to provide one of their daughters in marriage."

"That is good news?"

"Yes, my king. They will be a great asset in thwarting the senapati."

"I see."

"My sources tell me that three key people argued your cause."

"Is that so?"

"Yes. The former queen, your sister, and your friend Abaya."

"Tell me, Vizier, I am perplexed. Why does the former queen support me?"

"Because she is wise, my king."

"Wise? Vizier?"

"I am of the view she understands your circumstances. I think she believes her son Moggallana is not yet suitable for the role of king."

"Was there any dissent?"

"Yes."

"Who?"

"Moggallana, my king. He is hot-headed and ill-advised. He has absconded with the former queen's jewels, and together with his cousin Silakala, they have fled to Jambudvipa to raise an army against you. Also, there was an incident."

"An incident?"

"Yes, my king. Thinking there would be a reward for them, Moggallana's cook and manservant attempted to assassinate him. They failed and were put to death."

"I see. As I have said before, I do not wish any harm to come to my brother."

"Yes, my king. It would be wise, however, to keep a close eye on him."

"I see. Do you remember Varahadeva and King Harishena? We could call upon them to keep an eye on my brother. Also, send them both generous gifts from me, in appreciation of their hospitality during my visit there some months ago."

"I will arrange this, my king."

They reached a large pond in the middle of the gardens. A fresh blue lotus bloomed alone in the waters below. They turned around and returned to the audience hall.

THREE DAYS LATER, while in audience with the vizier and the chamberlain, Kasyapa asked, "Have you spoken to Abaya about the position?"

"Yes, my king. He is agreeable."

"Excellent. How does it affect the marriage prospects?"

"I discussed this topic with him at length. I also took the liberty to sound out the former queen on the subject. I hope you don't mind me doing so."

"Of course not, Vizier."

"There may be some problems with perception. Vis-à-vis, it may appear as a tradeoff. Be assured, my king, nothing of the sort was discussed. The Lambakanna are proud and honorable men."

"I trust your word on that, Vizier."

"I have requested for Abaya to meet you tomorrow."

KASYAPA HAD GROWN FOND OF WALKING in the royal gardens and conducting most of his meetings there. The fresh air helped him think. However, he didn't like having his visitors prostrating themselves before him on the gritty gravel pathways, so he always greeted them in his audience hall first.

Abaya arrived at the appointed time.

"Dear Abaya," Kasyapa said, rising from his throne with outstretched arms.

"Yes, my king," Abaya replied and prostrated himself before Kasyapa as was expected.

"Rise, Abaya," Kasyapa chided, touching him on his shoulder. "How have you been? I saw you at the ceremony the other day. Thank you for attending."

"You are an honorable man, my king."

"And you, Abaya, are a true friend."

Kasyapa escorted Abaya into the royal gardens and, as they walked, Kasyapa outlined what he had observed while traveling throughout the country in the past few years. Abaya listened. As usual, he said little.

"Abaya, I want to do things differently. Many of my plans will be controversial and may earn me enemies in high places. I wish to broach them with you before you take up your position."

"I understand, my king."

"My first orders of business are these: Reduce the rajakariya to the customary forty days a year and let the people go about their lives without vexations from their monarch. Return properties that were unfairly confiscated. Slow down monastic construction projects. Undertake more projects that directly benefit the people. These are the key foundations of my future policies." Kasyapa searched his friend's face for a reaction. There was none. "What do you think, Abaya?"

"My king, as your humble servant, I will faithfully execute your policies."

"Abaya, tell me as my friend. Do you see folly in what I propose?"

"The monasteries, we will have to approach with caution."

"True."

"No doubt you are aware there is already some antagonism from those quarters against you?"

Kasyapa laughed. "You are right, Abaya. I do not have my father's religious fervor. No doubt, the monks of the great monastery also hold a grudge against me for their loss of the Ambatthala Vihara at Cetiyagiri, which they attribute to my intercedence with my late father."

Abaya nodded.

"Having heard my intentions, do you accept the position?"

"Yes, my king. I will serve you loyally as your vizier."

"Will you also promise to advise me, as my friend, when you think I am being reckless?"

"Yes, my friend Kasyapa," Abaya replied with a dour, straight face.

Kasyapa hugged the big man. "Now, Abaya, are you aware that Dathapabhuti, your uncle, approached the vizier—the old vizier—with a request to be appointed the treasurer? I think we should turn his request down. What do you think?"

"Your opinion is a sound one, my king."

"But he is your uncle."

"I understand, my king."

"All right. I will ask the old vizier to let Dathapabhuti know of my decision. After that, we will announce your appointment. Also, you know people are in a hurry to get me married." Kasyapa laughed. "I understand you are aware of certain discussions with your family."

"Yes, my king."

"Now, as my friend, do you see any issues with what was discussed? Please be honest, Abaya."

"No, Kasyapa. There are issues of nobility, but this was resolved satisfactorily."

"Now, as my vizier, do you see any pitfalls in marriage into the house of the Lambakanna?"

"No, my king. But it is my duty to remind you, the Lambakanna have ambitions to regain the throne they lost some fifty years ago."

"Yes, I am aware. I will ask the old vizier to arrange this union. It frees you to worry about more pressing matters of state."

"I agree, my king."

"It's settled, then."

"Yes, my king."

Kasyapa escorted him back to the audience hall, where the vizier and the chamberlain were waiting for them.

"Vizier, I would like for Abaya to be your understudy. I have also advised him that I would like you to negotiate the marriage settlement. Chamberlain, you will be responsible for the ceremonies."

His ministers nodded.

"No doubt, when the time is right, someone will tell their king who he is to wed?"

They chuckled.

26

The chamberlain ushered the harem-keeper into the audience hall. Kasyapa had seen her often in the palace compound, and while she was always civil, at that time, she had never gone out of her way to gain his acquaintance. As far as she was concerned, he was not royalty and not worthy of her attention. Kasyapa was used to that.

"What is it, Harem-Keeper, that brings you here at this time?" Kasyapa asked as she entered the audience hall and prostrated herself before him.

"My king, the harem."

"The harem?"

"Yes, my king, the great king's harem. It is customary that upon the death of a prior king, his harem is disbanded, and the women's quarters refurbished for new occupants."

"I see no problem with that."

"But my king, the terms of severance?"

"Explain, Harem-Keeper."

"A concubine's exit-worth is determined by her position in the harem. The king's favorites and concubines with a male child from the king receive the highest payments, then those with female children, followed by those who had had intercourse with the king and finally those who had not."

Kasyapa studied the portly harem-keeper. From all accounts, she was a competent and fair administrator. He wished her to stay.

"Do what you must, Harem-Keeper. I trust you will serve me well," Kasyapa replied with a dismissing brush of his hand.

She stood and hurried toward the door.

"And Harem-Keeper?"

"Yes, my king?"

"Be generous and fair."

"Yes, my king."

As the chamberlain escorted the harem-keeper out of the building, she reached up to his ear and whispered. "Pardon my directness, Chamberlain; I am well pleased with the generosity of our new king. This means I don't have to be miserly with the severance payments to my girls. I tell you, Chamberlain, I have made up my mind right here and now. I will serve him faithfully with every breath in my body."

"Yes, Harem-Keeper, many of us share your sentiments."

27

Kasyapa guffawed as the sthapati entered the audience hall and performed the usual prostrating and salutation expected of a subject.

"Now, Sthapati, your belated visit to pay homage to your new king has been noted. You know, it is only the clergy who wait for the monarch to come to them." He motioned the sthapati to rise and led him to the gardens outside.

"As you are well aware, Ka—my king—I keep my nose out of politics."

"Yes, I know. However, I shall remember your slight," Kasyapa teased.

They laughed.

"Now, Sthapati, I have two topics I wish to discuss with you. Firstly, I would like you to stay on in your current position. Secondly, I wish to advise you that I am curbing all building projects. What do you say to that?" Kasyapa ribbed good-naturedly.

"Well, my king, you have told me two things. Firstly, you value my services, for which I am most grateful. Secondly, I may be out of a job," cackled the sthapati, tongue firmly in his cheek.

"You play with me, my dear architect."

The sthapati was a wealthy man. Losing his job was the least of his worries.

"You know Sthapati, I dislike this place, this palace. It has a ghoulish pallor to it. The only areas I find tolerable are my quarters—the same ones I occupied as a child, and the royal gardens where we are now."

The sthapati cast his eyes about and said nothing.

"The chamberlain advises me I will have to move to more suitable quarters if I am to have a queen."

"Aren't you billeted in the king's quarters?"

"No, I don't like them."

"So where are you now?"

"In the lodgings I used as a child. Let me show you."

They walked through the small gate leading to the compound, past the bathing well and into the little villa. It had remained unchanged, a single room furnished with a bed, a greyish-brown cupboard, a three-legged stool, and a table. They sat on the bed next to each other.

"What do you think, Sthapati?"

The sthapati let out a long, tortured sigh that appeared to deflate him physically. "My dear king, you can't live in a hovel like this."

"Why not? I like this place. I find it more comfortable than the accommodations in the king's quarters."

The sthapati turned to face Kasyapa. Gone was the jovial glint in his eyes, replaced instead was a firm-jawed stare.

"Because," he spluttered through his annoyance, took hold of himself, and continued. "Once upon a time, you may have been an insignificant nobody. But now you are a king. You must stop this weak, effete behavior of yours."

"That's a bit harsh, Sthapati."

"I will tell you this as your friend, my king. Stop acting like a mouse. Behave like a ruler." The sthapati's face was deeply colored. His voice rose. "Much as you may find pomp and ceremony immoderate, it is a vital vestige of kingship. You have certain handicaps to overcome. I do not need to elaborate. Suffice to say you have survived some six days so far. You may recall Sotthi-sena survived as the king for only half a day. So, rebellion does not seem to be a risk. The biggest threat facing you is the ongoing presumption of the illegitimacy of your rule. Rumors repeated often enough can soon be taken as fact. You must counter this perception. Nip it in the bud. If unchecked, it will grow like a cancer and blight your kingship."

The sthapati edged closer to Kasyapa, slapped him fondly on his knee. "So, my dear, dear Kasyapa, you need to be audacious—more daring than kings before you. Astound them with bravado. Dazzle them with flamboyance. Be bigger than life in everything you do. Use the goodwill of your subjects and the wealth of your kingdom to implement all those well-intentioned projects you discussed with me. But do so with gusto. Help the people. Build grandiosely. Manage the conversation, Kasyapa. Remember, my friend, if you want to be treated like a king, cast yourself as a demi-god."

"But a righteous monarch should be modest."

"A hen's ass!"

"A Dharmaraja should not indulge in self-aggrandizement."

"Says who? Only those who benefit from the king's self-inflicted paupery. Who will stop you?"

"Then, I ought to be Kasyapa the Magnificent? Not Kasyapa, the unpretentious, righteous king?"

"You are damn right. Be bigger than life. Yes, Kasyapa the Magnificent. Kasyapa the Munificent. Kasyapa the Benevolent. Be big. Be brash. Let the splendor of Kasyapa's reign dumbfound them. Let the conversation be of these things, and the rest will soon be forgotten."

A stingy ray of sunlight slunk into the room through the open doorway. Kasyapa sat in silence with his friend, watching the specks of dust dancing in the shaft of light illuminating the room. A feeling of melancholy drifted over him and griped him like a vise. The fear of rejection, of being the outsider, left him in constant anguish. His friend was right. He had to control the narrative of his destiny.

28

It wasn't long before the vizier arrived with a wedding proposal.

"My king, we have an offer," the vizier said.

"So soon?"

"Yes, my king, we must officiate your reign as soon as possible."

"I understand, Vizier."

"It is the Lady Sobhana, daughter of the aristocrat Roniguta."

"She is the niece of the former queen and the cousin of Abaya," the chamberlain interjected enthusiastically, apparently out of line because the vizier glared at him with a cocked eyebrow. The chamberlain sheepishly cast his eyes at the floor.

"I have arranged a visit for tomorrow," the vizier said.

*****

SOBHANA AND HER FATHER ARRIVED at the Royal Audience Hall the following morning. She walked three steps behind her father. They prostrated themselves before Kasyapa as expected of a subject.

"Arise, my friends," Kasyapa responded.

Roniguta and Sobhana stood up with their heads bowed.

"My king, may I introduce you to my daughter?" Roniguta said.

She wore a beige full-length dhoti and richly bejeweled to reflect her father's great wealth and prestige. She had a regal presence about her—elegant, serene, willowy, large-breasted, and wasp-waisted. After a short exchange of civilities among the men, the vizier ushered the chamberlain and Roniguta away.

SOBHANA STOOD ALONE before her king, her head slightly bowed, her eyes averting his. Kasyapa rose from his seat and stepped down to her. She lowered her head even further, dropping her handkerchief on the floor in front of him. Kasyapa picked it up and handed it to her. She blushed.

"Come Sobhana, let's walk outside."

She smiled, and taking small steps, she walked respectfully a few paces behind him.

The gravel path before them was still damp from the previous night's rain and had been swept into a neat crisscross pattern. A chorus of birdsongs filled the crisp morning air scented with the fragrance of flowering areka palm trees. The sun was already a ball of yellow above them, insinuating more warmth to come.

As he was king and it wasn't proper to strike up a conversation with the monarch unless requested, the dialogue centered almost entirely on questions Kasyapa asked. Like her cousin Abaya, she spoke little, preferring to listen, and commented only when asked. Kasyapa liked her responses. They were polite, measured, and showed the hallmarks of a keen intellect. He watched her from the corner of his eye as she accompanied him. Her complexion was caramel-colored and smooth. Her face was long with cheekbones that weren't high, and her nose was straight and narrow. She wasn't beautiful in the classic sense, but her imperfections nevertheless made her striking.

After walking toward the far end of the park, they sat on a bench by the pond.

"Do you understand the significance of our meeting today, Sobhana?" Kasyapa asked, turning to her and searching her eyes.

"Yes, my king," she said with a shy mellowness in her voice.

"What do you understand?"

This time she looked straight into his eyes. There was a hesitation in her movements that gave her a certain kind of mystery. A smile radiated across her lips, revealing a set of neat white teeth.

"I understand we are meeting to determine if we are suitable to be partners."

"And what do you think?"

"I think you are handsome," she said, fluttering a set of long eyelashes over a pair of almond-shaped brown eyes.

"Ha! Only handsome?"

Her eyes flashed.

"Nobody said you were handsome," she replied with perfect composure.

"Oh?"

"They only said you were a good man," she said as a well-placed smile danced across her lips.

"Oh, and who are they?"

"My cousins Abaya and Sakula."

"You've been making your own inquiries, I see."

She giggled with growing confidence.

"Of course. This is not a matter to be taken lightly."

"So, what do you think?"

She lowered her luminous eyes diffidently.

"I think I can be happy with you, my king."

"Sobhana, from now on, when we are in private, you may address me by my name, Kasyapa. In public, as required by royal protocol, you are to continue to address me as king."

"Yes, my king."

"Sobhana."

"Yes, Kasyapa," she replied with a sureness and self-confidence of a woman who understood her worth.

"That's better." He took her hands in his. They were soft, warm hands with long fingers. Kasyapa smiled with growing affection at this woman he just met.

"Do you want to be my partner, Sobhana?"

The playfulness in her voice fell away.

"Yes, Kasyapa, I want to share your bed and bear your children."

Kasyapa laughed.

She pulled her hands away and looked away, embarrassed.

"Oh, I am not laughing at you. I am laughing at myself. Sobhana, I don't have a proper place to bed you."

She twirled her handkerchief around her index finger and cast him a sideward glance.

"You see, I live in a small guest house in this large palace. You may not wish to marry me after seeing it," he joked and stood up. "Let me show you."

As they reached his compound, the guards snapped to attention and flung open the small gate.

"This is it."

She stood still and looked around, bemused. "This is where you live—the mighty king of all of Lanka?" She giggled.

"Yes."

"It is a humble dwelling indeed, my king. More fit for a hermit than a king," she replied with a mischievous, sideward glance.

"Are you disappointed?"

"No."

"I don't like the king's quarters. It haunts me."

"I see," she replied in her alluring voice. Her gaze now caressed his face with a gentle inner warmth as she spoke.

"You may take me as your wife wherever you chose to have me, Kasyapa."

Her directness, for a woman with such a demure appearance, took Kasyapa by surprise. He had expected a dull horse of a woman. Instead, here she was. Not necessarily beautiful, but most certainly alluring. A warming glow engulfed his body. Without warning, he stiffened for her. She grew more and more attractive with each passing moment.

"It's not all bad, Sobhana. The sthapati insisted I upgrade the facilities. He is demolishing the outhouses and putting up a new annex for me. Also, the queen's quarters in the harem, which I presume are sufficient, as I have not seen them myself, are at your disposal."

"Thank you for showing me your quarters, Kasyapa."

"Then it's settled?"

"Yes, I will love you as my husband, Kasyapa, and respect you as my king."

*****

LATE THAT AFTERNOON, Kasyapa asked, "How are the preparations for the consecration ceremony going, Vizier?"

There was a nervous shuffling of feet and a quick exchange of glances between the king's ministers.

The vizier spoke first. "We have a problem with the anointing ceremony, my king."

"What do you mean?"

"In the past, the consecration ceremony consisted of an anointing ritual of three parts. The first is by a virgin of the noble Kshatriya caste. The second by a member of the clergy. And thirdly by the head of the business guild." The vizier paused and eyed Abaya, who nodded.

The vizier sought to choose his words carefully, but Kasyapa was impatient.

"What is it?"

The vizier cleared his throat, the chamberlain looked down at his feet, Abaya watched on dour-faced as ever.

"My king, the fraternities are reluctant to officiate."

"Why? Is it because of my lowly birth?"

"Not exactly, my king. While the monks of the Thera School are unyielding, the others are more accommodating and are willing to turn a blind eye to this requirement of noble parentage."

"Then what is it, Vizier?"

"It is because they heard that you uttered the fatal words 'slay my father'. As you are aware, in our Buddist religion, the murder of one's parents is a cardinal sin, a heinous crime. For this reason, they do not wish to condone such an act by being part of the ceremony."

"But I never said that! I said, 'when do you intend to slay my father?' It was a question," Kasyapa shot back, slamming his fist against the arm of his throne.

The vizier continued, unperturbed. "The head abbot of the Dhammaruci sect—you know him, my king—is willing to help as he had heard differently, that you did not have a hand in your father's dreadful demise."

"Yes, I know him. He thanked me for arranging the gifting of the Ambatthala Vihara at Cetiyagiri to his fraternity. He is a good man."

"He is, my king. However, the abbot felt he would not be able to preside himself for fear of alienating his adherents, so he has suggested that a lesser monk officiates."

The air was brittle with tension.

"What about my uncle, Thera Mahanama?"

Kasyapa heard Abaya and the chamberlain suck in their breath.

The vizier remained unflinching.

"I have not broached the question with him, my king. I think it unwise. Whatever his personal views may be, we should not place him in a position where his religious convictions or loyalty are put to the test."

"Yes, I understand. Uncle always kept the secular and temporal apart. I will not compromise him. I must plot my own destiny."

Kasyapa slumped in his chair and stared at the checkered paving on the floor in front of him. He twirled the copper ring on his little finger. The glum shadow of melancholy soundlessly drifted over him. *I am never good enough. When I have proven myself, some twist of fate pulls me down again.*

A cooling breeze wafted through the audience hall, thrusting a large leaf noisily across the otherwise silent chamber and past its occupants hushed in contemplation.

Sensing Kasyapa's despair, Abaya broke the impasse. He cleared his throat and began, "Our first Buddhist king, Devanampiya Tissa, was anointed by only a virgin of the Kshatriya caste."

Kasyapa lifted his wistful glance from the floor. "Abaya, my friend, I see you studied your history lessons well."

"Why don't we eliminate the anointing by the clergy and setthi and return to the original rite?" Abaya said.

The vizier nodded.

"I will arrange it," the chamberlain said, relieved that an awkward situation had been averted.

Kasyapa soon regained his composure, but the slight by the fraternities only reaffirmed his dislike of them. He had refrained from paying homage to them, as previous monarchs had. Now, he was more determined than ever on asserting the authority of the king over the affairs of his kingdom.

At the conclusion of business, the vizier asked to speak to Kasyapa in private once again.

"Let's walk in the gardens. Now Vizier, what troubles you?"

"It is the consecration ceremony, my king."

"I thought we sorted it out?"

"We did, my king. But may I request to be excused from the ceremony? And may I also somberly request to relinquish my duties prior to that time? Abaya is ready. He will make an excellent vizier."

The gravel on the pathway crunched softly beneath their feet as they walked. Kasyapa understood the older man's distress. His presence would be perceived as though he had conspired with Kasyapa against the former king. Kasyapa had no desire to amplify his misery.

"Your wish is granted, Vizier."

The vizier nodded. "May I add some words of caution, my king?"

"Of course, Vizier."

"Be wary, my sovereign."

"What do you mean?"

"A man who cohabitates with a crocodile must always be vigilant. The creature may appear to be docile, but it can pounce at any moment with unimaginable ferocity. It owes loyalty to no one, not even to its own kith and kin."

"I understand, my dear, dear Vizier. Thank you. I have learned much from you. You guided me through my formative years. You supported me in our time of crisis. I will not forget you."

"Thank you, my king. I remain your loyal subject."

*****

THE ABHISEKA, OR THE CONSECRATION OF KASYAPA and his queen, took place on an auspicious day selected by the royal soothsayers. At mid-morning, to the sound of loud drumming and fanfare, Kasyapa and the royal entourage emerged through the massive *gopuram*. It was a three-storied ornamental structure the sthapati had erected to cover the entire front façade of the palace.

Kasyapa wore his characteristic white ankle-length dhoti and an un-adorned white blouse buttoned at the back. The only jewelry he wore was his little copper ring and the *Ekavali*—the pearl chain of one string. Behind him strode Sobhana, radiant in her white garments festooned with pearls. She wore her luxuriant black hair in a bun decorated with clusters of rubies, emeralds, and sapphires, that sparkled with every step she took.

As Kasyapa and Sobhana were not yet married, they stopped by a small poruva, a beautifully decorated wooden platform covered with a silken roof, outside the palace gates. As was the custom, Sobhana's eldest uncle officiated. He tied a silk thread around the little finger of their right hands and solemnized their marriage by pouring water on their joined fingers from a small golden vessel. As Kasyapa had no im-mediate relatives, he nominated Ayah as his representative. Trembling with happiness the little boy she had nurtured had bestowed such a great honor on her, she removed the thread and placed it in the same box she had given Kasyapa so many years ago to hold his precious little copper ring.

After the ceremony, Daya joined the royal couple and held the *Senachatra*—the white parasol of dominion—high above their heads. Abaya, the newly appointed vizier, followed, holding the *chowrie*, a fly-whisk fan made of the hair from a yak's tail. Two steps behind him, the chamberlain carried an unpretentious golden crown on a small cush-ion, and Migara followed with the sword of kingship.

The entourage walked to a large pavilion decorated with sweet-smell-ing jasmine flowers that gave it a mythical appearance. Kasyapa took his seat in a special coronation chair made from the wood of the Udumbara tree. Sobhana took her place behind him.

Clothed in the most elegant attire, a virgin of the Kshatriya caste took with both hands the sacred chank, a ceremonial sea couch shell, filled with water from the Ganges river, and raised it over Kasyapa's head. Then she slowly poured its contents over him while reciting the following invocation:

> *Sire, by this ceremony of abhiseka, all the people of the Kshatriya race and all of the people of the kingdom make thee their maharaja for their protection. Will thou rule over the land in uprightness and imbued with the ten royal virtues? Have thou for the people a heart filled with parental love and solicitude? Let them in return, protect, and guard and cherish thee."*

"I will—I do."

Then, to the applause of the assembled crowd, the chamberlain placed the crown on Kasyapa's head, after which Kasyapa stood to receive the ceremonial sword of kingship from Migara. Kasyapa was now the legitimate king of the land.

Soon after, Kasyapa took with both hands the same sacred sea chank filled with Ganges water, raised it aloft, and gently poured its contents on Sobhana's head.

"I anoint you my queen-wife," Kasyapa proclaimed.

"I will obey and serve you faithfully as my husband and my king," she responded.

Abaya, the new vizier, stood two steps behind and to the right of Kasyapa and read out the *danam*—the official proclamation of the king's largesse.

"It is proclaimed on this day by King Kasyapa that the mandatory days of service for the rajakariya will be reduced from fifty days to the customary period of forty days. Also recognizing the hardships endured by his people as a result of the recent drought, King Kasyapa decrees that the grain tax will be reduced by fifty percent for the next harvest." The vizier waited for the applause to die down and concluded, "King Kasyapa and his queen wish their subjects good health and good fortune."

The assembled dignitaries rose as Kasyapa made his exit.

Migara stood bolt upright, bowed, and snapped to attention. "Well, Kasyapa, you are king now," he remarked with an unmistakable note of cynicism.

"Yes, Senapati, I am king. I look forward to your loyal service." Kasyapa walked away without waiting for a reply.

SOBHANA DID NOT ATTEND HIS BED THAT NIGHT. For that matter, she did not visit until some days later to consummate their marriage. As was the custom at the time, the queen visited the king's bedchamber only on designated nights. These were the nights deemed most auspicious by the harem-keeper and always fell on those days when she was most fertile. As these nights had not fallen due as yet, Sobhana, her mother, and some female relatives spent their time settling into the recently refurbished queen's quarters.

As king and queen, they lived separate lives. She was free to engage in activities of her choosing both inside and outside the palace. Her interactions in the court were predominately through the harem-keeper and the chamberlain.

Besides their conjugal liaisons and official duties, they met each day for lunch. Afterward, they strolled the palace park together. Kasyapa enjoyed this time with Sobhana. They talked of many things besides the affairs of the household. He liked her intellect and valued her well-considered advice.

29

Soon after assuming the kingship, Kasyapa often donned a disguise and slipped out of the palace. Confident of his cover, he struck up casual conversations with passersby. In this way, Kasyapa believed he was keeping in touch with his people. On one occasion, he and his gatekeeper, Bodur, slipped out of the palace dressed as royal guards. Fronting up at the sthapati's house, they demanded entry into the premises. The sentinels at the gate hesitated. In his disguise, they did not recognize Kasyapa, but how could they refuse admission to the king's guards? They sent for the sthapati, who was entertaining his guests elsewhere.

"What do you want?" the sthapati snapped.

"We wish to join your party."

"What?"

"We wish to join your party, sir."

"Go away, you insolent fools," the sthapati snapped and was about to walk away when a voice rang out.

"Sthapati, it's your friend, Kasyapa."

"What?"

"It is I."

"Are you mad?"

"Why?"

The sthapati exited his front gate, dragged Kasyapa out of earshot, and slammed him up against the front wall.

"You could be killed roaming the streets like this. Go back to your palace!"

THE VIZIER AND CHAMBERLAIN GREETED KASYAPA at the gate when he exited his compound the following morning.

"You left the palace." The vizier's voice was firm and unyielding. A tone Kasyapa had never heard from his friend and chief minister.

"Yes, so what's wrong with that?"

"Do you realize the danger?"

"I only went to see the sthapati."

"But this is not the first time you have done this. Sneaking out."

"No, it's not."

"My king, this is a serious matter. You are the ruler of this realm. Do you realize what misfortune could befall the kingdom if someone assassinated you? Who will replace you? There is no one. The kingdom could quickly spiral into chaos and civil war. My king, you must assure us you will not behave like this again," the vizier said in a calm but stern voice.

Kasyapa knew they were right. He had put his safety and that of the kingdom in jeopardy. Gone were the days when he could roam the land at will. Gone were those carefree days of partying with the sthapati. He was back in a gilded cage, a captive of his destiny.

THE STHAPATI VISITED later the same day. He found Kasyapa uncharacteristically subdued.

"Greetings, my king," he chirped, pretending the events of the previous night had not occurred. But his mere presence at the palace, which he loathed visiting, was proof enough of his concern.

"Good morning, Sthapati. I appreciate your decision to visit me in my prison."

"A run-down one at that," the sthapati crackled.

After some inconsequential small-talk, Kasyapa began. "I have been thinking. Since I am forbidden from moving about freely and cannot attend your residence either, what if I were to arrange a regular gathering of the best and brightest here, in the palace?"

"Excellent idea, my king. Your patronage would encourage a cultural revival. Ahhh yes, I say, Kasyapa the Magnificent," the sthapati chuckled and waggled his eyebrows.

"Well, it wasn't my intention to win accolades for myself," Kasyapa said, brightening up. "Would you manage it, Sthapati? Since I know you will dither, I command you to undertake this task. Let's bring the most talented people of our kingdom together. Invite anybody. Whosoever you feel can contribute."

"Now, this is beginning to sound most exciting." The sthapati grinned, rubbing his hands with glee.

"There is one condition. The vizier and chamberlain must join us."

"Damn bureaucrats." The sthapati let out a sound somewhere between a moan and a pitiful sigh."

"Surely, Sthapati, how better to win their support? A large-scale resurgence needs the support of those who govern."

The sthapati mumbled subdued profanities and nodded.

KASYAPA SOON CONCLUDED the sthapati was enjoying his new role, more so than his position as the king's architect. He and the chamberlain were working together, drawing more and more talent into what became known as "The Gathering". Besides the intelligentsia, it also included singers, dancers, and reciters of epics and poetry. Agbo, the artist, often presented on the art and sculptures he had seen in Jambudvipa.

After one such gathering, Kasyapa said, "Why don't we organize traveling troupes to share these entertainers and our culture with the people?"

"A cultural revival! I will implement it immediately, my king," the sthapati said, eyeing the vizier, who concurred with his usual hallmark nod.

On another occasion, about six months into his reign, Kasyapa said, "We have reduced the rajakariya and are curtailing our building projects. Let us divert some of our resources for the benefit of the people. I want to build hospices and almshouses for the poor and construct a large park outside the city gates for the use of our citizens. Why must only the king have these parks? And finally, you may laugh at this idea, but I wish to plant mango trees."

"Mango trees?" the chamberlain, sthapati, and even the usually sub-dued vizier, replied in unison.

"Yes, mango trees. Let me explain. You know, I found it tedious trav-eling with the sthapati." He grimaced in good humor. "No, not because he was awful company, but because it was difficult to get one's bearings when traveling from place to place. Do you remember, Sthapati, how often we got lost? The only way to find one's way is to make inquiries along the way."

He paused and took a deep breath. "More often than not, the direc-tions given were inaccurate. Let's do something simple that serves two purposes. Let's plant mango trees on all main roads at a distance of five miles from each other, a walking distance of two hours. While this may seem flippant, it will be beneficial to travelers as these trees will offer them identifiable mileposts and also provide shade and sustenance on their journeys."

"Yes, my king," the vizier replied with a bow.

*****

IN THE SECOND YEAR OF KASYAPA'S REIGN, Sobhana gave birth to their firstborn, a daughter. As was customary, the naming rights for male off-spring rested with the father, and for females with the mother. Sobhana chose to name her Bodhi, after her maternal grandmother.

After lunch one day, while walking in the park with Sobhana, Kasya-pa ruminated.

"I rode past the Isuramenu Vihara this morning. It is dilapidated and in urgent need of repair."

"Built by Devanampiya-tissa, the king of the mango tree story. The story you recited some years ago."

"How do you know about my recital?" Kasyapa laughed.

"Sakula told me. She was very proud of you."

"Sobhana, this temple is over six hundred years old and the first

Buddhist temple to be built in this land. Why did my father overlook it and leave in such a poor state of repair?"

"Why don't you ask the former vizier? He is sure to know," she replied.

When he met the former vizier some months later, Kasyapa inquired, "It is not idle curiosity alone that makes me ask. Why didn't my father refurbish the Isuramenu Vihara?"

"There were two viharas your father did not repair. These were the Gonisa and Isuramenu Viharas. It was at the Gonisa that a fellow trainee monk named Damaruci threw cow dung at the young Dhatusena in an attempt to distract him from his meditations. The king never forgot the bullying and humiliation he suffered there as a child. He made no gifts to that vihara, nor to the vihara where the perpetrator of his humiliation now resides. The abbot at Isuramenu is Dama-rakita. That same Damaruci."

TWO MONTHS LATER, THE VIZIER advised the king of a dangerous trend.

"We are seeing rising unemployment, my king. Many are out of work."

"Why is that, Vizier?"

"I suspect it is a consequence of the scaling back of our projects."

"Yes, the temple-building works are coming to an end. Artisans will soon be out of work," added the sthapati, who was also present.

"I see."

"We could employ them to refurbish this dilapidated palace of yours. A few careful alterations here, some tasteful additions there," the sthapati chirped in, half-joking.

"No, I have little interest in this palace."

"Actually, there is little we can do with this place anyway without tearing it down and starting anew." The sthapati smirked.

"You would like that. Wouldn't you, Sthapati?"

"Yes, indeed."

"No. That's too ostentatious. I have no need of a palace."

The sthapati feigned great disappointment, but he knew Kasyapa still held onto his overarching desire to be seen as a righteous monarch, a Dharmaraja, a just Buddhist king. He frowned on any semblance of self-aggrandizement or extravagance.

"Why don't we refurbish Isuramenu?" Kasyapa asked.

"That may win us some credit with the fraternities, especially the Thera School," the vizier said.

"They still begrudge their loss of Ambatthala Vihara at Cetiyagiri. Maybe this will appease them." Kasyapa chuckled.

The sthapati was uncharacteristically subdued. Kasyapa suspected he was dreaming up some grand project.

The sthapati stroked his chin. "That won't be enough."

"What?"

"It will only take a small labor force to fix up the place. Why don't we do even better than that? Let's build a magnificent new vihara complex. Let's integrate the Vessagiri Vihara six hundred yards to the south with the Isuramenu, build facilities between the two, and also improve the Ranmasu Uyana royal park at the same time. Let's make this the first grand statement of your reign."

"Knowing your flamboyant ideas, Sthapati, it would indeed make a splendid statement and bankrupt your king," Kasyapa teased.

"What do you think, Vizier? Can the royal coffers withstand the onslaught of the sthapati's grandiose intentions?"

"You are fortunate, my king. The kingdom is prosperous. The recent drought has broken, and the late king's irrigation projects are reaping bountiful harvests. Duties and taxes are also contributing to the health of the royal exchequer."

"Moreover, the reduced generosity toward the religious establishments is also helping to swell the royal coffers." As usual, the chamberlain articulated what the others discreetly had left unsaid.

"Where is your tact, Chamberlain?" The sthapati teased, and the others chuckled and agreed.

"Let's do it. Let's refurbish Isuramenu and Vessagiri," Kasyapa declared.

He also had more personal motives. They were to repudiate his father's humiliation, expunge the deep remorse he still felt for the death of his father, and assuage the fraternities. Here was his chance to make good on all these things.

"Vizier, advise them of my visit. Sthapati, let's visit the place tomorrow. You often told me you wanted something interesting to do. Well, here is your opportunity."

Arriving at the Isuramenu Vihara, Kasyapa and the sthapati were greeted by the head abbot of the establishment. There was nothing distinctive about the man. He was neither tall nor short, fat nor skinny. He was just average and middle-aged, except for his shiny shaved head with a notable scar over his left ear. He did not have the air of dignity or grace of Kasyapa's uncle, Mahanama. Nor did he have the deportment of a holy man or even the gravitas of a teacher. On the whole, he was an unimpressive dot of a man. His name was Dama-rakita.

"Why is this vihara dilapidated?" Kasyapa asked.

Dama-rakita remained silent, staring at the ground and chewing on the corner of his lower lip. Kasyapa took an immediate disliking to the man.

"Let us be," Kasyapa ordered and dismissed the monk with the sweep of his hand. The sthapati noted the unusual timbre of the king's voice. It was one of disdain.

Turning to the sthapati, Kasyapa said, "Now show me."

*****

IN THE FOURTH YEAR OF HIS REIGN, the vizier advised, "We have a new report about your brother in Jambudvipa across the sea, my king."

"How is my brother?"

"He may have fallen into hard times. As you may recall, your brother Moggallana and his accomplice Shalika settled in a lavish villa in Madurai and then subsequently moved to less luxurious accommodations."

"Yes?"

"It seems he has pawned the last of his mother's jewelry and is eking out a meager existence in a run-down dwelling outside the city. I also have news that Shalika has left him to join a monastery."

Kasyapa was contemplative.

"Continue, Vizier."

"He is unmarried and spends his time carousing with friends of questionable character. He is living by his wits. Most importantly, he still hasn't given up trying to raise an army against you."

Kasyapa gently tapped his little copper ring on the arm of his throne. He said nothing.

SOME MONTHS LATER, Sobhana gave birth to their second child, another girl. Sensing Kasyapa's desire to name this child, she coaxed him to provide a name for her. He named his second daughter, Uppalavanna.

It was also the year in which the new vihara complex was nearing completion. The vizier arranged a meeting with senior monks of the Thera School to discuss the reconsecration and handover of the new complex.

When Kasyapa and the vizier arrived, the abbots of the Thera School remained some distance away with their backs turned to the royal party. Their insult did not go unnoticed by Kasyapa. "So, these monks turn their backs on their monarch, do they?"

Just then, a messenger came running to them. "Oh king, abbots of the Thera School do not wish to accept your gift."

Kasyapa was in no mood for their intransigence. "Bring them to me, Vizier," Kasyapa ordered.

Kasyapa watched as vizier hurried to the assembled monks. A heated discussion appeared to be taking place. Shortly thereafter, the monks approached him.

"I have learned of a reluctance on your part to accept my gift?"

The bhikkhus remained silent.

"Let me tell you this. Your choice is clear. Accept this gift from your king, or I will obliterate this place, raze to the ground, and convert it into rice fields."

The congregation of monks huffed and passed worried glances among themselves. What the king proposed was sacrilege? After all, this was the first Buddhist temple constructed in this land. Furthermore, they were not used to being spoken to in this way.

Kasyapa looked at them with a steely gaze.

"You will, like all my subjects, abide by the will of your king." Kasyapa mounted his carriage and rode away.

Abaya stayed behind. He was determined to resolve the situation once and for all. Being a tall man, he towered over them. "You have insulted your king. Reconsider your position. I give you fifteen minutes."

THE MONKS HUDDLED TOGETHER in the heat of the midday sun. Some exchanged nervous glances. Others hid their faces behind their oversized palm-leaf fans. They had provoked their monarch.

They were well aware of the consequences of offending a king. Their predecessors had done so in the time of King Mahasena, just a hundred years earlier. As a consequence, they lost their place as the pre-eminent fraternity of the land. That king had reduced them to poverty. Many monks resorted to eating grass to survive. They had also lost their magnificent Mahavihara and its treasures to their archrivals, the Dhammarucis. Now, they endured on the fringe of irrelevance. Again, they had taken up a controversial stance. They had declared they could not accept a gift from a patricide. It was Dama-rakita who was the most strident of them all.

The archabbot, the leader of the group, a frail old man with a hawkish nose, broke the silence. "What shall we do?" he asked, wringing his withered hands.

"Last time we rejected the work of the artist Agbo, at Cetiyagiri, the former king gave the vihara to the Dhammaruci," a skinny monk reminded his colleagues.

"But this place is so unorthodox, and the paintings are garish," a third butted in.

"What blasphemy. They have placed the Master, the Buddha, in darkness inside a deep cavern," another added in an indignant voice.

A young monk recently returned from Jambudvipa spoke out. "My brethren, if you visit the glorious temples at Ajanta in the land across the sea, you will see paintings and sculptures such as these. You will even see our first monarch, Vijaya, who reigned over a thousand years before, with his bride Kuveni depicted there. They are magnificent works of religious art. So are these. There is nothing salacious depicted here."

"Is that so?" the archabbot said.

"Yes. These paintings are certainly colorful and dynamic. But will these pictorial allegories, many from the Jataka Tales, not help us in our meditation? Will they not assist us in our reflection of the stories of our glorious past and of our Teacher? Let us make amends with this king; I beseech you. He has displayed great generosity toward us. What are we to gain by our obstinance? We already suffer from the absence of royal patronage from this monarch."

"You are a brave monk indeed, Buddha-datta, to speak out like this. I cannot fault your discourse. No doubt your foreign travels have made you more enlightened and outspoken than the others," the archabbot replied, stroking his hairless chin.

The moderate monk bowed his head rueful, for his intemperate outburst.

The archabbot continued, "This king did not visit us as previous monarchs did. This was, no doubt, because of our rebuff at his consecration. He has already forced us to comply with the reduced rajakariya, depriving us of ten days of free labor from each of the serfs toiling in our fields and properties. He has also returned properties handed to the fraternities, which were confiscated by his father."

The outspoken skinny monk spoke up once more.

"But Archabbot, the king applied these regulations, without favor, to all fraternities. We must, in true honesty, concede that while his actions were not favorable to us, they were fair to all. Are these not the reason for our lingering displeasure with him?"

The majority of the assembled monks agreed.

"But what about the decadence, music, and merrymaking this king encourages?" Dama-rakita added in a frenzy.

"True, true. Or is it that we are out of touch with the times?" the skinny monk reflected aloud.

"For decades now, the people have been drifting away from us," an emaciated monk to the left conceded.

"These are against the doctrine. These are dangerous precedents—scandalous heresy," Dama-rakita said.

The archabbot clucked his tongue at Dama-rakita.

"Dama-rakita, you have been the most virulent among us. What grudge do you hold against this king? Did you not also hold a similar grudge against his father?"

Dama-rakita sidestepped the question and addressed his response to that of decadence.

"We are adherents of the true doctrine. Our path is one of abstaining from all kinds of evil. We do not advocate a life of frivolity and pleasure." He bristled.

The archabbot grew impatient and clucked his tongue once more. "Release yourself from your hatred Dama-rakita," he admonished, knowing all too well that this man's bile ran thick with malice.

The rays of the noonday sun glistened off their shiny bald heads, as the monks stood unable to agree on what to do. It was Buddha-datta who broke the impasse once more.

"Let us accept the king's generosity in the name of the Supreme Buddha."

"What do you mean, Buddha-datta?" the archabbot asked as the others gathered eagerly around the young monk.

"We can remain true to our position and accept this gift on behalf of the Supreme Buddha. The gift then belongs to the Master, the Buddha himself, and not to the fraternity or its bhikkhus. Who are we to refuse something gifted to our Master?"

The monks, all except for Dama-rakita, concurred. The archabbot straightened himself up and ambled over to the vizier to broach the compromise with him.

"This is not an ideal outcome, but it will suffice. You will public-ly and most graciously accept the king's gift on behalf of the Buddha. Take note, Archabbot. You have raised the ire of your king. My advice to you is to tread with great caution, for you know not what you may reap," the vizier responded and departed.

The head abbot watched glumly as the vizier's carriage disappeared from sight.

THE VIZIER FOUND KASYAPA in the Audience Pavilion, pacing back and forth like a caged leopard, twirling and twisting the little copper band on his finger.

"I have no patience for these petty-minded men," Kasyapa said, as the vizier approached him.

"I have made up my mind. I will no longer pander to these ill-advised fundamentalists in their stultified establishments. They lack imagina-tion, stifle progress, and meddle in every aspect of life. I will be my own man. My principles will guide me. I will exercise the powers vest-ed in me as I choose." The tone of Kasyapa's voice would have halted a stampeding elephant in its tracks.

"It will be the king's vihara. Vizier, dismiss the abbot at this vihara. We will give this vihara to the Dhammaruci." Without turning around, he stormed out and returned to his compound.

30

Kasyapa was exhausted. He stood at his bathing well, lowered the bucket into its depths, and dowsed himself with its cold, refreshing water—once, twice, three times. Then four, five, six times. Seven, eight, nine times, until soon he lost count. He couldn't stop. Repeatedly, obsessively, he tried to wash away the inequities and hurt in his life. He stopped when his arms ached, and he couldn't haul the bucket up anymore. He walked to his room, dressed in the fresh clothes laid out for him, climbed into bed, and curled up into a ball.

It was then the world started spinning around him, faster and faster. He was falling, falling into a bottomless pit. Darker and darker it grew, sucking him down. There was no end to it. He blinked and blinked again, but the light was fading, growing dimmer and dimmer until he was alone in a dark, empty space. In the inkiness of his mind, demons danced. Their shrill voices reverberated around him, bouncing off the walls and slamming against his head, which wanted to explode. He wanted to disappear, to rid himself of this nagging torturous torment, this ever-present anguish.

Everything around him grew ugly, flat, and sinister. Everything wanted to engulf him. Everything seemed wrong. His life was wrong. Life was meaningless. Everything was meaningless. He was always an outsider. Never accepted. Constantly rejected. It was as though one eye was looking into his past and the other into a future that offered no comfort—only misery, regret, loneliness, and more humiliation. He was alone.

Throughout the night, his mind's eye looked into a dark abyss. He was wholly consumed by it. He wanted to climb back toward the light, but he didn't have the strength to do so. The safest place seemed here, within himself, alone.

He didn't wake up at the usual time the following morning. He heard Daya open the door, peek into his room, and close the door again. A few hours later, Daya was back. This time, he tiptoed into the room, placed his hand on Kasyapa's forehead, and withdrew.

Kasyapa didn't get up for lunch. Then the queen came to see him. She said nothing and touched his forehead. Satisfied he had no fever, she sat on his bed for what seemed like hours. Finally, she coaxed him to drink some water. In the later afternoon, the royal physician arrived and examined his patient. He concluded the king wasn't suffering from any physical ailment.

Toward evening, she woke him again and coaxed him to eat. He wasn't hungry, but he couldn't refuse her tenderness, so he ate a few mouthfuls and went back to sleep. He heard her say she would stay with him that night. He wanted to be alone, but he was grateful she chose not to leave him. She remained in the room next door. He knew her bed there wasn't comfortable. It was a small, narrow bed, the same one he had used as a child. She came and looked over him many times that night, touched him, kissed his forehead, and sat by his side. He felt her doze off. He wanted to offer her a place in his bed, but he couldn't make himself do it.

On the second day, the chamberlain and vizier came to see him. He strained to hear their garbled voices. But to him, they were in another world, and he was in his own—in a bubble of impenetrable aloneness. Sobhana remained with him all day. She kissed him often. He heard her cry. He wanted to comfort her, but he was trapped, held down, immovable, and voiceless.

That night, Kasyapa dreamed of his mother. He didn't think of her anymore. It was so long ago now. But on that night, she came to him. She sat next to him on their favorite rock, hugged him, laughed, and told him stories. He remembered her hardships and grief. He recalled how the villagers ostracized her. He recollected how she had always risen above her adversity to find joy. She comforted him, smiled, and left him to his restless slumber.

On the third day, Kasyapa woke up early and slipped outside. The air was cold and damp against his face. Grudging rays of sunlight pierced the morning, illuminated the world in a surreal monochromic haze, amplified by a wispy mist rolling sullenly over the palace gardens. He was alone, only accompanied by the sound of freshly swept sand crunching beneath his feet. In the distance, shadowy grey figures, obscured by the fog, swept crisscross patterns across the footpath he was traveling on.

As he approached them, the sweepers, startled by his presence, stepped off the path onto the dew-drenched grass and prostrated themselves as he walked by. Usually, he would have greeted them and inquired after their wellbeing. But this time, he wanted to remain invisible. He walked past them in silence. He sat on the bench by the pond as the sun's yellowish-orange disc lumbered into the sky, predictable and indifferent to the travails of mere mortals such as him.

He sat alone for an hour, maybe two, when Sobhana joined him. Seated next to him, she took his hand in hers. Feeling the coldness in his fingers, she rubbed them with her hands. He was glad she did. She looked tired and drawn.

"I am sorry, Sobhana, for putting you through this ordeal."

She tapped his hand with hers. "What troubles you, Kasyapa?"

He did not answer her. She did not goad him. They sat on the bench by the pond in silence as the sun followed its measured trajectory through the sky, casting a soft, diffused golden glow on the two of them.

"Those monks rejected my gift. They dared to say they would not accept a gift from a patricide."

"They are thoughtless men, Kasyapa."

"How am I to be exonerated, Sobhana? I did not murder my father."

She kissed his cheek. "You will, Kasyapa, with strength, perseverance, and good deeds."

"At every turn, they attempt to stymie me, to humiliate me, and bring me down."

"Kasyapa, you are a good man. Your people will support you. You are one with them. If need be, if it gives you succor, ignore those imprudent men. Work with those who support you. Avoid those who are vexations to your spirit. You, my dear Kasyapa, my dear king, my dearest husband, will prevail."

Kasyapa remained silent, watching the ripples on the surface of the pond. They had purpose. They had direction, persistent and pervasive. He took a deep breath, filling his lungs with the fresh morning air.

"I am thinking of naming the new complex after our daughters Bodhi and Uppalavanna."

"It is your wish, Kasyapa. May I suggest you add your name to it also?"

"Why?"

"So no man forgets it is the work of a great king."

"What about your name too, Sobhana?"

"I bask in the glory of my husband and king. I don't need anything more." She glanced up and smiled.

Kasyapa looked at his wife, kissed her, and got up.

"Let's go, Sobhana." He escorted her back to her quarters.

THE STHAPATI VISITED THAT AFTERNOON. He had tried calling in earlier, but the vizier and chamberlain dissuaded him from doing so. Kasyapa was happy to see him. This man had a knack of bringing out the best in him. Like his dear mentor and friend, the bubble man chamberlain had.

Talking about this and that, they walked in the park for hours.

As the sthapati was preparing to leave, Kasyapa pulled him aside. "I must get out of this place, Sthapati."

The sthapati left the meeting perplexed. This was the second time Kasyapa had said this to him. He wasn't sure what his king meant.

31

On the appointed day, the royal entourage traveled to the new complex for its re-consecration as the *Isuramenu-Bo-Upulvan-Ka-sub-Vihara.* Isuramenu was more conventional, with a dagoba, bodhi tree, outbuildings, and a cave temple dug out from under a large boulder. Being the more historically significant of the two, Kasyapa commenced his inspection there.

The sthapati met the king at the entrance and escorted him to the most noteworthy new feature of Isuramenu, a large upright boulder sheathed in an awning.

"Behold! I present to you the new image house," the sthapati proclaimed as the workmen pulled the awing away.

Kasyapa laughed.

"Ahhhh, Sthapati, you have such a penchant for theatrics and surprise."

Chiseled deep into this large upright boulder, about six yards above ground, was a cave with a well-articulated archway. The sthapati escorted Kasyapa up a white stone staircase and to its entrance. On either side of the entrance were two carved reliefs, depicting the god Kuvera astride mythological creatures known as *Makaras*—symbols of good luck, wealth, and prosperity.

They proceeded to an antechamber hewn deep within the rock. Fashioned into its rear wall was a beautiful shrine with a statue of a seated Buddha in meditation.

"Carved by Agbo. The first of its kind in all the kingdom," the sthapati said.

Kasyapa turned to Agbo, who was close behind.

"I commend you. It is indeed beautiful. You have excelled as a sculptor also."

Agbo beamed, his hallmark crooked grin, from ear to ear.

When they exited the image house, Agbo beckoned Kasyapa to the right. There he pulled aside another awning, revealing a small bas-relief of a man seated in a maharajalila royal pose, gazing upon a frieze of elephants frolicking by the pond below. Behind him, looking over his shoulder was his horse.

Kasyapa had his suspicions, but in good humor, he asked Agbo, "Who does this depict?"

"Why, my king, it is you, of course."

"It's Agbo's statement of defiance," the sthapati added.

"Defiance?"

"Yes, my king, for the clergy's affront to you earlier," Agbo replied and tittered.

The symbolism in the sculpture wasn't lost on Kasyapa.

"No one will doubt this is indeed the king's temple," he whispered to the queen who nodded and smiled.

From the glint in the sthapati's eyes and the spring in his walk, Kasyapa suspected his chief architect had something noteworthy in store at Vessagiri, on the other side of the park. Taking a circuitous route, he escorted Kasyapa to a courtyard at the rear of the complex.

"Now turn around, my king."

The base of the several giant boulders was scooped out and decorated into shelters and meditation cells. From a distance, these little pockets appeared to be were ablaze with color, gleaming like glittering gems amongst the verdant green vegetation.

"How did you do it?"

"Frescoes my king, like at Ajanta, but even better," Agbo boasted.

"Outstanding, Agbo. From this day, you are the chitrakar, the chief artist of the kingdom. Let us all work together to bring about a revival of culture and civility in our kingdom."

THE ARCHABBOT AND HIS BRETHREN monks who had assembled at Vessagiri were kept waiting. They were not invited to join the royal tour.

The handover was a simple affair; at the designated time, the monks accepted the complex on behalf of the Buddha. Notably absent was Dama-rakita. In his place was a new abbot. His name was Buddha-datta.

Kasyapa did not know the details of the negotiations that had taken place since that fateful day two weeks earlier. Nor did he know the vizier had set stringent conditions on the management of this royal vihara. The king's vihara was bequeathed to Buddha-datta, the new abbot, and not to a fraternity as was usually the case. Buddha-datta was directly accountable to the vizier. Unbeknownst to Kasyapa, he had an ally in Buddha-datta. But alas, it was too late. Kasyapa had resolved to walk his own path and find his own peace.

Migara was also in attendance that day.

"Well done, my king. It is indeed splendid," the senapati commented, a supercilious smile playing on his lips.

Kasyapa accepted the compliment without comment.

32

Life soon returned to normal for Kasyapa. Affairs of state filled his day. He spent leisure time with his young family. And as was customary, he spent his nights with a woman of the harem.

About three months after his episode, at the meeting of The Gathering, Kasyapa beckoned the sthapati.

"Come, join us, my friend."

It was a rare occurrence indeed when king, vizier, chamberlain, and sthapati sat together at these gatherings. The chamberlain clapped his hands. A bevy of attendants materialized from thin air, laying an extra place for the sthapati and replenishing platters brimming with sweetmeats and morsels. The sthapati rinsed his hands in a copper bowl and sat on a cushion opposite the king. At the flick of Kasyapa's wrist, the attendants disappeared on scurrying feet.

"The vizier here tells me since the completion of the Isuramenu-Bo-Upulvan-Kasub-Vihara, we again have many laborers and artisans without work."

"This is true, my king." The sthapati picked up a morsel and tossed it into his mouth. He rolled it with his tongue and munched on it with relish while the others watched with bemusement.

Kasyapa continued. "He also informs me the recent bad weather has aggravated the situation, with the peasants idle also."

The vizier and chamberlain concurred.

"We have engaged as many men as we can on rajakariya duties, repairing reservoirs, roads, and so forth, but this labor is free. It doesn't help the populace. If we were to pay these workers for their free labor, I am advised by the vizier here we would set a dangerous precedent where a wage would be expected in the future too. We could build more reservoirs. But this will take time and require mostly unskilled labor. We have already cut taxes," Kasyapa said.

The assembled audience remained silent.

"Do you have any suggestions, Sthapati?"

The sthapati gulped down a mouthful of food.

"Do you wish to hear my frank opinion, my king?" the sthapati replied with his usual brazenness. It was obvious to all, he was eager to speak his mind.

Kasyapa looked around to make sure no one else was within earshot.

"I am keen to know."

The sthapati leaned over and winked with a conspiratorial smile plastered across his face. The rest joined in the huddle.

"You are in an enviable position, my king. The rajakariya provides you with all the labor you require for the upkeep of the public works. By my humble estimation, the royal coffers are overflowing. You can only amass so much treasure. What are you going to do with your wealth? Build more viharas?"

"No."

Throwing caution to the wind, the sthapati continued, "You are rich like Kuvera, the god of wealth, the regent of the Dikpala and a protector of the world."

"But Sthapati, Kuvera is a plump character, carrying a money pot and a club. I am nothing of the sort."

"A mere travesty, my king." The sthapati continued with a roguish grin. "Kuvera reached heaven through generosity. His city, Alakamanda, built atop a divine mountain, embodied all prosperity."

"Sthapati, I sense a scheme brewing."

"Rich like Kuvera," the sthapati mused out aloud as though to himself, but clearly, it was intended for his companions.

"Oh, the melodrama, Sthapati. You have missed your vocation in theater," the chamberlain piped up.

"We need a palace worthy of such a king. And I know just the place," the sthapati said with a triumphant cackle, adding to the emerging sense of mystery.

"You are provocative, Sthapati. Are you serious?"

"Yes, very serious, my king, and as for the location," he paused and held his breath, waiting for Kasyapa to take the bait, which, as expected, Kasyapa did.

"Where?"

"Let me take you there."

Kasyapa looked at the others, who traded blank stares. The sheer audacity of the sthapati's proposal had them flabbergasted.

*****

THE STHAPATI AND THE KING SET OUT on their journey a month later. This time, however, their retinue numbered over five hundred, and there was no procurer of women.

"Oh, how I miss the delectable pleasures trips such as this once offered," the sthapati said with a twinkle in his eye.

"You are in the company of the king, Sthapati. No dalliances."

The sthapati laughed.

"Yes, yes, I have reconciled myself to my deprivation. Suffice to say the lavish creature comforts provided by you, my king, more than recompense."

The sthapati had planned the trip meticulously. The first night, they camped at the base of the Arittha Pabbata, the highest mountain range in the region. After a visit to a temple nearby the following morning, they proceeded in a southeasterly direction. They arrived on the banks of the Thakote Wewa lake after sunset. Since it was late, the travelers retired to bed.

WELL BEFORE SUNRISE THE FOLLOWING MORNING, an incessant banging on his tent awoke Kasyapa.

"Get up. Get up," the sthapati shouted, clearly forgetting he ought not to be addressing his king in this way. But the excitement had gotten the better of him.

"What's the urgency, Sthapati?" Kasyapa inquired on exiting his tent.

"Follow me. There is no time to waste. Hurry." The sthapati beckoned, leading the king down a freshly cleared path to a body of water. There, on the verge of the bund of the lake, was a seat.

"Sit here. Wait for the sunrise."

"You brought me here to see the sunrise?"

"Yes, yes. Be patient," the sthapati's voice cracked with excitement.

The twilight sky spread before them into a convexed infinity, twinkling with a million blinking pinpricks. A crisp morning breeze lifted a silvery mist off the inky waters of the Thakote Wewa and wafted it against the assembled crowd. Slowly, the top of the sun cleared some unseen horizon and soared skyward as waters of the lake morphed into a viscous syrup of onyx, gold, and silver. Then, bracketed against a brilliant mango and pomegranate sky, a massive black silhouette appeared in the distance across the lake. Squat and brutish, it poked out of the surrounding forest plain and thrust itself boldly into the morning sky.

"There! Alakamanda!"

"Are you serious?"

"Yes, most certainly. Like nothing ever built before."

Kasyapa sat in silence.

"Let's visit the place," the sthapati said, unable to contain his excitement.

Since the sthapati did not ride, they scrambled into the king's carriage and hurried to the site. On reaching the base of the chosen rock, they clambered out.

"This spot offers the best view of this remarkable sight."

Kasyapa positioned himself at the center of the clearing, placed his hands on his hips, and craned his neck skyward. "You are right, Sthapati, but how are you going to climb this monster? It must be at least six hundred and fifty feet high and made of solid rock."

"Doable," the sthapati said with a self-assured wave of his wrist.

"Have you been to the top?"

"No."

"Has anyone been to the top?"

"Yes. I sent an exploratory team to the summit."

"And?"

"Very difficult to climb. We nearly lost a fellow when he misplaced his footing and almost fell to his death."

"And?"

"There are approximately four acres of useable land at different levels on the top. We will build the Sky Palace there. The abode of King Kasyapa the Magnificent."

"Sky Palace?"

"Yes."

"And what would you call this place?"

The sthapati's eyes twinkling with excitement. "Kasyabgiri—Kasyapa's Mountain, of course."

Kasyapa laughed. "Of course."

In a clearing on the western side of the rock, the sthapati had constructed a large, smoothed-out sandpit. Using a well-honed ebony walking stick with an elegant ivory handle, he quickly sketched his master plan for the royal palace. The king and his architect spent the rest of the day together, fine-tuning their vision. By day's end, it had grown into a plan for a new city.

That night, they camped to the east of the rock and watched the sun set behind this imposing monadnock. Secretly, Kasyapa hoped to find solace in this place, away from the constant rancor and ire of the fraternities.

33

Kasyapa returned to the old palace three days later. During his usual walk with the queen, he outlined his vision for his new city. She listened and, true to her Lambakanna roots, said little.

"What do you think, Sobhana?"

"Your vision is grand, and your ambition great, Kasyapa."

"Yes, I know."

"I am sure it will be better than this dilapidated old place, and certainly an improvement on your modest quarters here." She delicately covered her mouth with her hand and giggled.

Kasyapa couldn't agree with her more. "Yes, this royal palace is indeed a ramshackle place. Hemmed in on all sides by a hodgepodge of buildings and neglected for decades. I dislike it. I must get away from this oppressive place, Sobhana."

She remained silent for a long time and placed a warm hand on his.

"I understand. Do what you must, Kasyapa."

"Of course, I would like you to be involved with the design of the palace."

"Of course, my king."

THAT AFTERNOON, HE CALLED IN THE VIZIER. As usual, he listened. His face was impassive as ever. He nodded to acknowledge this or that point and said nothing.

"Your thoughts, Vizier?"

"It is a massive undertaking, my king. To move the entire capital some fifty miles inland is no easy feat. We have never undertaken such a large project before."

"Yes, that's what makes it exciting. What concerns you, Vizier?"

"My king, you know our culture, especially our religion, frowns upon self-indulgence and self-aggrandizement."

"What are you saying, Vizier?"

"I am saying, I support the wishes of my king. I must, however, warn him of the ramifications of his actions."

"Yes, yes, I understand. Let's walk outside, Vizier."

On stepping out into the garden, Kasyapa turned to his friend. "Abaya, am I foolish?"

Abaya mulled over his answer.

"Well?"

"I can share your vision, Kasyapa. I worry we may be setting our sights on more than we can achieve. I also fear we may have damaging commentary from the fraternities."

"Abaya, I am tired of those pompous, self-righteous men who live in opulence and duplicity. I will no longer be beholden to them. They will be subject to the will of their king. Let them not forget this. Let them not dare speak ill of their king. Let them covert my displeasure at their peril. I am resolute."

Abaya nodded obediently.

"As the sthapati pointed out and you affirmed the other day, our coffers are full, if not overflowing. What am I going to do with my wealth? Although no one is starving yet, it could soon happen if we do nothing. Let us use their labor on this project. It will be the largest construction project ever undertaken, Abaya. I will put my people to work. I will give them jobs."

Abaya listened in silence. He crossed his arms and rocked back and forth on his heels and said nothing.

"My intention is this. I will spend eighty percent of the royal revenue on the wellbeing of my people. In this instance, to construct a new city and provide them employment during these hard times. I will spend the rest of my income at my discretion. After much lobbying and cajoling by the sthapati, I have decided to spend it on a new palace. You must admit, Abaya, I am more generous than kings before me. I am spending my wealth on my people."

Abaya uncrossed his arms and nodded.

"I am turning my back on this place, Abaya. I am abandoning Resplendent Anuradhapura, the capital of my kingdom for over a thousand years. A new city will be constructed in that isolated place, away from the corrosive influence of those who think ill of me. I will move my government there."

Abaya said nothing.

KASYAPA KNEW THERE WOULD BE TALK when word reached the monks of the fraternities. No doubt, behind their oversized palm-leaf fans, they would tut-tut about the low-caste patricide king and his foolish earthly folly. They would whisper about his lack of generosity to the fraternities and clergy.

But Kasyapa no longer cared.

MIGARA MARCHED INTO THE AUDIENCE HALL. His voice was potent with malice. "You are moving the city?"

Migara always walked a fine line bordering on insolence. Kasyapa ignored his failings.

"Good morning, Senapati. I take it you are in good health?"

Since becoming king, Kasyapa never addressed Migara by his name and remained unruffled by Migara's outbursts. This, he knew, irked Migara and threw him off balance.

"Ah, yes, I'm in good health, my king," Migara said, adjusting his posture to a more conciliatory one.

"Now to respond to your earlier outburst. Yes, that is true. I am moving the capital."

"Why?"

"May I remind you, Senapati, it is the prerogative of your king to do as he pleases. As I am the king, I am accountable to no one."

"Why do you want to leave this magnificent city, the capital of our kingdom, the center of our religion for nearly a thousand years?"

"The city has outgrown its usefulness."

"Usefulness?"

"Yes."

"What usefulness? Everything works."

"Senapati, this city is overbuilt. There is no room for expansion or improvement. It is stultified."

"It has served us well all these years."

"Yes, that is true. But now it is time for a change."

"What about the army?"

"The army will move with us. You will move with us to new facilities. Of course, you will personally specify the army's requirements."

"I see."

"I have also allocated one of the finest residential blocks in the new city for you. Imagine what you could do with a new residence. That hundred-year-old house of yours surely can't be comfortable for a man of your stature, Senapati?"

"Yes, it is somewhat of a hovel, I admit. And I can't expand it. The lands adjacent belong to the temples. They are not willing to part with their possessions."

"The vizier will keep you informed of developments," Kasyapa said, tiring of the conversation and wanting it to come to an end.

"All right, then." Migara eyed the vizier and chamberlain with disdain, pivoted on one heel, and exited without bidding his king or the ministers goodbye.

The chamberlain whistled and wiped his brow.

Kasyapa sat on his throne, nibbling on his thumbnail. "What do you think, Vizier?"

"We need the man, my king."

"Do we still lack sufficient support?"

"The Senapati has not caused us any trouble over the years. Is it prudent not to test our strength, my king."

"True. He has been exemplary. Will he cause us grief over this?"

"I don't think so. It was wise of you to offer him lucrative incentives. I think he will enjoy billeting his army in new facilities. I fear it will be expensive."

"Chamberlain, your thoughts?"

"My king, you know of my deep distrust and hatred for that miserable toad."

"Strong words, indeed, Chamberlain."

34

It was a foreboding place indeed, this location Kasyapa chose for his new city. In the thick of the wilderness, it was teeming with wild elephants, snakes, leopards, bears, mosquitoes, hornets, and other vermin. The challenges were daunting, but Kasyapa had the determination, courage, resources, and workforce to fulfill his grand ambition.

Tens of thousands of workers toiled in the construction of the royal citadel and palace alone. Four hundred and thirty elephants were mustered from throughout the land. Supplementing these mighty beasts were two thousand bullocks with their carts and drivers. Over a hundred and twenty million bricks and hundreds of thousands of stone blocks were used in its construction. In four years, it was ready.

On the auspicious day nominated by the royal soothsayers, a large contingent of musicians, dancers, and banner bearers lead the procession down the broad boulevard to the western entrance of the citadel. Kasyapa and the queen, dressed in their royal finery, were transported in gilded palanquins carried by four pole-bearers. Kasyapa's senior ministers, noblemen, and dignitaries followed.

The procession first crossed the massive forty-yard outer earthen rampart and moat to an equally wide middle rampart. There, the procession halted. Ahead lay a wide cooling moat filled with deadly crocodiles, placed there to deter would-be attackers. Kasyapa smiled mischievously at the nervous hush these crocodiles elicited from his guests.

On the opposite side of the moat was a three-tiered inner rampart painted in white, with a narrow footbridge and stairway leading up to an ornate, multicolored, multi-story gopuram-style entrance. At the appointed time, the ornate gates of the gopuram flung open. Kasyapa proceeded over the bridge, up the flight of narrow steps, to an elaborate cleansing hall. The floor of this hall consisted of a paved wading pool with flowing freshwater designed to cleanse the feet of those who entered the sanctuary of the king.

Kasyapa stood on the landing as a virgin of the Kshatriya caste chanted incantations for good fortune and slowly poured a decanter of perfume into the shallow water. Kasyapa then walked through the water, followed by the queen, the royal family, and their visitors.

When the guests exited the cleansing hall and entered an open courtyard on the other side, they were agog. There in front of them were brightly colored buildings and pavilions with brazen copper roofs set among gardens vivid with color, cooled by soothing ponds, pools, and streams reflecting a radiant sun. Some rubbed their eyes in disbelief.

The white apparition many had seen from a distance earlier, now looked like a gigantic wisplike cloud floating just above the treetops. Atop this magic cloud, almost hidden from view, was the gleaming palace of Kasyapa, the king. At the highest point was a tower sheathed in gold and mounted with a massive crystal that refracted sunlight into shafts of iridescent light that radiated into the sky.

"It is as though we have entered paradise," remarked his friend Varahadeva, the chief minister of the Vakataka kingdom, who had traveled especially for the occasion.

"Thank you, Varahadeva. Many of my inspirations were gained while visiting your country as a young man."

"I have seen nothing as picturesque as this anywhere," the envoy from Cina added.

"There is no palace in the sky in my country," the ambassador for Persia noted.

Many of the assembled dignitaries agreed.

Migara was flattering also. "Extremely beautiful. But do you need such an opulent residence, Kasyapa, oh King? Is it not self-indulgent?"

Kasyapa smirked. He had no intention of letting Migara's barb go unnoticed. "My dear Senapati, I note the dwelling you have constructed on the main street is the most lavish. What say you to that? It outshines all others by far."

"Thank you for the compliment," he countered and walked off with his hands clasped behind his back.

Kasyapa turned to the sthapati and chitrakar. His smile broadened into a happy grin. It was indeed the creation of genius, the epitome of magnificence, the ultimate embodiment of royal power celebrating Kasyapa, the king, and the wealth and power of his kingdom.

They had recreated on earth—*Alakamanda*—the city of the gods.

35

Seven years had passed since Kasyapa moved to this place. He never returned to Anuradhapura. Nor did he engage with the fraternities. He had no intention of doing either.

Kasyapa did, however, remain spiritual. He practiced his religion alone and governed his life by a strict code of ethics. These included the Ten Royal Virtues he had learned as a child and the Five Precepts of Morality. On the Uposatha days, he fasted and abstained from worldly pleasures. He meditated twice a day. He had found peace.

Since the incident at Isurumuniya, Kasyapa undertook no further religious projects. Instead, Kasyapa and the vizier reduced the burden of taxation on the people. He continued his good works with new alms halls and hospices for the poor. With Kasyapa's patronage and the sthapati's enthusiasm, the arts flourished. The chitrakar continued to hone his skills as an artist and sculptor.

Migara had also moved to the new city; however, he still favored his residence in Anuradhapura and returned there often to indulge in his secret vices.

Over the years, the vizier received regular reports on the whereabouts of Moggallana.

"My king, we have received news your brother has fled from Madurai to avoid his creditors. His whereabouts are unknown," the vizier advised.

"Fled?"

"Yes, he has disappeared."

Kasyapa sat on his throne, twirling the copper ring on his little finger. "You know, Abaya, we used to play together as children."

"Yes, I remember. You were very fond of each other."

"He must be about twenty-seven years old now. I am often troubled. I snatched away Moggallana's birthright and relegated him to a life of exile and poverty, while I rule as king and am called a patricide and a usurper.

"You had no choice, Kasyapa."

"Didn't I? I can understand Moggallana's bitterness. It saddens me."

PART THREE

36

At about the same time, in far-off Kapisa, in north-central Afghanistan, near present-day Bagram, a sixteen-year-old servant girl named Amira was scrubbing the gloomy corridors of the royal palace.

The daughter of a goat herder, she was the oldest of five siblings, and the only one with striking blue eyes and red hair. She had been twelve-years-old when her father brought her to this dreadful palace and sold her into slavery. Abandoned by her family, she was alone. Just a grubby little waif—a forsaken little nobody.

It was cold in the hallways of this crumbling edifice. Her face was numb, and her fingers cherry pink from her exertion. To keep her mind off her drudgery, she sang to herself a song she had picked up from the royal singing troupe. It was the only one she knew.

On that day, a royal courtier happened to be walking by and overheard her singing. "You have a fine voice," he said. "We will train you to be a singer and dancer."

Some months later, the second time she performed, the king clapped his hands and called her to him.

"You are a good singer and dancer, young girl," he said.

"Thank you, my king." She curtsied nervously. Amira was so pleased to hear that from the king. No one had ever complimented her before. She was happy.

Then, about a week later, a man came for her. He placed a leather collar around her neck, attached it by a long rope to the back of his camel, and took her away. No one bade her goodbye. No one cared.

"You are lucky," the man grumbled and spat on the ground. "You have your own camel because you belong to the king." He was a gruff and smelly man. "Now, don't do anything foolish. The king will murder my entire family if anything happens to you."

Yes, she was lucky. Other women in the caravan had to travel on foot. They whipped those who fell behind, and in the night, some were taken away by the men and used. One woman had tried to run away, but they caught her. They beat her on the bottom of one foot till it bled. The wounds on her foot festered, and she couldn't keep up with the caravan. So the men used her over and over again and dumped her on the side of the road. Amira didn't know what happened to her. Maybe she was eaten by wolves.

The slave trader guarded her at all times and kept other men away from her. He didn't speak to her much. It was as though he didn't like her, but then, in her mind, nobody else seemed to like her much either. She didn't remember much else about the journey at all. Only that she was always hungry and just sat on her camel, rocking from side to side, daydreaming of being a princess, or maybe a concubine, with lots of jewels and beautiful clothes.

A servant had once told her anyone could become a concubine if they were good-looking and caught the king's eye. Nobody had told her she was pretty. Besides, why would a king like her? Nobody else did. Often, she wondered what it would be like to be dead.

When they reached a place called Hormuz, they put her in the bowels of something called a ship. It was worse than being on a camel. It tossed and lurched about, squeaking and thudding in a big blue lake where the water was salty and never still. She couldn't see much of the outside at all, only what was visible through a small crack between the planking of the ship. Each morning, they let her onto the top deck to empty her slop bucket and wash her face. After that, they locked her up again amid bundles of smelly dried fish.

ABOUT THREE WEEKS AFTER they had left Hormuz, the ship stopped at a city by the side of the sea called Desinganadu. Soon, there was a loud commotion onboard, and the captain and a man in a flowing robe came below deck to look at her. They spoke to each other in a language she didn't understand and went away. The captain returned later and said he had a job for her. She feared the worst. She had seen what happened to slave girls. She was about to cry when he slapped her across her face.

"Listen to me. I have a job for you. You will come to no harm if you behave. Do you understand?"

Amira's eyes filled with tears. She nodded.

"You are going to a wedding."

"A wedding?"

"You are going to pretend to be a princess. You should be able to do that. You worked in a palace. You know how they act."

She nodded again. Yes, she had seen them in their beautiful clothes.

"That's all you have to do. Don't talk. Just sit, smile, and look pretty. I will be there to guard you and make sure you don't do anything foolish. Do you understand?"

"But how can I look pretty in these dirty clothes?" she asked in a meek voice, pointing to her tattered clothing, which she hadn't changed since leaving Kapisa nearly six months earlier.

"Don't worry," he said and left.

Two days later, the captain said she was going to the city.

He brought his face close to hers. His breath stunk as much as the dried fish he had in the hold of his ship.

"Now don't do anything stupid. Or you will be dead. Or in a brothel. You don't want that to happen, do you?"

Amira shook her head.

When she set foot on land after so many weeks at sea, she was pale as mountain snow and wobbled to the edge of the dock, almost falling into the sea. The captain grabbed her by the arm and laughed. He led her through the streets using a rope attached to her collar. Passersby stared at her as she stumbled behind this gruff man.

He took her to a well-to-do-looking house. There, he introduced her to a large, fat woman and removed her collar before leaving. The woman gave her a bucket of water and a small cup and watched over her as she cleaned herself the best she could. That evening, the captain returned to collect her.

"You look pretty," he muttered and wrapped a large scarf around her neck to hide her collar.

"I don't feel pretty, even though the clothes that woman gave me are very pretty," she replied.

ON THE CENTRAL DAIS WERE SIX LARGE CUSHIONS. Amira lowered herself gracefully onto one, imitating what she had seen of the king's courtesans back in Kapisa. The captain sat behind her. Next to her sat a man. They introduced him as a prince from a place called Sin-a-lad-vip-a.

He was impeccably dressed and wore a stylish turban with a large gem at its center. The man himself was shorter than her, and skinny with a dark, sallow complexion. His eyes were small and sat below straight eyebrows on a gaunt, acne-scarred face. His nose was average, and large chapped lips stretched over his buck teeth. He curtsied as she took her place. She smiled politely and averted his eyes. Amira wondered if he, too, was an actor like her.

As the evening wore on, he tried to make conversation with her. She didn't understand what he was saying. Besides, she found his nasal voice unmanly. There was something ugly about the man—on the inside. The way he stared at her made her skin crawl. He tried to touch her hand. The captain put a stop to that, leaning over and whispering something in the man's ear. He left her alone after that.

She enjoyed playing a princess, even if it was only for a few hours. As she walked back to the ship, she wondered what payment the captain received for this elaborate charade. But she didn't mind. It was amusing.

ABOUT SEVEN DAYS LATER, SHE ARRIVED at some place. She didn't know where. She thought her father would have liked this place with all the lush green plants for his goats. It was hot and sticky.

They locked her up in a dingy room and fed her through a hole in the wall. They allowed her out twice a day to go to the toilet in the back.

Amira spent her days in this darkened room alone.

Why is my life like this, penned up and tethered like a goat in my father's flock, bought and sold and abused?

But then, her life had always been this way. She knew no other.

37

The manifest from the king of Kapisa read: one box of lapis lazuli, one jar of opium, three fish-shaped jars containing the best Kapisayani Madhu wine, and a young dancing girl—a virgin with blue eyes and red hair, with an excellent disposition, guaranteed healthy and not liable to run away. In exchange, the Kapisan king requested a hundred pearls for which the resplendent island of Lanka was famous, and any other items the king of Lanka deemed seemly.

The vizier judged a reciprocal gift was appropriate. The chamberlain determined the only place suitable for a gift such as her was in the king's harem. And the harem-keeper agreed. It was settled. The vizier set her exchange price: one hundred pearls as requested, one bundle of peacock feathers, one bundle of cinnamon, one bag each of nutmeg, cloves, and cardamom, and a small bag of assorted gems of inferior quality.

Amira was now the property of King Kasyapa.

*****

AROUND MID-MORNING, about a week after Amira had arrived, a man dragged her into a courtyard. She blinked wildly as her eyes adjusted to the bright sunlight. She sniffed herself. The stale odor of dried fish wafted up from her clothes and into her nostrils.

A short, plump woman with saggy jowls and a belly that flopped out of her clothes stood a short distance away. She had a no-nonsense look about her and carried what appeared to be a short whip.

The plump woman walked up to Amira, grabbed her by her cheeks, forced open her mouth, and sniffed her breath.

"*Humph*," she grunted.

The woman's hands were small, with stubby, businesslike fingers that dug into her cheeks. The woman had a roundish face on which sat a large nose and thick lips. She had a receding hairline and wore her hair in a small bun on the back of her head.

The plump woman peered into Amira's eyes and said nothing. To Amira, she was looking in two directions at once. She had one straight eye, and the other a lazy one that looked elsewhere.

The plump woman grabbed Amira's hair and moved it away from her face and ears and studied them for defects.

"*Humph*," she grunted and said something.

Amira blanched; her eyes darted from left to right.

The plump woman stuck her elbows out like wings and called out to a tall, masculine-looking woman. This woman, who looked as strong as an ox, wore large bracelets covering her arms. She had a sword slung from her waist and carried a pointy spear. She grabbed Amira by the back of her neck and shoved her forward.

Then the tall woman squatted, stood up, jumped, touched her toes, and bent over backward. She motioned Amira to imitate her.

Her thick, dirt-encrusted brocade blouse and heavy skirt clung stiffly to her body as Amira did as instructed.

The plump woman then motioned Amira into a building. As she followed, with each step, her terror grew more and more acute. *Why are these terrible things happening to me?* Her hands trembled uncontrollably at her sides.

The plump woman gestured to Amira to take off her clothes.

Amira shook her head vehemently.

The plump woman tapped her whip on her thigh. The tall woman rattled her spear. Tears cascaded down her cheeks as she took off her grubby brocade vest.

The plump woman grunted, gesturing to her to remove all; the tall woman growled. So, Amira took off all her clothes and stood naked. She had never been naked in front of anyone before. The plump woman squeezed each of Amira's breasts and said something to the other woman. They laughed.

Then she walked around her and tapped her shoulders and her buttocks with her whip. She squeezed her buttocks and thighs, then stuck her hand between them. She got the tall woman to bend Amira over and examined her from the rear.

Then came the worst part. She made Amira sit on a large box in the corner of the room and ordered her to spread her legs. With tears streaming down her face, she shook her head and refused. The plump woman slapped her and shouted something.

Before she knew what was happening, the tall woman knelt in front of her and grabbed both her ankles, lifted them up, and forced her legs apart. She was certain she would fall off the box. It was painful too, but she could do nothing. The plump woman came over and inspected her vagina and said something to the other woman. They sniggered. She squatted in front of Amira and stuck two fingers into her. Amira writhed in agony, more of shame than of pain. The woman wriggled her fingers inside, took them out, studied and smelt them, and made a disgusted face. She got up, made her *"humph"* sound again, and walked out. The tall woman followed.

Amira waited for a few moments and put her clothes back on. She sat on the floor and begged her gods that this would end. *Why is my life like this, one of endless suffering and humiliation? What did I do in my past life to deserve this?* She wrapped her arms around herself, rocked back and forth, and sobbed.

ABOUT HALF AN HOUR LATER, THE TALL WOMAN RETURNED and beckoned her to a carriage outside. Amira had never been in a carriage. She didn't know where it was taking her. She peeped out of a small window. It was a large city, with wide streets and colorful buildings.

Once they had cleared the city gates, the tall woman pulled out something that looked like a hand with many thick yellow fingers. She broke a finger off and gave it to the plump woman, who snapped the top off and peeled the yellow skin, revealing a white tubular structure inside. She took a large bite and happily chomped away.

Amira noticed the plump woman and the tall woman both had a dainty three-ringed tattoo on their necks—like a permanent necklace.

Realizing Amira was watching, the plump woman leaned over, patted her leg, and gave one of these finger-like things to Amira. Seeing she was confused, the plump woman took it back and peeled it by breaking its top and gave it back to Amira. Amira cautiously took a small bite, and her taste buds exploded. She had never tasted anything so delicious in her life. So sweet and tangy. She smiled keenly at the plump woman and her friend and ate it all. They shared many more on their trip until there were none left.

The women were a lot nicer to her now and laughed at her often, especially the tall one. Even though she appeared scary and spoke with a man's voice, she sounded carefree.

That night, they stayed at a house. The food they ate was different. Not dry like what she was used to. They also had lots of different dishes. She watched the plump woman and the tall woman eat and did as they did. The food had many unusual tastes. Some were very hot and made her mouth burn and her eyes water. They laughed at her and pointed to foods that were not so hot. Back home with her family, they had little food. All she had to eat there was bread and stuff from goats— goat meat, goat milk, goat cheese, goat ghee, goat curd, maybe a turnip, and a few leaves of spinach. At the palace, she had eaten food scraps. She had to compete with the other servants for it. So, she usually went hungry.

They shared a room that night. They gave Amira a corner with a mat. The women had held their noses and indicated she stank. Amira curled up on her mat and slept well, even though the plump woman snored all night, making loud sounds like a camel.

The following morning, she woke to an unusual noise. She opened the door a crack and peered outside. There was water falling out of the sky—buckets and buckets and buckets of it. The branches and leaves of trees sagged from the weight of swollen drops of water falling on them. The fresh smell of rain filled her nostrils. Amira sat cross-legged and watched the downpour for hours.

The tall woman woke up and soon started jumping about because she wanted to go to the toilet, but she couldn't go there in the rain. Finally, she opened the door and stood outside under the eaves, lifted her dhoti to her thighs, parted her legs, and did it into the rain. Amira did too, but she wasn't as good at it. Her thick and heavy pale blue skirt, richly embroidered, soiled, and frayed in many places was hard to lift, so some of it went down her leg.

By mid-morning, the sun came out, and the sky was blue once again. It became hot and sticky. There was a commotion outside, and extra people joined their caravan. They left at about noon, but the journey was slow because the ground was muddy. When it got dark, the additional people who had joined them lit lanterns, waved burning torches, and banged their drums. Amira later learned this was to scare off wild animals.

Towards midnight, Amira gazed out of the window. In the distance was a shimmering mountain lit by the brightest moon. *Such an odd mountain, sticking out of nowhere, looking like a giant white ball of cotton or maybe even a cloud.* Then she saw the tops of buildings. Just their roofs poking out from the top. *Strange indeed.*

AMIRA AWOKE TO THE SOUND of whispers. She assumed she was dreaming, but there were no pictures. She cracked open a sleepy eyelid and peeked. Then she opened the other eye and found herself surrounded by beautiful, bright-eyed, dark-faced girls seated on the floor observing her.

"Look at her red hair," whispered one to another.

"And her eyes are blue—very odd," another chimed in.

Their whispers sounded so soft, gentle, and musical. Amira lay on her side, not sure what she ought to do. She peered at them. They looked like concubines Amira remembered seeing back home. So clean and elegant, with such pretty clothes.

"Can she see with those strange eyes?"

"She smells."

"Where did she come from?"

"Oh, poor thing. Look at that terrible collar around her neck and look, they have tied her to the post."

"All right ladies," the plump woman clapped and shooed the giggling girls away. "This is Amira. She is from across the sea, from a land far away. She is a gift from a king."

"But she is too dirty and smelly to be a gift from a king."

"Now Siripali, you would be too, if you had traveled as far as she has."

The plump woman came close to Amira and wriggled her nose and grimaced. She fiddled with Amira's collar, made her trademark *"humph"* sound, and clapped her hands. Two assistants, lesser dressed than the others, but still pretty and shapely, came up and unshackled her. A glint of sympathy flashed across the plump woman's face when Amira touched her neck, which she hadn't felt for months.

Amira's mind was racing. *Where am I? This place looks like a harem. These pretty girls must be concubines, and the plump woman must be the harem-keeper. I am in a harem somewhere!*

"Come. We need to bath you first." The harem-keeper beckoned with her hand.

Amira followed her timidly, happy to be free of that terrible collar and rope.

First, the harem-keeper took her to a building that had a mildly repugnant smell. There, along the wall, were a row of large blocks set into the floor. Each had a hole at its center with two elevated footprints. *That's odd. What were they for?* She thought. The harem-keeper, annoyed by Amira's ignorance, pushed her aside, lifted her clothing to her waist, placed one foot on each footpad, and squatted. Now she understood. *These are fancy, indeed.* The harem-keeper took a cup, dipped it in a bucket close at hand, and motioned that certain parts of the anatomy to be washed like so. Everything down the hole, the harem-keeper gestured. The girls piled up against the doorway sniggered through stifled giggles. *Back home, we did it wherever it was convenient. In the warmer months, it was in an outside courtyard. During the colder months, it was inside and then covered over with some sand. Washing? Never!*

The harem-keeper chased the girls off and left Amira alone for a while. When she emerged, the harem-keeper marched her to a building with a high wall decorated with delicate floral patterns and a veranda all around. At its center was a paved courtyard with a large elevated fountain under a large pergola.

She couldn't see where the water entered this fountain, but it brimmed over and cascaded down its fluted sides on its own accord. Amira traced the cascading water with the tip of her finger. So much water. Back home in Kapisa, water was scarce and carried in buckets. If you saw a bucket full of water, it was a noteworthy event, let alone a whole tank of it flowing so wastefully into a covered drain below.

The harem-keeper beckoned Amira to take her clothes off. Amira looked around and shook her head. Why did that woman want her to take her clothes off again? In public! She hoped this wasn't like before. She was just beginning to like this place.

The harem-keeper was losing her patience. She slapped her ever-present whip against her thigh. She yelled something to her assistants, who grabbed a pail, filled it with water from the fountain, and doused Amira with cold water. She had never had water on her whole body in her entire life. Never!

She stood there dripping while they all laughed at her. With her hands on her hips, the harem-keeper ordered Amira to remove her clothes. She demurred. The harem-keeper motioned to her assistants, who descended on Amira and pulled off her clothes. First, her shawl. Then their fingers undid her thread-worn brocade blouse. Amira grasped it across her breasts, but it was to no avail. The harem-keeper yanked it off her and added it to the pile on the ground.

The girls giggled. "Oh, look at those," one said to another. "So small and pointy and pink. So white!"

Then the assistants undid her thick skirt and let it fall to the ground. Amira didn't protest anymore. It was pointless. She stood there naked, her lithesome pale body glowing in the morning sun. Her matted and dirty red hair hung loosely on her shoulders and back. The assistants covered their mouths and sniggered, pointing at her dark-orange triangle and perky breasts with erect pink nipples. They had never seen such before; theirs were black. The harem-keeper chuckled, too, sharing their amusement. Amira blushed.

Then they got to work on her. The harem-keeper supervised as two assistants, while prattling away at each other, scrubbed Amira from top to bottom. *So strange, all this water and wetness on my body—so soothing.* They shampooed her hair with shikai extracted from the acacia plant. They rubbed smelly liquid they called reetha all over her and used a round scrubbing stone to strip away years of accumulated grime. They were too shy to scrub the delicate parts, so they indicated to Amira what she needed to do. She followed their instructions. Finally, they rubbed her down with a large white linen sheet and wrapped it around her. The curious spectators gathered around clapped merrily.

As Amira followed the harem-keeper out, she couldn't stop sniffing her arms. They smelled fresh, with a delicate fragrance that was new to her.

Taking her to another building, the harem-keeper rummaged through several large wooden trunks. Pulling something out, she looked at Amira with her lazy eye, returned it, and searched some more. Finally, she found something appropriate. The blouse was of muslin cotton fabric that only came down to her midriff. The harem-keeper laced it up and pinched the blouse where her breasts should have filled out. She made the usual sound, "humph."

Clearly, Amira didn't fill out the blouse as the harem-keeper had expected. She was relatively small-breasted compared to the enormous breasts she had noticed among the harem girls. She blushed.

For her lower attire, the harem-keeper held up a large piece of white cloth, about five yards in length and a yard wide. No doubt Amira's bewilderment showed, the ever-helpful assistants jumped in and grabbed the cloth. "Dhoti, dhoti," they giggled as they demonstrated how one was worn. One of the assistants ran off and returned with a small metal mirror and held it in front of Amira. Amira's eyes widened, and she broke out in a broad smile. She looked so clean and even beautiful. She never imagined herself as being attractive. For that matter, she had never seen herself in a mirror before, only her reflection in a bucket of water. *Maybe I could have had bigger breasts,* she thought.

THE HAREM-KEEPER EMPLOYED A PERSIAN WOMAN, the wife of a horse trader, to teach Amira the local language. These classes took up most of her day.

In her first week, Amira reported to the infirmary each morning for a checkup. They made her drink a thick, green concoction. "To rid you of worms," the woman there said. She was certain the worms would hate it as much as she did.

Amira also reported to the menstrual house, where the attendant recorded the dates of her periods and checked her private bits. Amira had by now gotten used to exposing her body bits. Nobody here seemed to care. She too walked about with her body barely hidden beneath her clothes. It made sense. In the heat, it was more comfortable this way.

"Amira, you sound like a crow—*caw caw,*" the harem-keeper joked one day, flapping her arms like a bird. "You need to speak like a songbird, gentle, soft, and melodical," she said, wagging her finger. The harem-keeper loved wagging her finger at everyone.

As her language skills improved, Amira attended classes in voice training, reading, writing, counting, reciting poetry, singing, dancing, playing musical instruments, grooming, etiquette, and civility.

*****

SOME MONTHS AFTER her arrival, the harem-keeper dressed Amira in a beautiful light green dhoti and blouse. She set her long red hair in a braid decorated with sweet-scented flowers.

"Where are we going?" Amira asked, her voice quivering, and her heart thumping.

"You are going to meet the queen. Make sure you make a good impression," the harem-keeper said.

The queen and certain members of her family had separate quarters within the harem. The two princesses, Bodhi and Uppalavanna, and four older females related to the queen usually stayed in their quarters in the harem. The queen rarely stayed but visited often.

"This is Amira, a gift from the king of Kapisa," the harem-keeper said and bowed.

"You are very pretty, Amira, with your red hair and blue eyes."

"Thank you, my queen." Amira bowed and blushed.

"Oh, you turn pink too," the queen said and laughed. "I have an appropriate nickname for you. It's *Nilupulesi*—one with eyes like blue water lilies."

"Thank you, my queen."

"You made a good impression," the harem-keeper said as she accompanied Amira back to the women's quarters.

"Thank you, Harem-Keeper. The queen seems like a very nice person. The queen in Kapisa often beat and punished the concubines in fits of jealous rage."

"Oh, our queen would never do that. As long as you don't break the rules, Amira," she said, brandishing her ever-present wagging finger.

*****

THE FIRST TIME AMIRA MET SIRIPALI, she was seated cross-legged on the floor, having her eyebrows plucked. Siripali had thick-lashed brown eyes, shapely eyebrows, and a straight, narrow nose. She was darker than most of the other concubines but very beautiful. Siripali looked up and patted the floor beside her. Amira sat next to her and crossed her legs too.

"So light-skinned, red-haired Nilupulesi."

"How do you know my nickname?"

"News travels fast in the harem." She smiled and shrugged a shoulder. "So, do you like our harem?"

"It is much better than the one back in Kapisa, where I come from."

"Is Kapisa like here?"

"Oh no, this place is a lot hotter, nicer, greener, and stickier."

"Are all your people like you?"

"They are mostly pale. Some have different-colored eyes, grey or brown, and sometimes green or blue. Their hair is usually dark, but sometimes golden or red like mine."

"The people here are all the same. Just darker or lighter," Siripali replied in a playful offhandish voice. "Welcome to our harem. I will look after you," she said, tapping Amira on her knee.

Amira flashed a meek smile.

38

As they had always done, Kasyapa and Sobhana continued their regular afternoon walks. Their preferred route was along the meandering paths of the Boulder Gardens, laid out at the base of the rock.

"You know, Kasyapa, we do not have a vihara close to our palace."

"Does that trouble you, Sobhana?"

"No, but it may be good for our children. While you and I know the teachings of our religion, our children have no such experiences."

"Could we not engage a bhikkhu to tutor them, like I was?"

"We could. If this is your wish."

They walked in silence for a short distance, and Kasyapa stopped. "When I built this city, a group of hermit monks occupied many of the caves under these massive boulders of our garden. As you can see, the sthapati decorated them lavishly and incorporated them into the grand design of the gardens."

"Yes, I often imagine a garden in paradise to be like this. With multi-colored pavilions, decorated caves, waterfalls, songbirds, flowers, and shade trees."

Kasyapa smiled. "I relocated those ascetic monks to Niyyanti Park over there. At the time, I promised I would build them a vihara. I have been remiss. Let me make amends with them and also fulfill your wish. We will build a vihara and name it the Bo-Upulvan-Kasub-Vihara of Niyyanti Park."

"You are a virtuous man, Kasyapa." She smiled and touched his cheek.

ONCE WORD REACHED THE FRATERNITIES that Kasyapa was building a vihara at Niyyanti Garden, they too had ideas. The monks thought to themselves; perhaps the king had a change of heart. Soon, the vizier was receiving representations for the funding of other viharas. The vizier raised the subject with the king.

"Oh, do they suffer, Vizier? Are they in hardship? Are their viharas dilapidated? Are the monks starving?"

"No, my king."

"You know my position. They must support themselves from the generous grants they received from my late father and from the donations they receive from their devotees."

The vizier did not pursue the matter any further.

While walking with Sobhana a few weeks later, Kasyapa said, "The monks of the viharas have come to me with their begging bowls."

"I see."

"These men who ostracized me and called me a patricide, now curry favor with me. I have no desire to have anything to do with them. Why should I help them?"

"Kasyapa, it is true they riled you in the past, but is that a reason to carry this grudge into the afterlife? You have stymied their power and influence and curtailed their stipends from the royal purse. Listen to their plaint, my dear king, and be magnanimous if their grievances are genuine. Extract from them certain undertakings if you wish. Do what bodes well with your conscience."

Kasyapa said nothing. She was his trusted partner and confidant.

*****

"MY KING, YOU MAY RECALL A CONVERSATION we had regarding the viharas some months ago."

"Yes, Vizier, and I made my view clear."

"I support your view, my king. However, I think we should consider the Isuramenu-Bo-Upulvan-Kasub-Vihara in fair Anuradhapura as a special case."

"Why so?"

"We didn't fund it sufficiently to be self-sustaining. Since it is the royal vihara, it may be prudent to maintain it to a good standard. May I suggest you meet the abbot of this vihara? I am certain you will find him interesting."

"If you wish."

A WEEK LATER, WHILE KASYAPA WAS WALKING in the gardens adjoining the public audience hall outside the citadel, the vizier and the abbot of the royal vihara joined him.

The vizier, ever the astute statesman, had orchestrated the meeting place carefully. As the abbot was a bhikkhu, specific deferential protocols needed to be observed by king and commoner alike. The vizier knew, however, Kasyapa would never agree to this. In fact, he had not spoken to the clergy since that incident some twelve years earlier. The mere fact he was willing to meet the abbot was a significant shift in his position. The vizier needed to tread cautiously.

"My king, this is the abbot Buddha-datta of the royal Isura-menu-Bo-Upulvan-Kasub-Vihara."

Kasyapa was gracious. "Greetings Buddha-datta. I hope we find you well?"

"Yes, my king. I am well. I hope we find you well also."

Kasyapa nodded.

The vizier put on his deadpan smile. "My king, do you not recognize the bhikkhu?"

"I don't believe we have met."

"This is Sumana-datta, who now goes by the name of Buddha-datta. He was in school with us."

"Yes, I was. Much younger than both of you and the ferocious Miga-ra," Buddha-datta added.

Kasyapa grimaced. "Ahhhh... Migara. Everyone remembers Migara."

"Oh yes, and the day you punched him in the face. It was a sight to behold. We all supported you for putting a bully in his place. Oh, and the drama that followed. I remember it so vividly. Like it happened only yesterday."

"Yes, it was an episode indeed. One I have had the good fortune not to repeat, thanks to the guidance and intercession of the vizier here."

"Buddha-datta is also a good friend of the queen," the vizier added.

"Yes, we grew up as neighbors. We are about the same age."

"I see. Now Buddha-datta, the vizier tells me your vihara is run down"

"If I may correct you, my king. It is your vihara."

"Yes, yes, I see. It is mine, indeed."

"Sumana-datta became a bhikkhu after leaving school. He has studied in Jambudvipa and has visited Ajanta," the vizier added, keen to set the groundwork for a cordial relationship between the two men.

"Oh, we must talk about your visit there some time," Kasyapa replied, warming to his new acquaintance on discovering their shared interests.

During the ensuing discussion, additional fields and villages were gifted to the vihara to ensure its proper upkeep. After the meeting, Kasyapa added, "Buddha-datta, join the queen and me this afternoon. I am sure she would be pleased to meet you, and I would like to hear about your visit to Ajanta and other matters."

Once Kasyapa departed, the vizier turned to Buddha-datta. "Now Thera, you have made a good impression on our king. You are privileged to be invited into the royal citadel. I would caution you in the strongest words not to reveal what you see and hear inside to anyone. As you know, many seek to besmirch this king."

"I understand, Abaya."

AFTER REMINISCING WITH HER OLD CHILDHOOD FRIEND, the queen retired with her ladies-in-waiting.

"Let's walk in the Western Precinct, Buddha-datta," Kasyapa said, leading the way. "I would like to share with you the view from a vantage point of these gardens. It is my favorite," Kasyapa added as he climbed a stairway at the rear of a large boulder in the Terraced Gardens to a pillared multi-colored circular pavilion on top.

"I see what you mean, my king, the vista is breathtaking, proportional, and spectacular."

"Yes, it's the sthapati's work. He always yearned for a project like this. If not for his persistence, I doubt I would have had the courage to undertake such a monumental undertaking. While I had considerable misgiving about it at the start, it helped the people during hard times and has brought me much solace."

While they spoke, two attendants rushed up the stairs with refreshments. Since it was already past noon, and monks did not eat after that time, Buddha-datta took only the water offered to him. In consideration for his guest, Kasyapa also took only the water.

"Come, let me show you the chitrakar's latest project."

They walked down a flight of steps and through a tunnel created by two boulders resting against each other. They headed west toward the formal gardens and paused by a large open-air building with a multi-tiered tiled roof and brightly colored pillars located at the center of the gardens. Kasyapa called out, "Chitrakar, we have a visitor."

Out came the chitrakar, dressed only in a loincloth and covered from head to toe in a powdery coat of dust.

"Buddha-datta, you may remember the chitrakar. He did most of the paintings at your vihara and the carvings of the image house too."

"Yes. I remember the chitrakar."

"I have been telling the chitrakar we need to create unique local art. Don't you agree, Buddha-datta?"

"Most certainly, my king. We have many gifted artists in our kingdom. No doubt, the first among these is the chitrakar."

The chitrakar lowered his eyes to the floor. Even though he was now the king's chief artist, he was unable to shed his innate shyness.

"Chitrakar, show the bhikkhu your work."

The chitrakar's face lit up. He rubbed his stubbly chin releasing a small puff of dust and ushered them behind an awning. There, on a large incomplete block of stone, was a sculpture in high relief of a man in a royal pose with a woman seated on his thigh.

"This is the king and queen when they were first married, with the king seated in a royal half-lotus pose and the queen seated on our king's thigh," the chitrakar announced. "The inspiration for this sculpture was the painting of the great love story of Udayin and Gupta in Ajanta."

"Yes, indeed. I have seen that painting at Ajanta." Buddha-datta nodded. "I can see the resemblance."

"See what I mean, Chitrakar? You are copying."

"Beautifully executed, Chitrakar," Buddha-datta said. "To be fair, my king, this sculpture is similar, but it is far superior to the painting across the sea."

"Yes, this is true," Kasyapa said.

Then chitrakar rushed off to the other side of the building and unveiled his latest work. Again set in a large unfinished block, it was of a family. The chitrakar cleared his throat. "It is of the royal family."

Kasyapa studied the sculpture in silence. "Now Chitrakar, this is indeed a fine work of art, original, flattering, and realistic. I like it."

Buddha-datta agreed. The chitrakar simpered, wringing his hands with pride.

LEAVING THE CHITRAKAR, they continued their walk through the lavish gardens of the royal compound.

"Now Buddha-datta, you no doubt are aware the fraternities frown upon this city. They claim it is the fanciful work of a deluded megalomaniac. The work of a king who squanders the wealth of the kingdom on self-aggrandizement. What think you?"

Buddha-datta reflected on the king's question for several moments and replied. "My king, our religion does not see wealth as inherently evil. Nor does it assert nirvana is more difficult for a rich man to attain. To some extent, our religion associates one's financial wellbeing in the present to acts of charity during one's previous lives. Wealth itself is not problematic, as long as it is obtained without deceit and used munificently for the benefit of the needy. On the contrary, the rich are in an enviable position of being able to practice the great virtue of generosity. By all accounts, you have been generous to your people."

Buddha-datta waited, allowing his king to reflect on his monologue and continued. "Some in the religious establishments encourage charity to themselves to accumulate spiritual merit for future lives. I see you do not do this. This does not make you sinful. What is important, is that you show compassion to the less fortunate. This, on all accounts, you have done."

They walked into the Pavilion of the Four Ponds, a massive structure that straddled the main thoroughfare. Standing at its center, a cooling breeze blowing around them, the thera continued.

"Fear not the barbs of spiteful men, my king. Do what is meritorious. Undertake personal devotion and practice what is virtuous. Reflect on the teachings of the Enlightened One. 'What you are is what you have been. What you will be is what you do now.' In this way, find peace for yourself."

"I am grateful for your candid insights, Buddha–datta."

39

"A large force of Pandyans landed on our island at Jambukola in the north," Migara announced as he quick-marched into the audience hall.

"Why so Senapati?" Kasyapa asked.

"The army of the Kalabhra has invaded the land of the Pandyans. As a consequence, a displaced Pandyan chieftain has fled to our shores with his army. They captured Jambukola port and are headed south. We must push them back into the sea."

"Vizier, do you agree?"

The vizier nodded. "Yes, my king."

"What do you propose, Senapati?"

"I suggest we annihilate them," Migara said, banging his clenched fist into the palm of his hand.

"Yes. Let us send a clear signal. We, in this kingdom, will not be trifled with," the vizier said.

Migara looked at Kasyapa obliquely. "Why don't you join us and see for yourself what real men do?"

"Why not, Senapati? Let your king see for himself how his senapati spends the royal revenues," Kasyapa replied, deflecting the Migara's insinuation that he was less than a man. "Also, let the people see their king safeguarding their realm."

The vizier's eyebrows shot skyward. "Senapati, do you propose to take our king on this expedition of yours?"

"Vizier, you stifle our king."

"May I remind you it is your duty and mine to protect our monarch? How do you propose to ensure our king's safety?"

"Why, Vizier, he has a splendid army to protect him."

The vizier looked down at Migara with disdain. "May I remind you, Senapati, our kings only fight adversaries of equal rank? A petty war-lord has mounted this incursion. Am I correct?" the vizier said in an unusually raised voice.

"I believe so."

"How strong?"

"No more than a thousand men with their families."

"They are mere riffraff unworthy of a kingly encounter. Therefore, I demand our king refrains from leading his army. You, Senapati, may lead the army as its commander. The king, may if he wishes, accompany you as an observer. You are to personally guarantee his safety. Is that clear, Senapati?"

"As you wish, Vizier."

In secret, Migara despised the vizier. He remembered Abaya from their school days. He found it much easier to get his way with Kasyapa in the vizier's absence.

"It is agreed, then. I will join my troops in battle."

"An advance guard from Anuradhapura will be dispatched immediately to carry out any holding action. The main force will accompany us north. We should be ready in five days. The journey north will take us another five," Migara said.

The vizier crossed his arms across his chest as the meeting ended.

*****

MOUNTED ON A FINE TURKMENE STEED, Kasyapa made a grand exit through the eastern gates of the citadel.

"Come, Amira. Come look at our king," Siripali yelled.

By the time they reached the harem gates, the crowd of onlookers was at least five deep. Amira, being taller than most, could see over their heads. Siripali, on the other hand, was much shorter and jumped up and down to get a view.

"Why are you jumping like this? You have seen him before," Amira teased.

"Can you see him? Can you see him?"

"No, I can't."

"Never mind, you will see him soon enough," Siripali said playfully as they walked back to the courtyard.

Sɪʀɪᴘᴀʟɪ ᴀɴᴅ Aᴍɪʀᴀ sᴀᴛ ᴜɴᴅᴇʀ ᴀ sʜᴀᴅᴇ ᴛʀᴇᴇ. "That girl over there, with the black hair and yellow skin, is foreign like you. She comes from a land called Cina. She brags a lot," Siripali said, pointing to a girl standing alone near the fountain.

"Where is Cina?"

"I don't know. Someplace far away, I guess." She shrugged. "Girls in the harem are mostly daughters of nobles, chieftains, and high-class families. There are a few girls from ordinary families too. And of course, there are also gifts from foreigner rulers, like you. We don't have any slaves, though."

"I was a slave girl in Kapisa," Amira responded.

Siripali looked surprised. "*Shh*, there is no reason for you to tell anyone that. Tell no one. It will be our secret."

Amira nodded innocently.

It was the hottest day by far for Amira. The languid air hung like a limp cloak. She fanned her crotch to cool herself and giggled. Siripali laughed too.

"The harem-keeper seems to like you, Siripali," Amira said, not looking up from the doodles she was drawing on the ground with a twig.

"Yes," came her direct reply, for Siripali was a forthright person. "My mother and the harem-keeper were childhood friends. The harem-keeper was once married to a wicked man. My mother told me so. Anyway, that man used to get drunk and beat her, and then he died. He left her destitute, and her family refused to take her back. My mother spoke to the old chamberlain—they killed him, you know—and got the harem-keeper this job. So, she looks after me."

THE FOLLOWING DAY, A LARGE BULLOCK CART LOADED to the brim with green, yellow, and orange-colored fruits rolled into the harem compound.

"Come, Amira," Siripali shouted. "Let's go, or we won't get any. Grab as many as you can and tuck them into your clothes," she yelled, lifting her dhoti to her knees and racing ahead of Amira.

Siripali rummaged through the fruits, sniffing them and throwing her selection over her shoulder for Amira to catch and tuck into her dhoti.

"What are they?" Amira yelled.

"Mangos," Siripali shouted back over her shoulder. She stopped midthrow. "What are you doing?" she asked, laughing, noticing Amira's dhoti was bulging with mangoes.

"Stop. I am losing my dhoti," Amira screamed.

Siripali tucked a few more into her own clothing, and they ran to the shade of a large tree.

"What do you do with these?"

"I'll show you."

Siripali bit into a fruit, peeled its skin with her teeth and sank her teeth into the exposed yellowish-orange flesh. Following Siripali's lead, Amira indulged herself. Sweet nectar trickled down her chin and fingers as she feasted on the most delicious fruit she had ever tasted. When they had satiated their appetites, Siripali leaned over and rubbed her juice-drenched fingers all over Amira's face, got up, and ran to the central fountain. Amira gave chase.

Amira screeched to a halt. "Siripali, it's against the rules to wash in the fountain."

She giggled, scooped up a handful of water and threw it at Amira, and ran off again. Amira too quickly rinsed her hands and washed her face in the fountain, and gave chase.

A FEW DAYS LATER, WHILE DRYING themselves after their afternoon bath, Siripali told her another story. Siripali loved telling stories. She had a mouth that was never out of stories.

"One girl ran off with a harem guard. A bit odd, don't you think?"

"Why?"

"Because the guards don't have a 'thing.' It's been cut off."

Amira stared at her, confused. "What thing?"

"Their man thing," Siripali pointed to her crotch. "You know the thing men have there."

"My brothers had those. They looked like worms." Amira giggled.

"Anyway, the girl ran off with a pandaka, a eunuch, and they were caught. Do you know what they did to them?" Siripali didn't wait for a reply. "Threw them both into the crocodile pond."

"Oh, that's awful. I don't believe your story, Siripali."

"It's true. Ask anyone."

Siripali was full of extraordinary stories. She was smart too and knew a lot. One day, while Amira was staining Siripali's hands red with alta paste, she told Amira of two girls doing it.

"Doing what?" Amira asked.

Siripali laughed. "They were kissing and touching each other. The harem-keeper found out, and they got whipped and thrown out of the harem. Luckily for them, they were not concubines, or else they would have been branded with a hot iron—like they do for cattle—before being sent away in disgrace. That is the biggest disgrace for a harem girl and also her whole family—to be branded."

Siripali also loved teasing Amira about her hair and eyes and other bits. Another day, they were seated in their room, filing their fingernails with a filing-rocks. She said all the girls were curious to know what Amira looked like down there.

"Ha! You want to see? Come on, admit it." Amira could see Siripali was shy now, but she was in a playful mood too, so she spread her legs and showed her.

Siripali gasped. "Oh, it's so pink," she said.

"Now show me yours. Come on, I showed you mine."

Siripali demurred for a moment, but then showed Amira hers.

"It's so dark. You can't see anything. Everything is hidden by black hair."

They giggled. They had become inseparable.

40

The weather was mild as Kasyapa and Migara rode northward.

"Did you hear about Moggallana?"

"What do you mean, Senapati?"

"They almost killed the pissant in Jambudvipa. He had to flee Madurai. Did you know Moggallana has fled Madurai?"

"Yes, I heard."

"He was up to his neck in debt. I hear they threatened to kill him if he didn't cough up. He had to part with all his treasure. The one he stole from his mother. My sources tell me he escaped only with the Precious Red Ruby."

"That's tragic."

"Tragic! Wait till you hear this." He snorted. "The only reason he saved the Red Ruby was that he stuck it up his ass." Migara laughed a cruel mocking laugh. "Now that's tragic indeed. Maybe I should call him sore-ass from now on." He sniggered, slapping his thigh.

Kasyapa shifted uneasily in his saddle and winced.

"Did you know he has moved to the west coast of Jambudvipa?"

"No, I didn't."

"Well, that's where the little sore-ass is now. In the town of Desinganadu on the west coast."

SETTING UP HIS DEFENSIVE LINE two miles inland from the lagoon in Nagadipa, Migara constructed a watchtower there and mounted it with a white awning. He stationed a thin line of infantrymen five hundred yards ahead of this tower. Mistaking the white awing, for a royal parasol hoisted over the watchtower, the invaders raced to capture it. As the enemy approached, the line of defense crumbled and fell back from their positions. Migara waited until they were within striking distance of the tower, ordered it pulled it down, and retreated toward another tower further inland. The foe followed in hot pursuit.

This tower was the vantage point from which Kasyapa observed the battle unfold. As required by the Kshatriya code of chivalry, mounted on its pinnacle, was the royal standard, the white parasol of dominion—the Senachatra of the king.

As the foe approached this tower, Migara raised his arm, signaling a halt to the retreat. He spun his horse around, dug in his heels, and started his counterattack. At the head of his cavalry, he executed a well-coordinated pincer movement.

Seeing Migara's forces closing around them, blocking their retreat, the chieftain's ragtag army made a last-ditch effort to capture Kasyapa. But before they could get within striking distance, they stopped in their tracks and startled out of their wits by the sudden appearance of a wall of war elephants Migara had hidden from them. Panic gripped the invading army as these fearsome mammoths lumbering toward them with archers on their backs, hailing arrows which whooshed overhead and struck them down with impunity. They fled in all directions.

Migara wheeled his horse and galloped into the thick of the battle. "No one is to be spared. Kill them all before they reach the sea."

Soon the battlefield was thick with the carnage of war. The gory remnants of dismembered dead and the screaming dying littered the battlefield. The chieftain's bloodied soldiers picked their way through scattered corpses, only to be brutally mowed down by Migara's soldiers.

They captured the chieftain and hauled him before Migara. Brandishing his sword with flawless precision, Migara leaned over on his horse and swung his weapon, lopping off the man's head with a single fell swoop. Spouting blood and flapping his arms almost comically, the man ran a few steps headless and dropped dead.

Kasyapa watched with numbed horror. After the battle, he congratulated Migara and his soldiers and hurried back to the citadel.

*****

RETURNING TO HIS PALACE, Kasyapa rushed to his bathing pavilion in the Sky-Palace. Dismissing the bathing attendants, he doused himself over and over again with water. But no amount of bathing and cleansing could erase the haunting memory of war and the memory of that cowering man, decapitated with ruthless brutality.

Kasyapa remained secluded in his palace, praying and meditating. On the third day, he joined Sobhana for their regular luncheon walk.

"I found the war, the stench of death, the suffering unbearable, Sobhana," he said. "I am appalled by it all, and at the joy the senapati took from it. He reveled in the misery of others."

Sobhana said nothing. With her head bowed, she walked closer to her husband. As they approached the Pavilion of Four Ponds, she pointed to a bench close by. They sat under a large shade tree.

Kasyapa observed the shimmering waters of the pond below. A cormorant perched on the rock in the middle of the pond, dived into the water and emerged with a small fish in its bill, gobbled it up and flew away.

"You know, the only act of violence I was ever involved in was punching Migara in the face some twenty-odd years ago."

"I wish I had been there to see it," Sobhana half-chuckled trying to lighten his melancholy mood.

Kasyapa smiled wearily. "Sometimes, I am thankful Migara relieves me from these horrid choices. Violence is evil. It debases humanity."

Sobhana tapped his arm, smiled weakly, and said nothing.

"Migara also told me Moggallana is now living in Desinganadu, a coastal town in Jambudvipa. This was something I didn't know."

"How does Migara know so much, Kasyapa?"

"I didn't ask."

*****

BUDDHA-DATTA VISITED THE KING A WEEK LATER. He visited Kasyabgiri often now, and Kasyapa enjoyed his company.

"It is good to see you again. How is my vihara, and its abbot?" Kasyapa asked.

"All is well, my king. I hear you had a great victory."

Kasyapa nodded and pulled the monk aside. "Buddha-datta, my mind is troubled. The war in the north resulted in the death of countless people."

Looking into his king's eyes, the monk spoke softly. "Your unease is praiseworthy, my king. As you know, the principle of *ahimsa* is at the heart of Buddhist teaching and behavior. Avoid killing or harming living things. It is the first of all precepts."

"It is."

"There is no correct answer to your quandary. Never, even in the most extreme circumstances, can acts of violence be seen as righteous or good. Sometimes, it is necessary to defend our nation and its people. This cannot, in itself, be seen as wrong. However, to lash out with excessive force or harbor hatred toward one's foes is always reprehensible. This is still poison."

In the distance, a few wayward clouds drifted across a powder-blue sky. Gentle ripples skittled over the surface of the large pond as they walked past.

The monk continued. "There are no righteous wars. There are no good wars. Sometimes, there are regrettable wars. The fact that you show contrition is commendable."

"I heard later my army massacred the wives and children of my foe also."

"My king, did you order it?"

"No. But maybe I could have prevented it."

"Your fault is you did not act to forestall it from happening. It is my belief you had no idea such an atrocity would take place. It was a tragic oversight on your part. You must reconcile this failing yourself, my king."

41

The Harem-Keeper held her head high, bounced up and down on her ample frame, and clapped her hands with delight. "You are ready to meet our king! It has been hard work, but I have turned an uncouth camel into a graceful swan."

Amira smiled wide-eyed and dashed off to tell Siripali the news. She ran so fast her feet barely touched the ground.

Seated on the floor in her room, Siripali was staining the tips of her fingers with a bright red Alta dye, when Amira arrived. She tapped the ground with the palm of her hand, as she didn't want her painted fingertips ruined. Amira sat in front of her cross-legged.

"I am ready," Amira said, breathless and dizzy with excitement.

Siripali, who had already been with the king several times, fluttered her eyelashes and flashed a playful grin.

"So, now you will get to experience the pleasures."

"Pleasures?"

"Yes, you silly chicken. The pleasures of his 'thing.'"

"Oh. I don't believe your stories, Siripali."

"Ask anyone then," Siripali pursed her lips and screwed up her face like she'd chewed on a raw tamarind fruit.

Amira was never sure if she should believe Siripali's tales. She definitely wasn't sure about her stories about sex and the 'thing.'

"I have never been close to a man. Well, except for my father, the slave trader, some random smelly men, and that prince," Amira said, pulling on a strand of her red hair.

"You will love it."

"I once heard my father and mother do the sex thing. It sounded like a pig grunting and scuffling, and it didn't last long."

Siripali tossed her head and laughed.

"It seemed like an odd thing to do—this sex thing."

"Oh, you will love it, Amira. Trust me, you will love it," Siripali said with a know-it-all laugh.

AT MID-MORNING ON THE DESIGNATED DAY, the harem-keeper said.

"There is a celebration at the Sky Palace. We will be attending."

"Sky Palace?"

"Yes, the one located up there," she said, pointing to the big white rock. "We are going there today. We are presenting you to the king."

Amira bounced on her toes, clasped her hands against her chest, and pirouetted in front of the harem-keeper. In those days gone by, while traveling tired, dirty, and unloved through the desolate desert and the big blue ocean, she had fantasized about meeting a prince. Never in her wildest dreams did she imagine she would meet a king.

AS AMIRA WAS ABOUT TO LEAVE THE HAREM, Siripali and two hand-maidens rushed up to her. Chattering and laughing, they draped a large translucent shroud over her.

"What this for?"

"It's to hide you from prying eyes," the handmaid said, giggling.

"Don't worry," Siripali chirped in. "The king is handsome and elegant and gentle. You will love it."

Amira took her word for it. She trusted Siripali.

A pair of guards and four baggage porters carrying four large wicker baskets packed with all the necessities of a concubine then joined them.

From the moment she exited the gates, the harem-keeper grumbled. "I hate going to the Sky Palace, even though it is the most beautiful place on earth. It is so hard on these ancient legs of mine." As they climbed a long, steep staircase, she pointed to her left. "That's called the Cobra Rock because it looks like the head of a snake," she called out.

"Oh, look at those caves decorated with paintings," Amira remarked from under her shroud. "There are even benches to sit on. And look at those pavilions on the top of the large boulders. They look like many-hued mushrooms."

"And mind you," the harem-keeper said, "this is the rear entrance we are passing through."

As they climbed, Amira called out to the harem-keeper, "Now I understand why you hate going to the Sky Palace. It is hard work, especially with this big sheet over my head."

They laughed.

"There are one thousand, eight hundred, and twenty-four steps from the harem to the Sky Palace. I counted them once," a handmaiden said.

"I don't care. To me, it seems like fifty thousand," the harem-keeper grumbled as they reached the top of the stairs and proceeded along a corridor suspended from the side of the rock. On the right was the rock face, painted white. On the left was a wall with a mirror-like sheen, also in white.

"This is the Mirror Wall," a guard said, bringing his face close to it. "See, my face reflecting off the wall?"

"I can't see anything," Amira said sweetly from under her shroud.

"Stop fraternizing with my girls," the harem-keeper scolded.

A guard laughed. "She is a clucky old hen. She always tells us off."

About a third of the way along, the harem-keeper stopped at a lookout point. She elbowed the others aside and pulled Amira along with her so they could get the best view.

"There are two of everything," Amira commented.

"Yes, everything down there is in twos—one for the king and one for the queen. See the large ponds far away near the entrance? One on the left and one on the right."

Amira nodded.

"See those smaller, longer ponds with those curvy streams flowing into them in front of the big ponds? See the Lake Palaces over there? Two of them. Everything is duplicated and mirrored. One for the king and one for the queen, one on the left and one on the right."

"The queen is lucky; the king treats her so well. Back in Kapisa, where I came from, the king had all the luxuries. The queen didn't have anything except her quarters in the harem, which wasn't as well-appointed as here."

"Yes, she is treated well. He is a good king," a guard said, and the assembled party concurred.

"Now that's enough. We have a long way to go." The harem-keeper clapped and hurried the party along.

As they approached the end of the corridor, another steep staircase confronted them. The guards led the way. The harem-keeper followed, huffing and puffing as she hauled her ample body upward. A guard, seeing the harem-keeper's plight, circled around her and attempted to push her from behind.

She slapped his hand away. "How dare you touch a lady on the backside, you rascal," she scolded. "What is the world coming to these days? There is no respect," she blustered.

The guard chuckled, abandoned his effort, and dashed to his position at the front of the procession.

"Will no one help this miserable old lady?" she said with a soulful groan, holding the small of her back. A handmaiden took the harem-keeper's hand and escorted her up. "How lovely it is to know my girls care for a rickety old lady like me."

Amira and the handmaidens giggled.

"I am so tired of climbing." Amira groaned from under her shroud.

"Only a few more steps, Amira," her handmaiden coaxed.

At long last, they exited onto a small plateau. Ahead were two open-air pavilions with ornate pagoda-like roofs.

"This is the Plateau of Red Arsenic. It's called that because of the color of the sand on the ground. Now close your eyes, Amira," her handmaiden whispered.

Amira closed her eyes. The handmaiden placed her hands on Amira's shoulders and spun her around.

"Now, open your eyes. It's the Lion's Gate."

"It's amazing. It's gigantic!" Amira squealed through her cloak. In front of her was a sphinx-like lion, made of brick and plaster at least thirty-five yards tall. Painted in red, yellow, orange, and black, with its large menacing eyes and its mouth agape, it appeared ready to devour anyone who dared approach it.

"Isn't it incredible?"

"Yes. Yes." Amira nodded enthusiastically from under her sheet.

After a moment, the harem-keeper made her usual "humph" sound, signaling that it was time to keep moving.

As if on cue, the guards stationed in front of the fearsome lion flung open two doors built into its chest, revealing a narrow marble staircase.

They inched up the narrow winding stairs shielded by another mirrored wall similar to the one they had traveled along earlier. Amira was sweating profusely. The harem-keeper cussed equally profusely.

"We will reach heaven before this climbing ends," Amira lamented.

Just then, the handmaiden exclaimed, "We are here."

"I couldn't have lasted a minute longer. I am exhausted." Amira moaned, sweltering under her covering.

The harem-keeper caught her breath and walked Amira to the edge. "Look, Amira."

The view was spectacular in every direction. The city, with its tidy gridded streets, lay below them. There were green fields as far as the eye could see, dotted with vast reservoirs and clusters of small villages around them.

The harem-keeper clapped her hands and shooed the party along the outer perimeter of the complex. Amira didn't see much of the palace. What stood out in her mind was the dream-like nature of the place, the steps, the walls, the terraces, the roofs; they were all gleaming white. It reminded her of the snow-covered mountains back home in Kapisa.

They proceeded to the rear of the complex, where a special area had been set aside for the harem.

"Now, eat something and rest. You have a busy evening ahead," the harem-keeper said.

42

The harem-keeper approached with exaggerated solemnity and prostrated herself before her king. Amira worried that her beautiful green dhoti with its elaborate fantail ruffle would get dirty, but she too had to follow protocol. So, she prostrated herself and waited until the harem-keeper stood before she did the same. The harem-keeper pushed Amira forward and positioned her before the king. He sat in a dignified royal pose, his arm resting on a large silk cushion.

"My king, I present Amira, a gift from the king of Kapisa," the harem-keeper announced, lifting Amira's veil with melodramatic flourish.

"I hope we reciprocated his kindness, Harem-Keeper?"

"We did, my king, most generously."

The king nodded and turned to Amira. A gentle smile played on his full lips as his large brown eyes engaged hers and held her captive in a soft caress. "Welcome, Amira."

Amira stood transfixed. That's all she seemed capable of doing. His voice was like honey, strangely melodic, and oh so sensual. A magical tingling overcame her. Her heart pounded with such force she feared her pearl necklace and large jeweled pendant would bounce on her chest. It was as though this man was reaching inside her and was playing with her soul.

He smiled and dismissed her with a casual wave of his hand.

Amira returned to her seat. Had the king liked her? She hoped he had. She had put so much effort into preparing herself for this. Siripali and the harem-keeper had assured her she looked beautiful. Siripali had even loaned her some jewelry for the occasion.

KASYAPA NOTICED HER INDEED. About five-foot-six, with a well-formed figure, ivory-colored complexion, and flaming red hair decorated with a garland of jasmine flowers, she was celestial. He loved the smell of jasmine. Her face was longish, with a well-proportioned nose. The curves of her eyes were bracketed by eyebrows, plucked and shaped into perfect arches. When she smiled, her thin lips, tinted red, revealed a set of porcelain-white teeth.

What he found most alluring about her was her striking blue eyes with cat-like irises that gazed out on the world like iridescent star sapphires brimming with innocence.

AMIRA TOO HAD BEEN EYING THE KING. She caught his gaze. Her body tingled. She dropped her eyes and blushed.

When she sensed it was safe, when she was certain he wouldn't notice, she let her eyes wander over him once more. He wasn't as tall as the girls had told her, but he was indeed dark and very handsome. His brown eyes, sitting beneath thick eyebrows, were mesmerizing. And he had captured her heart.

AFTER THE EVENING'S ENTERTAINMENT, the king retired for the night, or so Amira thought. Soon after his departure, the harem-keeper hurried Amira off to the harem quarters.

"You have to change quickly, Amira," she spluttered.

"Why?"

"Because you are going to see the king, that's why."

"Oh," Amira heard herself say as she slipped out of her clothes. The harem-keeper ran her fingers between Amira's legs and sniffed them.

"*Humph*," she grunted, dressed her in a translucent beige robe and ushered her out the door.

The whole enchanting place glowed in moonlite luminescence as it drifted through the night sky. The steps, the walls, and the buildings, they all sparkled as Amria and the harem-keeper made their way toward the highest point of the Sky Palace. The only sound that disturbed the eerie stillness of the place was the soft swishing of Amira's robe. And the harem-keepers muffled groans each time she navigated a flight of stairs, of which there were many.

As they climbed the final flight of steps to the king's quarters, the harem-keeper whispered, "Now Amira, don't be afraid. Remember, I am here. I will be sleeping in the little hut over there."

Amira nodded.

They halted at the top of the stairs, and the harem-keeper settled Amira's clothes. "You only need a smile, Amira. Go in. Go in now." She pushed Amira toward the door and vanished into the night.

AMIRA'S HEART THUMPED like a drum as she climbed the final steps in semi-darkness, her fingers tracing over a doorframe textured like tiny slippery white pebbles. Then she noticed, in fact, thousands of embedded pearls.

She took a deep breath, turned the gem-studded handle, and pushed open the solid timber door.

A warm whiff of perfumed air rushed past her as she slid into his chamber, lit by subdued golden lamplight. At the far end of the large room was an elevated platform. There, resting on one arm and watching her as she entered, was the king himself.

It started at her fingertips, a numbing sensation that spread across her translucent skin like wildfire. The more she looked at him, the more her panic grew. Goosebumps raced along her neck and back. Her breath became tortured and shallow. She stood, shaking like a leaf.

The king looked at her from under his full eyebrows. A smile dangled from the corner of his lips as he rose from the bed and walked to her. He looked into her desolate eyes, wrapped his arms around her, and held her tight against his warm, firm body. "Don't be afraid, Amira," he said as his breath brushed against her neck, setting her afire.

She took a shuddering breath, and then another, and the trembling waned. Her senses returned, but only for a moment until she remembered who held her. Then her heart raced for different reasons, her body softened, and a warm glow radiated through her. Something hard rubbed against her thighs.

He released his hold, placed his index finger under her chin, and lifted her face to his.

"You are beautiful," he whispered when she fluttered her auburn-colored eyelashes over her lapis-lazuli blue eyes. They were like angel wings opening and closing the doors to paradise. He placed a soft, fleeting kiss upon her lips.

The only sound that escaped her lips was "Ohh."

No man had ever told her she was beautiful. Now a king was telling her so. Her embarrassment was telling. It spread in a warm glow across her cheeks, chest, and breasts, matching her flaming red hair.

His eyes flashed. "You are so pink, Amira," he said with a lighthearted chuckle, watching her transformation with amusement and surprise.

He grappled with her robe. She helped him. Her long graceful fingers eagerly untied it herself and let it fall to the floor. She was naked for him. She wanted to be.

He moved her hair away from her small and well-shaped ears and slid his fingers slowly down the side of her neck, her shoulder, her chest, her breasts, and her excited nipples. When he cupped his hands over her breasts and caressed them, she almost jumped out of her skin.

She felt her breasts compress against his well-formed chest as he held her tight. He kissed her and ran his hands over her soft, willing body. She was breathless.

Her hands moved swiftly. She fumbled with his dhoti, and let it fall to the floor. He pressed his body against hers. Something slippery and hard slid between her thighs and against her wet lips. Then he stopped and moved away. She saw his thing; the one Siripali often talked about, large black and straight, and oh so desirable. Not at all like the little worms she had seen on her brothers.

He took her hand and walked her to his bed. She lay down, her chest heaving. He lay beside her and looked into her eyes and ran his hand down her body toward her legs. She parted them impulsively for him, opening wide. He touched her. She gasped and arched her back.

He smiled and climbed on top of her, kneeling between her legs, he kissed her breasts and then her lips. Then his body was against hers, and before her brain could register the events taking place, she felt him slide into her.

A tinge of pain shot through her body. She held her breath. But it disappeared almost instantly. Instinctively her hands clutched his back as she felt him deep within her, replacing her anxiety with an incredible pleasure she had never experienced before. She was riding to heaven.

"AMIRA! AMIRA!" SHE HEARD THE DISTRESSED VOICE of the harem-keeper outside. Amira looked around. It was morning already, and the king was no longer in her bed.

"I am here, Harem-Keeper, I am here," Amira replied.

"What are you doing, still in the king's chamber? Come out at once."

Amira wrapped her robe around herself and exited the chamber, blinking wildly in the bright sunlight.

The harem-keeper gazed at her and breathed a hefty sigh, and rushed Amira to the little hut she had spent the night in. "Now, sit on the bed and spread your legs."

Amira did as she was told.

The harem-keeper took a linen cloth and dabbed it between her legs and examined the light pink stain on its surface. She sniffed it and beamed.

"You have done well, my girl."

Amira's face lit up, dreamy, and content.

THE GIRLS JOSTLED AROUND when she returned to the harm later that morning, keen to hear some salacious gossip about Amira and the king.

"Did you like it?" someone asked.

A girl laughed. "Oh. She is embarrassed. She's turned crimson again."

Amira swayed gently and stared at the floor.

"Come. Come," the harem-keeper beckoned and took her to the bathing pavilion and poured the first bucket of water over her head.

"You are a concubine now, Amira." She grinned, her lazy eye pointing somewhere else as usual.

Siripali was waiting for her outside the bathhouse. "Tell me. Tell me. Don't keep me in suspense," she pleaded in a high-spirited babble.

"*Shh,* not here."

When they were out of earshot from the other girls, Amira broke out in song. "It was wonderful. It was heavenly." She rose to the balls of her feet and twirled.

"Did you like his thing?"

"I did. I did. It was so big and slippery." She wasn't shy to tell her best friend these things.

" Of course it is. What did you expect?

"But Siripali, I forgot all my training. I didn't do any of those things we are taught about pleasing a man."

"Oh, don't worry. I know the king would have loved having you."

I hope so, Siripali. I really liked it—the feel of a man, his smell, his body."

Siriplai laughed her know-it-all laugh. "Now they will give you a tattoo. It hurts a bit, but it is worth it. It is a pretty tattoo. See mine. I am worth a lot since I got it," she said, strutting in front of Amira.

Amira shrugged. She was too happy to care.

"Ha! Don't shrug your shoulders. Not all the girls here get to sleep with the king."

"Siripali, I noticed that girl, Mitiya, looked at me oddly when I returned today. She seemed very hostile."

"Oh, Mitiya thinks the king belongs to her. She got into trouble with the harem-keeper about this before and has been warned. The harem-keeper said no girl had a right to the king."

A FEW DAYS LATER, the tattooist appeared. She made Amira sit in the sunlight in the far corner of the courtyard.

"Stop wriggling, girl, or you will end up with a tattoo on your nose. How will you look then, huh? Stay still," the tattooist scowled.

Amira gritted her teeth and sat motionless until she finished.

"Let's see. Let's see," the girls shrieked, pushing and shoving each other. Siripali elbowed herself to the front. She gasped and took a step backward.

"Oh, oh."

"What? What?" Amira begged.

"Oh. Oh."

"What! Tell me?"

"You have a crow tattooed on your neck."

"What?"

"A crow. That means the king didn't like you."

"Noooooooooo."

"Yeeeees."

"I don't believe you, Siripali."

"See for yourself." Siripali laughed and handed Amira a mirror.

Amira gazed into the mirror. Her neck was rose pink, but the tattoo was indeed beautiful, three attached circles on a narrow necklace.

Later, when they were alone, Amira said, "The harem-keeper said I would get my own cubicle and handmaiden."

"So, what's wrong with that? You should be pleased."

Amira looked down at her feet and said nothing.

Siripali tickled her. "Oh, Amira, don't be sad. This is the way of the world. We will always remain friends...forever."

AMIRA THOUGHT ABOUT THE KING OFTEN. In fact, she thought of nothing else. She played and replayed that evening in her mind. daydreamed of him kissing her lips, her neck, her breasts, and lower down her body. Each time she did, she became wet and wanted him there again. The waiting was killing her.

But it wasn't that simple. She couldn't just walk up to him and ask for more. Now could Amira go to the harem-keeper and ask for more either. If she did, the harem-keeper would surely think she was mad, or even worse, that she was too wanting. Amira was sure the king had his favorites and asked for them more often. She hoped she would be one. She had to wait.

THE HAREM-KEEPER HAD WHAT SHE CALLED HER "FEELING," and Amira rated well on the feeling scale. She was certain the king enjoyed the young harem girl's company. After all, she had spent the whole night with him. That was highly unusual. The king liked to sleep alone and usually dismissed his bedmate once he finished with her.

The harem-keeper decided she would hold Amira back until the following month. She had her reasons. She knew her job well.

43

The sthapati was much displeased to discover a bhikkhu at the meeting. But he was a servant of the king, so he held his tongue.

The king arrived late. The vizier, chamberlain, sthapati, and Buddha-datta were in a heated discussion when he approached. Their babble died away as he climbed to the audience hall.

"Now, what was this toing and froing I heard among you?"

"We are discussing the role of religion in art. Namely, is art's sole purpose the glorification of religion?" the chamberlain said.

"I see. And who says it is?"

"We have concluded that this is not the case. Art's purpose is to glorify the creativity of man. One manifestation of this is his conscious choice to celebrate his religion in art."

"A sound discourse indeed." Kasyapa settled onto a cluster of soft silk cushions on the royal couch at the far end of the audience hall. "My learned friends, I have an item for discussion. Something I have been mulling over for some time." Kasyapa looked around him. These were his friends and confidants, some of the sharpest minds in the land. "My question to you is this. How can we inspire culture, knowledge, and wisdom amongst our people?"

The chamberlain was the first to speak. "We could increase the number of troupes visiting the towns and villages. They are very popular with the people. Many walk for miles to see them."

"Chamberlain, the king talked of wisdom and knowledge," the sthapati responded. "The troupes we are sending out are dancers and musicians. Also, they only visit sporadically and don't reach a vast proportion of the people."

"This is correct. The king wishes for universal enlightenment," the vizier added.

The chamberlain persisted. "Well, we can attach teachers and storytellers to these troupes and increase the number and frequency of their visits."

Kasyapa reclined himself on the royal divan, gazing across the open-air audience hall to a trickle of water tumbling down the side of a boulder close by and splashing into a small ablution pool below. He smiled and turned to his friends. "I hear you talk of teachers. So, if I may surmise, we need to provide education. Am I correct?"

The assembled huddle looked at each other and nodded. Kasyapa had gotten to the heart of the issue and elucidated their thoughts in one simple word.

"Good. My next question to you is this. How do we educate?"

"We could send out teachers to visit the villages from time to time, as the chamberlain suggested," the sthapati said.

"But we have very few of those, I am afraid, and they are mostly tutoring the elite. We would have to train a vast army of them. This will take time and money," the vizier added.

"And where would these new teachers conduct their classes?" Buddha-datta asked.

The chamberlain scratched his head. "In the village squares, I presume. For all those who wished to attend."

"But what about during inclement weather, especially during the rainy season?" Buddha-datta said.

"We could build schools," the sthapati replied.

"Another huge undertaking," the vizier said in his cautious voice.

"Would this be for only the children or the adults also?" the chamberlain asked.

"If we were to take adults away from their work, there would be an impact on the economy. That wouldn't be a good idea. Besides, there would be resistance," the vizier warned.

"I agree. We should concentrate on the children," the sthapati said. "They, in turn, can pass on what they learn to their older relatives."

Again, Kasyapa had remained silent and listened. Then he clapped his hands. "Gentlemen, gentlemen, is the answer not obvious?"

They looked at each other and then at Kasyapa. Whatever Kasyapa had in mind wasn't apparent to them at all.

Kasyapa leaned forward from his couch. "The temples and viharas."

The sthapati's jaw dropped. "The temples and viharas?"

Kasyapa paused to draw out the sthapati's anguish. "Yes, the temples and viharas. These are the only institutions with the reach and the skills to carry out this task. Buddha-datta, don't you agree?"

"Most certainly, my king. The monks are well educated and have the requisite skills and the facilities."

"There you have it. Let us engage them in our splendid enterprise. Vizier, arrange for the senior bhikkhus of the fraternities to see me."

With that, Kasyapa left the audience hall.

44

Located in a rectangular park on the south side of the western precinct was a circular lake with an elevated island. On the brow of this island was the Lake Palace. It wasn't a particularly large building as such, a two-storied structure but exquisitely proportioned with a glazed tile roof. From a distance, it appeared white, with the slightest tinge of grey, like the color and texture of pearls.

Amira walked behind the harem guards to a causeway at the rear, which was the only access to the island and palace. There, the guards turned around and returned to the harem. Her heart pounded in her ears as she crossed the causeway and climbed a small flight of steps to the palace.

A handsome black eunuch with glistening skin stood in front of an ornate entrance. The center of each door was embossed with a multi-petaled lotus flower design. These petals were inlays made of mother of pearl lined with red gems. Amira assumed these were rubies. At the center of the flower was an incredibly large golden cymophane, a cat's eye gem, with a sharp and centered eye that moved with the light.

The black eunuch opened the doors and pointed to the stairs at the rear of a spacious hall with ornate pillars and furnishings. The entire place glittered with precious metals and gems.

An audible gasp escaped Amira's lips as she entered the king's private quarters. Having just ventured through such opulence in the hall below, she expected the same in the king's quarters, but the room was stark, containing only a large sleeping platform in the far corner, and four brass lamps to illuminate the room.

Amira found the king on the balcony with his back toward her. She approached him, almost gliding, making no sound at all. Sensing her presence, he turned around. His large brown eyes fell upon her once more, caressing her from within as he had done before. She shuddered.

"It's been a while?"

"Yes, my king, one month."

"Come here, Amira. Look at the magnificent sunset."

He remembered her name. A warming glow radiated through her Taking small strides, she approached him with her head bowed and stood a few steps behind him.

"Come stand next to me."

She obeyed her king.

"Look at the sky, and the way the light plays on the white surface of the rock."

"It is wonderful, my king," she replied in her demure, newly trained sing-song voice.

The sun was dipping towards the horizon, its golden rays bouncing off overcast candy-floss clouds, imbuing them with colors of scarlet and amethyst. Remnants of daylight lingered on, like an afterthought, turning the surface of the rock chalky yellow, orange, and mauve, and then into a shadowy, ghostlike apparition as sooty darkness finally enveloped the sky.

Mosquitoes nibbled at her arms. She brushed them away, not wanting to draw attention to herself. As she stood next to him, a sense of overwhelming oneness engulfed her. She wondered if he had similar feelings toward her. Could he sense her ache, her desire? But why should he? The king had many women.

As they walked into the residence, Kasyapa turned and asked, "Can you read Amira?"

"Only a little bit. Only what I have learned since I came here."

"Didn't you learn in Kapisa?"

"No, my king. Girls were only taught to cook, clean, and look after the goats."

"What about boys?"

"They were taught to herd goats and beat their wives."

"Seriously?"

"Most of the time." She made light of her remark, but it was true.

"I see."

"I like learning. Now I can read some books in the harem library. You can learn so much from books. My friend, Siripali, she can read and write and do numbers as well. She helps me sometimes."

"So, the education you receive in the harem is good?"

"Oh, yes, my king."

THAT NIGHT HE TOOK her body on a journey to paradise. In the morning, he was gone. Atop her clothes lay an intricately inlaid box brimful with sparkling jewelry.

As soon as she returned, she showed her present to Siripali. They both squealed and jumped up and down with joy.

"The king likes you, Amira," her best friend said. "Now, after you have admired them, remember to give them to the harem-keeper for safekeeping. She will store it for you in the strong room."

Amira pouted. She was reluctant to part with her gift. It was the first present she had ever received. And it was from a king!

SOON WORD WAS GETTING AROUND the harem that Amira was spending the whole night with the king. The gossip in the harem was she was the king's favorite.

The harem-keeper pooh-poohed the matter and wagged her finger at her girls. "Jealousy and salacious gossip will not be tolerated in my harem," she said, placing her hands on her hips with her elbows extended out like jug handles.

Of course, she knew what was going on. It was her job to know these things. She knew the king was fond of Amira. She had even heard from the black eunuch that Amira addressed the king by his first name. That too was highly irregular. In her view, however, if the king liked this beautiful swan, she would do everything in her power to facilitate his desire.

"I am jealous," Siripali said one day, wiggling her eyebrows. "I think it's because of your pink bits."

"Siripali, you are so forward." Amira blushed. "Actually, we just talk."

Siripali rolled her eyes in exaggerated circles. "What's there to talk about with a delicious man like him?"

Amira knew her best friend wasn't jealous. But she knew others were, especially Mitiya.

45

On her designated nights, which usually occurred twice a month, Amira continued to visit the king.

Once, during a thunderstorm, Kasyapa jumped out of bed and dragged her to the balcony.

"You said you liked the crystal spire on top of the Sky Palace."

As Kasyapa spoke, a bolt of lightning arched through the rain-drenched sky and struck the spire. The sky lit up. The earth shuddered beneath their feet, and the air filled with an ear-splitting crackle. Amira trembled and pulled her clothing tightly against her body. He smiled, stood behind her, and wrapped his arms around her.

"You know the spire was designed to do that. To absorb lightning strikes and protect the Sky Palace."

"Incredible, Kasyapa. The sound is like a cracking horsewhip. Back home, when the Kapisan horsemen held their riding displays, they used to make a similar sound with their whips. But this sound is a thousand times louder." She lent her head against his shoulder. "I was a servant girl then. I wasn't allowed to watch the horsemen's displays, so I stood on a stool and peeked out of a kitchen window. That was all so long ago."

He kissed the back of her neck and pulled her tighter against him. The tiny bristles of his face scratched against her cheek.

"You aren't a servant anymore, Amira."

She snuggled closer to him.

AMIRA HAD BEEN SEEING THE KING on her designated nights for over six months now. They stayed up late into the night and frequently slept in the following morning. But on this particular morning when she woke up, he wasn't there.

She found him in the garden, rocking back and forth on his heels, gazing out at the rock. The moist morning air kissed her cheeks with the delicate fragrance, jasmine, citron, and lime as she approached him. A peacock screamed some distance away.

"This rock has confounded me for years," he said.

"What do you mean, Kasyapa?" She loved the sound of her voice when she called out his name—Kasyapa—and the way he responded to her. She also loved the feeling of him dripping in her the morning after. His voice quickly brought her back from her thoughts.

"This composition has no life, no vibrancy. Something is missing."

Amira stood next to him and studied the enormous white monolith dominating the vista in front of them. Yes, it was indeed striking, with the shining copper rooflines of the Sky Palace visible on top of the rock. She loved the cascade of sparkling light from the crystal-spire-tower when it caught the morning sun.

Amira sauntered on the damp grass to the edge of the lawn and peered into the moat below. In its still waters was the reflection of that imposing white rock once more. She reached into a nearby Kadupul scrub, known as the queen of the night flower—because its flowers only bloomed once for a few hours at night. Its soft, tired petals came off readily in her hand. Swinging her arms and humming a tune, she skipped along the edge of the garden tossing the petals high into the air. She knew Kasyapa was watching her. She liked teasing him. She was well aware he loved her body.

"Stop!" Kasyapa sliced the air with his hand.

Amira froze mid-stride, one foot poised in the air, thinking she had offended him.

"That's it. That's it. Stand there."

Amira did as she was told.

"What is it?" she asked softly.

He grinned, walked to her, and kissed her forehead. "Trust me. You will love it. Come, I must speak with my ministers right away."

*****

KASYAPA PACED THE ROYAL AUDIENCE HALL. He noticed three tassels of the Persian carpet out of place. He arranged them with his foot.

"I have an idea," he exclaimed as the vizier, sthapati, and chitrakar were ushered in. He was impatient and gestured to them to be seated. The vizier took up his usual advisory position on Kasyapa's right. The sthapati and chitrakar sat on the large silk cushions on the floor in front of the royal settee.

"You know this magnificent rock has confounded me for years. There is something amiss. The views from the Western Entrance and Lake Palace are uninspiring. This morning, I had an inspiration. I know what is needed."

Kasyapa paused, waiting for the suspense to build. The sthapati knew how to play Kasyapa's game, he feigned disinterest and casually tugged on his earlobe. The vizier remained expressionless, as usual. The chitrakar, on the other hand, sat upright, rapt with excitement, and unable to contain himself. Aware he lacked the finesse and stature of the others, he sat on his hands and forced himself to remain still.

Kasyapa's eyes twinkled as he leaned toward his audience. "We should paint frescoes."

"Where?"

"On the side of the rock."

"Can be done," the sthapati said with his usual assuredness. "But paint what? The Jataka Tales, geometric shapes, and such have been done before."

"Your favorite subject, Sthapati."

"What?" The sthapati was impatient.

"Women."

"Women?"

"Yes. Women."

"Women as in females?"

"Yes, Sthapati. Women."

A titter rippled across the audience hall. The vizier and chitrakar were well aware of the sthapati's fondness for the fairer sex.

"Doing what?" the sthapati asked, ignoring their sniggers.

"Throwing flowers, maybe?"

"Throwing flowers at passersby below them, along the Mirror Wall walkway?"

"Yes. That sounds good. I like it."

"But what sort of women?"

"I don't know. I am not sure."

"Apsaras? Maybe?" the vizier said.

"Of course." The sthapati's eyes sparkled. "Apsaras, yes, yes. Apsaras, beautiful celestial nymphs who inhabit the skies and heavenly cities—muses of the gods—yes, yes, perfect for Alakamanda. Yes. That's brilliant. How many?" the sthapati said.

"Hundreds."

"Yes, yes. Hundreds. We must fill our canvas. Yes, one massive, breathtaking tapestry extending from the rear of the rock all the way to the Lion Gate on the other end, covering the entire face of the rock." The sthapati's face lit up. He jumped up and paced the floor. "But what will these nymphs look like?"

"I don't know," Kasyapa replied.

"I know." The chitrakar bounced in his seat, flashing an asymmetric grin. "Why don't we use the ladies of the harem as our models?"

"Brilliant," Kasyapa said. After all, his inspiration had come while watching Amira in the garden that morning. But it hadn't crossed his mind to use his ladies as the models for this work of art.

"That will work," the sthapati said. "After all, the ladies of the harem are the most beautiful women in the kingdom."

"How would we do it?" Kasyapa leaned forward in his seat.

"Well, just below the waist of the rock, where it is most rounded, we could incise a drip ledge. That will prevent water from dripping on the frescoes. Then we can paint below it in the midriff of the rock, as you suggested."

"Chitrakar, can we paint up there?"

"Yes, we can, my king, but it will be tricky. We have to keep the plaster wet while we paint frescoes. And we must use only mineral dyes because they don't fade in direct sunlight. We have painted many frescoes before, so we have the skills to do this."

"Gentlemen, it's time Kasyabgiri had a refurbishment," Kasyapa said, leaning back in his settee and placing his arms behind his head.

"I want it done in time for the Water Festival."

"But that's only ten months away."

"Well, there's your challenge, Sthapati."

The chitrakar spoke up. "When we transformed the black rock into this gleaming white megalith, we cleaned and painted it by dangling workers on ropes strung from the top of the rock and down its side. This approach will not work for fresco painting. Large areas of the rock must be covered with multiple layers of plaster and painted on while still wet. The plasterers and artists will need steady platforms to work on.

"All right. Let's build a scaffold about three hundred and fifty feet high. No. Let's go all the way to the top—six hundred and fifty feet high, along the entire face of the rock."

"That's over two hundred and thirty yards long on each side, Sthapati," Kasyapa said with a concerned frown.

"It's been done before, albeit for dagobas. But the same principle will work here. We will need tens of thousands of bamboo poles to construct this scaffold."

"Vizier, you have been silent. Can we afford this?"

"As you wish, my king."

"Let's tell the chamberlain and harem-keeper. Summon them."

"AH, HAREM-KEEPER," Kasyapa called out as she trundled up the stairs to the audience hall. "You no doubt know of the sthapati and the chitrakar."

"Yes, my king," the harem-keeper replied with a deep bow.

"Chamberlain, welcome. Join us. We have a proposition for you."

Seated beneath the linen canopy as a cooling breeze wafted through, the assembly listened to their king as he outlined his plan.

"It will surely enhance the appearance of Alakamanda, my king," the chamberlain agreed.

"Harem-Keeper, what do you think?"

The harem-keeper hadn't had much interaction with the king in the fifteen-odd years she had served him. All she knew was that he was a polite and generous man who treated her girls with respect. She was feeling edgy.

"Speak your mind, Harem-Keeper. You are among friends."

The harem-keeper's eyes darted around the hall. She cleared her throat to rid herself of the lump lurking there. "My king..."

"Yes, Harem-Keeper? Speak your mind without fear."

"May I humbly suggest we include all the ladies of the harem?"

"Why so, Harem-Keeper?"

"They are all your ladies, my king. We should not favor one over the other."

"Of course, Harem-Keeper, you are right. We will include all the ladies. All the ladies will be included in the grand tapestry, including you, of course, in a prominent position." He grinned.

The harem-keeper looked down at the luxurious Persian carpet to hide a happy flush engulfed her. She hoped those present didn't notice.

The following day, Kasyapa shared his plans with the queen. She agreed it would enliven the rock.

****

AMIRA AND SIRIPALI WERE PLAYING the leopard and dogs board game when a short, skinny man with wild hair entered the harem.

The girls were curious. Except for the royal physician, the controller of the harem purse, and young male children of the king, no males were allowed into the harem. The harem-keeper soon announced that he was an artist and would be painting portraits of all the ladies of the harem for recordkeeping purposes.

When it was Siripali's turn, Amira stood outside and made faces at her. Siripali giggled and fidgeted.

"Why are you painting our portraits?" Siripali asked.

"None of your business." His eyes remaining fixed to his rectangular painting board.

"You know, you are the luckiest man in the whole kingdom to be allowed to be so close to us pretty girls. I hope you aren't planning to sell our portraits at the local market. You could fetch a good price for them." She niggled him.

He glared at her in exasperation. "Young lady, I am on the king's business. If you don't stop fidgeting and teasing, I will paint you with a jackal's head."

Siripali thought about it for a moment. "I don't care," she said defiantly and continued her reckless teasing.

Just then, the harem-keeper appeared. With a stern stare and furrowed brow, she put an end to their shenanigans.

46

As a sign of deference, it was customary for a king to sit at a lower level than members of the religious fraternities. So, the abbots of the three fraternities were indeed surprised when they entered the public audience hall and found Kasyapa already seated on his elevated throne. He didn't rise to greet them. There were no seats for them.

The abbots bounced glances at each other. Some scratched their heads. "This is not the way things were done," they murmured and shook their heads.

They had little choice. The message was clear. Like all subjects, they too were to remain standing before this monarch. The vizier smiled to himself. He had avoided a similar situation many months earlier when he had arranged for Buddha-datta to meet the king in the park. There, he had orchestrated that both men were standing.

Kasyapa raised his hand to command silence. "So, abbots, which of you wishes to address their monarch first?"

The most senior abbot by age raised his hand and spoke.

Kasyapa shut his eyes and listened to the man's litany of hardship and woe. Prices had risen, income from the monastic estates had declined, more recruits had joined, viharas were in disrepair, and so forth. The vizier observed the king from the corner of his eye. Kasyapa was gently tapping his ring on the arm of his throne. A thin smile on his lips conveyed feigned interest. He was tiring of the conversation.

Kasyapa raised his hand and stopped the abbot in mid-sentence. The abbot looked about flabbergasted and bobbed in place like a squirrel. Nobody interrupted a bhikkhu from speaking. This was most irregular.

"Do your monks have an education?" the king asked.

The monks laid eyes on each other, perplexed. They couldn't see the relevance of the king's question.

The senior abbot spoke on their behalf. "Yes, my king, some of them to the highest standards. All can read and write."

"Can they read the common vernacular?"

"Yes, my king."

"Can they write the same?"

"Yes, my king."

"Are the monks capable of counting?"

"Of course, my king."

"What about history? Do they know our history?"

"Yes, my king. You may recall your learned uncle, the great Thera Mahanama himself, recently completed the *Mahavamsa*. An excellent piece of work, I must admit."

Kasyapa acknowledged the monk's flattery with a nod. He slowly twirled the copper ring on his little finger. "What do they do with their time?"

"They carry out the duties of the monasteries and temples, oh king."

"What are these duties, Abbot?"

"Alms gathering, temple cleaning, self-confession, chanting and meditation, reflection, caring for one's preceptor, Dhamma studies, attending to oneself, and undertaking behavior worthy of respect." The abbot was noticeably confounded by the king's questioning.

"These duties occupy their whole time?"

"Yes, my king."

The vizier watched in quiet amazement. He knew Kasyapa was about to spring something on them.

"My proposition to you is this," Kasyapa said. "The king will offer you one coin, one silver Kahapana, for every child you educate in reading, writing, counting, and history."

The abbots were aghast. Some fanned themselves in disbelief.

"But...But my king, this is highly improper. Monks do not work like common laborers."

"What do you mean, Abbot?" Kasyapa feigned genuine concern that he may have offended their sensitivities.

"It is highly improper for monks to have paid employment."

Kasyapa leaned toward them. "Dear Abbot, you misunderstand your king. Forgive me if I have not conveyed my thoughts clearly. I do not offer to pay monks. I am giving alms. I am making a donation to their temples in exchange for a benefit. Is this not fitting? When a monk receives alms, is he not bound to repay the generosity? Surely, my dear Abbot, you would agree by passing on knowledge, a monk is recompensing with something far more valuable than anything he receives through alms?"

The assembled monks eyed each other anxiously. They could not fault his discourse. So, they nodded.

"Dear Abbot of the Mahavihara. Does your fraternity not have thousands of monks in fair Anuradhapura alone?

"Yes, my king."

"Could you not spare a few to teach the children?"

The delegation of abbots was dumbfounded and incapable of presenting a counterargument. After all, for a small compromise on their part, they would receive a significant injection of funds from the king. They had little choice but to accede to his request.

"Vizier, we are to set up a new ministry. Let us call it the Ministry of Awareness. Its responsibilities will be to provide the curriculum and guidelines for the education of our children. From the ages of six to ten, all children are to be educated."

"All children, my king?"

"Yes, all our children, both male and female."

"Yes, my king."

THE QUEEN GIGGLED when Kasyapa told her of his meeting.

"I am glad you are engaging with the fraternities, Kasyapa, and more so because you are doing so on your terms. Very fair terms, I might add. Mostly, I am proud of you for looking after all children."

When Kasyapa told the sthapati of his plans, he reacted with affable flourish. "Brilliant. So that's what you were scheming up the other day at our meeting. I am glad you are pursuing the social reforms you talked about in our oh-so-carefree days gone by." He paused for effect, filled his lungs with a deep breath, and declared, "So now we are to witness the greatest largesse of Kasyapa the Munificent."

They laughed.

47

Amira had been in the harem for over two years when Siripali told her the news.

"You can't leave me, Siripali. Who will I have?" Amira couldn't help herself as tears cascaded down her cheeks, her face flushed crimson with grief. "I don't want to lose my best friend," she said, in between sobs, which sounded like soft hiccups. "The only friend I've ever had."

Siripali's eyes brimmed with tears too. She touched Amira on her shoulder. "Amira, we must all leave here sometime. We must all leave things we love and the people we care for. Change is inevitable. This is the impermanence of life. Things come, and things go. Now it is time for me to go, but I will always be your friend, Amira."

"I know I am being selfish. I know I should be glad for you, Siripali. You are going outside, going to a new life with a husband and children. Who will I have?"

Siripali hugged her friend as she trembled against her.

*****

AMIRA WAS SILENT, her eyes downcast when she next visited the king. He placed his index finger under her chin and lifted her face to his.

"Tell me why you are sad, Amira?"

It took Amira a moment to find her voice. "My friend Siripali is leaving the harem," she murmured, her eyes clouding with tears.

"I see."

"She is my only friend."

"She is a charming girl from a good family. She will be happy."

"I know. I know. Inside me, I know. But I am so miserable. I will never see her again. What will happen to me when I am discarded from this harem? I have nothing. I have nobody. Where will I go? Who will marry me? Perhaps it isn't about Siripali. It's about me. Maybe this is why I feel so bad." Amira hugged herself and sobbed.

Kasyapa remained silent and took her to his bedchamber. She started undressing, but he stopped her.

"Come, lie with me, Amira."

He hugged her as she sobbed herself to sleep.

WHEN SHE RETURNED TO THE HAREM, she asked the harem-keeper for her collection of jewelry. The old woman searched Amira's face with her straight eye.

"I want to give Siripali a present, Harem-Keeper."

The harem-keeper broke into a smile, walked over to her, and wrapped her arms around her. "You are a good child, Amira. Your friend will appreciate your kindness."

After they had selected a piece of jewelry for Siripali, the harem-keeper said in a low whisper, "It is highly improper to give away the king's jewelry. Each of these jewels is priceless. Be discreet. I will turn a blind eye to it."

THE DAY SIRIPALI LEFT WAS THE SADDEST in Amira's life. She stayed awake all night, crying. As morning broke, she reconciled herself to the inevitable, even though it tore her heart apart to see her friend go. She knew her life would never be the same again.

TWO MONTHS AFTER SIRIPALI LEFT, a letter arrived. Amira rushed to the harem-keeper and showed it to her. The harem-keeper nodded. She already knew its contents.

"Can I go, Harem-Keeper?"

"That would be highly unusual, Amira," she said, shaking her head.

Amira was crestfallen. She couldn't attend her best friend's wedding.

*****

"I HEAR YOU ARE GOING TO YOUR FRIEND'S WEDDING," Kasyapa said a few months later as Amira walked into the Lake Palace on her appointed day.

"You know? You didn't tell me you knew about the wedding," she said. "Did you arrange it? You didn't tell me you would arrange it. The harem-keeper said it was impossible," she babbled. "You are a bad boy, Kasyapa," she teased and chased him around the hall.

"Stop it. Stop it," he said as she caught up with him and tickled him. He grabbed her from behind and pressed her against his body and whispered in her ear. "My special gift to you, Amira." His words made her nipples stand up.

"Oh, Kasyapa," she whispered.

He cupped his hands over her breasts and sent her into another space. Her heart wanted to burst.

THAT NIGHT IN BED, HE WAS MOST REFLECTIVE. He lay there with his arms behind his head, gazing at the ceiling.

"You know, Amira, I have no best friend."

She lifted herself onto her elbows and looked into his eyes. They were sad, tortured eyes. She kissed him gently and moved his hair away from his face. She noticed a tiny crystal teardrop in the corner of his eye.

"It must be nice to have a best friend. I have never shared everything with anybody. Maybe men are like that. Maybe women are different. I have friends. Abaya is one of the oldest. Then there's the sthapati, the chamberlain, and so forth. They are dear, dear friends. But no best friend. Abaya is certainly a true friend. I know he would stand by me at all costs—like he did when we were children. But no, not a best friend."

He was silent for a long time. Amira didn't know how to comfort him other than to be there with him. She coaxed him to place his head against her breast and held him close. She ran her fingers gently through his hair.

He smiled and added. "You are my best friend. I tell you more than I have told anyone else."

"Me?"

He smiled and gazed into space. She nuzzled his chest then found his lips with her own. She climbed over him, gliding her erect nipples over his chest, and kissed him. He pulled her down, rolled her over, and entered her. She purred.

*****

AMIRA AND THE OTHER HANDMAIDENS STOOD to attention as the queen walked to her carriage. As she approached, Amira curtsied.

"Ahh Nilupulesi, you are coming with us to your friend's wedding, I understand?"

"Yes, my queen. Thank you."

The queen knew. Of course, she did. She knew of Kasyapa's particular fondness for this harem girl. He had told her so himself.

The harem-keeper, who was chaperoning Amira to the wedding, let off her signature "*humph*" sound. "So Amira, you sit in the third carriage while I must ride in the donkey cart at the rear," she joked half in jest as she headed toward her carriage at the rear.

On the way to the city, Amira sat by the window and often peeked outside. "Why are people running to our carriage and not the queen's?"

"They are curious because you are so white and have red hair," her companions replied between giggles.

WHEN THE TWO FRIENDS MET, they hugged and laughed and hugged and giggled and were inseparable once more.

"I saw this funny-looking black animal with big flappy ears, Siripali. It must have been ten times bigger than any animal back home. You are not going to believe it. It had its 'thing' on its face." She giggled. "Very strange indeed," she said, rubbing her chin.

Siripali laughed. She held her belly and laughed even more.

"Why are you laughing? What's so funny?"

"You silly girl, Amira. That wasn't its 'thing.' That's between its legs like all animals. What you saw was its nose."

"A nose?"

"Yes, a long nose, Amira. Now, once I get married, we can't talk about the 'thing'," she continued, in-between fits of laughter.

"Why?"

"It's not considered proper," Siripali squealed, still holding her sides and laughing.

"Oh." Amira covered her face and giggled.

"I hope my husband has a nice one like the king," Siripali added. "I noticed it stood up once when I was talking to him. It looked promising."

They both laughed themselves silly over it. They talked late into the night. It was Siripali who did most of the talking. She was a flood of words, speaking on and on until she was out of breath.

At long last, she stopped and studied Amira's face. "What is it, Amira?"

"I miss you, Siripali."

She hugged Amira. "I am here, so tell me."

"You promise you will not tell anyone?"

"Have I ever let you down, Amira?"

"No, you are the best friend anyone could have."

"And you are my bestest, bestest friend, Amira, the red-haired, blue-eyed, crazy girl," she teased, tossing her head about.

"I think he tells me everything, Siripali. And the harem-keeper is sending me to him more often than the other girls. I think he asks for me."

"Then you are a lucky girl, Amira. Trust is an important thing. You must keep what he tells you in your heart and tell no one—not even me. His trust in you must remain absolute."

Amira nodded.

"So, what does he tell you?" Siripali asked with a twinkle in her eyes. Amira peered at her, confused.

"I am teasing you, Nilupulesi. I meant what I said. Tell no one."

She wished she could tell Siripali about all the things he spoke of. How he told her about his childhood, his mother who had died young, the father he had never spoken to, the bubble man, and the giant. How he didn't like the senapati because he was a cruel-hearted man who always made him feel inadequate and reminded him of his inferior birth. How he loved the company of the sthapati, and how they used to go carousing whenever they traveled. That the vizier was a good and honorable man who he would trust with his own life. And about the chamberlain who had helped him become king. Many times he told Amira he loved his queen dearly, but he had never had the same feelings for the queen as he had for her. She wished she could tell Siripali all these things.

But she knew Siripali was right. These confidences were only between the king and her. Siripali would have died laughing if she told her the king said he liked her bits. She smiled, imagining that.

"What are you smiling about?"

"Nothing." Amira rolled her eyes and flashed a sweet, amiable smile.

"Ha! Maybe I should have told you not to tell me anything after you had told me all the juicy gossip. Now I am bursting to know."

"Ha, ha."

Siripali grimaced.

"Oh, but I can tell you something else though," Amira teased and blushed crimson. Siripali giggled and pressed her finger against Amira's cheek. She loved to do that and watch the blood drain away from the spot where her finger had pressed, turning Amira's pink skin white. Amira didn't mind. She laughed at her friend.

"So, tell me."

Amira hesitated. "I have incredible feelings for the king, Siripali. Like I want to burst. Like I want to be inside him. To be a part of him forever. Like I want to have his baby."

Siripali put on her know-it-all face. She prided herself on knowing all things important. "There is a word for your feelings, Amira," she said, resting her finger beneath her chin. "It is the most wonderful feeling in the world. It's called love."

"Yes, I must be in love."

"But my dear friend, to love the king can be dangerous. You are still a harem girl. Your position, your very existence, is at the whim of the king. He could tire of you and discard you like an old rag."

Amira sulked.

"And if he loved you back, it can be even more dangerous."

"Why is that?"

"Because he is bound by convention. The whole system works on convention. He can never make you his queen, or even a lesser queen because you are not of noble blood, especially in the case of this king. You know, the system works because he is meant to show no favoritism. It is the harem-keeper who manages his women, and of course, the queen. You know, the queen oversees the harem. She has a lot of power if she chooses to use it. If the king falls in love with a concubine, things could become complicated. So be careful, my dearest friend. I am warning you for your protection. Stop sulking. You are here for my wedding." Siripali said, poking her in her ribs.

It was nearly midnight when the harem-keeper broke up their happy chatter and accompanied Amira back to the old palace, where they were staying.

WHEN IT WAS TIME TO LEAVE, it was again one of the saddest moments of her life. She couldn't stop crying. Siripali called her aside. They sat alone in the courtyard of Siripali's father's house.

Siripali took Amira's hands in hers. "I must tell you something important. You must never forget it. Promise?"

"Yes." Amira nodded.

"Did you wonder how you were allowed to come to my wedding?"

"Yes. The harem-keeper said it was impossible."

Siripali wore her know-it-all face. "It's because you are my sister."

"Your sister?"

"Yes, my sister?"

"I don't understand, Siripali."

"My father adopted you, Amira. You are legally his daughter and my sister now."

"Why did he do that?"

"Because I told him you were my best friend, and I was worried for you."

"Thank you, Siripali, but I don't understand."

"My father spoke with the chamberlain, and they came to an arrangement.

"Arrangement?"

"Father bought you from the king. He adopted you as his daughter."

"Did the king sell me?"

"No, Amira. He did not sell you in his heart. Legally, he sold you to protect you and allow you the freedoms I enjoy. You are no longer a slave girl. You are the daughter of Yasodara and the sister of Siripali."

Siripali's father and mother walked over at this time. Amira stood and bowed her head as was customary for a child in the presence of a parent. She had seen Siripali do that. Siripali's father smiled at her and touched her on the top of her head like she had seen him do to Siripali.

"Welcome, my daughter," he said.

Siripali's mother held Amira's cheeks in her hands and cried.

Once her parents had left, Siripali continued, "You are safe now, Amira. You will always have a home. If you ever need any help, if you are in any trouble inside the harem, get in touch with the linen attendant. Do you know her?"

Amira nodded.

"She is my former ayah's daughter. She will convey your messages to my father or me. We will always be here for you, my bestest friend," she added and corrected herself. "My sister."

Amira sobbed louder. Siripali joined in.

ON THE MORNING THEY WERE TO RETURN HOME after Siripali's wedding, Amira tugged on the harem-keeper's arm.

"Oh, Harem-keeper, I so want to see our king's cottage. The one he occupied as a young child."

"No. No, I can't do that." The harem-keeper pooh-poohed. But when she looked at Amira, her heart softened. "Come. My child, I will take you there."

They entered the palace compound through the harem gate. Finding a guard the harem-keeper knew, they gained access to the compound. The harem-keeper broke into a smile and winked as the guard opened the gate and let them in. The little compound was overgrown with weeds. But it was as Kasyapa had described it, with the bathing well and small villa.

"I will stay out here," the harem-keeper said as Amira pushed open the door. It creaked wretchedly, reluctant to give up its secrets. Covered in cobwebs and dust, there was the little bed, the stool, the table, and cupboard as Kasyapa had described. Amira sat on the stool and gazed around her. She got up and peered out of the window at the nondescript wall Kasyapa had told her about. This was the genesis of the man she loved. She was one with him in this place and at peace.

"Come, daughter, it is time to go," the harem-keeper called out from outside the door. She was indeed a kind-hearted soul.

48

In the fifteenth year of Kasyapa's rule, Migara took gravely ill. Consumed by a fever, he lay bedridden for over two weeks when his friend Palikada came to visit.

Palikada tip-toed into the room and sat next to Migara's bed. "How are you, my friend?" he whispered at the wasted shell of a man lying before him.

Migara's eyes fluttered, and he hauled open his eyelids. "Palikada." Grasping his friend's arm in his fevered delirium, Migara began. "Palikada, I am haunted by terrible nightmares. They are of my dear mother roasting in hell, her flesh afire, and howling in agony. She keeps talking to me, but I can't hear her."

"It is the fever, Migara. It will all pass."

"No. No, Palikada, this is different. My dear mother was trying to talk to me. She was warning me. Warning me of the karmic retribution awaiting me in hell." Migara clutched Palikada's arm even tighter. His overgrown fingernails dug into his friend's flesh.

"You know, Palikada, I am no saint. In all these years, I have belittled our religion and the Ten Grand Precepts. In fact, I have broken them all. I have berated bhikkhus, calling them orange-robed beggars. I have killed and maimed with great pleasure. I have indulged in all the vices known to man. I am a sinner of the vilest sort. I will roast in the eighth hell. The worst hell of them all."

The pace of Migara's speech faltered and slowed to a slur. His eyelids flickered. Palikada held his breath thinking Migara would breathe his last, but no, Migara continued, "I swear, Palikada, if I survive this affliction, I will follow a path of righteousness. There is little time left. I must make amends and gain merit for my afterlife."

Migara released his grip on his friend's arm, his eyes rolled, and his body convulsed uncontrollably.

The doctor rushed in and ushered Palikada away.

KASYAPA HADN'T SEEN MIGARA for nearly two months. He watched as the senapati marched in, noticeably slower than he had in the past. His face was drawn, and his skin was pasty and scaly, like the underside of an iguana.

"Welcome, Senapati. I am glad to see you are recovered."

"Thank you, my king."

"What brings you here?"

"I wish to build a *parivena*, a residence hall, for monks of the Thera School."

"Where do you wish to build it, Senapati?"

"At the Mahavihara in Anuradhapura. I wish it to have a hundred rooms."

"That is rather lavish."

"Yes, and I intend to name it after myself."

Kasyapa tapped his copper ring on the arm of his throne and turned to the vizier. "Do you see any issue with this request?"

"No, my king."

Turning back to Migara, Kasyapa said, "Your wish is granted."

THE SUN FOLLOWED THEM THROUGH THE TREES LIKE a leopard stalking its prey as Kasyapa and Sobhana walked in the palace gardens later that day. Taking shelter from the heat, they rested on a bench in the Night Sky Grotto in the Boulder Gardens. Kasyapa was particularly fond of this cave shelter. About thirty feet wide and fifteen feet deep, its walls and ceiling contained a night scene painted by the chitrakar himself. The ceiling was covered with thousands of tiny stars that filled a dark night sky. Painted on the walls at the rear, and both sides were a jungle scene of grazing spotted deer and langur monkeys sleeping in the trees.

A short distance away in front of them, two house sparrows busily ruffled their feathers in a dust bath, chirped at each other, and took off to perch in a nearby tree.

"Husband and wife, you think?" Kasyapa quipped.

The queen laughed. "Maybe lovers. Or just good friends."

"By the way, the senapati came to see me today. He claims to be a changed man. He wishes to follow the path of righteousness and build a parivena."

"Can a leopard change its spots?"

"I too, doubt it."

A crow squawked and flew off into the distance.

49

Shortly after Amira returned from Siripali's wedding, Mitiya, attacked her in the latrine block.

"You white she-devil," she shrieked, yanked Amira by her hair, spun her around, and flung her to the floor.

Amira slipped and hit her head against the paving, and her foot went into the hole of the latrine.

"You red-haired demon," Mitiya yelled and kicked Amira, sprawled on the ground.

Fortunately, some other girls heard the commotion, rushed in and dragged Mitiya away. But she fought to break free of them, flailing her arms and legs, cursing and swearing, and frothing at the mouth.

The harem-keeper materialized from nowhere, her hands firmly planted on her hips. "What's going on here?"

"She attacked Amira, shouting out that the king belonged to her," one of the concubines said.

"I think she is mad," added another.

"I will not tolerate this sort of behavior in my harem. Attendants, take her to the punishment post immediately," the harem-keeper shouted. Seeing Amira staggering about, she added, "Take Amira to the bathhouse, clean her up, and then take her to the infirmary," she ordered and marched off.

The attendants dragged Mitiya to the public flogging post in the central courtyard and tied her there. Not long after, the tall enforcer woman and an equally powerful looking helper woman entered the compound, pushing a small cart. The tall woman and her helper stripped off Mitiya's clothes and tied her taut to the punishment post. Then the tall woman opened the cover of a small brazier built in the cart and pulled out a red-hot branding iron. She held it up in the air for all to see and pressed it firmly against Mitiya's right buttock. It made a hissing sound, and Mitiya let out a long bloodcurdling scream.

When the tall woman removed the branding iron, there was a large red oozy mark on Mitiya's buttock. Mitiya's father came and collected her from the harem soon after.

About a week later, an attendant pulled Amira aside and whispered. "Have you heard the news about Mitiya?"

"No."

"Her father killed her."

"Why?"

"Because by her actions, she disgraced her entire family and made them outcasts."

SEEING AMIRA STANDING ALONE IN THE COURTYARD, the queen said, "Why are you so red, Nilupulesi?"

Amira demurred and absentmindedly touching her face. Tears welled in her eyes once more. She couldn't control them; they had just flowed and flowed these past few days.

"Tell your queen what's wrong, young girl. Are you sick?"

Amira shook her head.

"Come here."

The queen never sat on the ground, so she found herself a seat and folded her hands in her lap. Amira sat at her feet.

"Now, tell me," the queen said.

"I am miserable because of what happened to Mitiya. All on account of me. I don't want to hurt anybody," she mumbled and burst out weeping once more.

The queen looked down at her with gentle reproach. "It is not your fault, Nilupulesi. You didn't do anything to harm that girl. She brought it on herself. Surely, nobody foresaw this awful outcome." The queen's voice was gentle but assertive. "Look at me, Nilupulesi, when I speak to you."

Amira did as she was told.

"Mitiya was just a harem girl like hundreds of others. She had no claim on the king. Every morning, each of you renews a sacred vow. Tell me what the vow is, Nilupulesi."

"It is not to be envious or jealous of another." Amira sniffled.

"Take me, for example. I am the queen. If I were jealous and spiteful, I could have any of the girls in this harem executed. But I would never do such a thing. Now stop crying and listen to your queen."

Amira sniffled, dried her tears with the back of her hands, and looked up at her queen.

"Jealousy is the root of many evils. Do you understand?"

Amira nodded.

"Wanting what is not yours—claiming something that is not yours to claim—demanding something not freely given. These are all evils that corrupt us. We cannot demand love. It must be given. Do you understand, Nilupulesi?"

"Yes, my queen." It was a timid and tentative response.

"Do you follow the teaching of the Radiant One, Nilupulesi?"

"Yes, my queen. But I don't understand as you do."

"It is a path that is hard to understand and even harder to practice. It is not always easy to be selfless. To be concerned more with the needs of others than with one's own. We must rise above our personal needs and desires."

The queen fell silent. The unrelenting glare of the sun shimmered off the white sand of the courtyard. At the far end of the yard, a group of harem girls kicked around a wicker ball. A distant shriek and their occasional laughter punctured the still morning air.

"The king asked me why you have not visited him," the queen added. "I told him of the attack and black and yellow marks all over your body. It is my duty to keep the king informed. He was concerned for you."

Amira stared wide-eyed at her queen. The queen knew so much but showed no resentment towards her.

"Yes, Nilupulesi. The king is fond of you," the queen added with serene calm.

Amira didn't know how to respond; she didn't know what to say; so she bowed her head and remained silent. After all, the king was the queen's husband.

"I understand my relationship with the king, and I am aware of his fondness for you." A faint and inscrutable smile drifted across her lips. "You are a lucky girl."

Amira felt a soothing warmness sweep over her body. The air was still with anticipation. The two women, one a queen and the other a harem girl, sat in silence.

"This is the guidance your queen gives you. Be virtuous. Be loving. Always do what's right, Nilupulesi. Now, stop this sulking."

She clapped her hands and dismissed the harem girl.

*****

THE HAREM-KEEPER HADN'T BEEN STANDING IDLY BY. From a distance, she had observed the queen and Amira with her wandering eye. Her feelings told her what she needed to do. She had to double—no, quadruple—her vigilance. No harm could come to Amira ever again.

50

In the sixteenth year of Kasyapa's reign, Migara approached him with a new request.

"I want to build an image house to enclose the Abhiseka Buddha."

"Isn't that the statue late King Dhatusena, this king's father, restored with exquisite jewels and gold?" the vizier asked.

"Yes," Migara blustered and stuttered, annoyed at the vizier's interjection.

Kasyapa called the vizier over for a private consultation.

"Do we see any harm in this, Vizier?"

"No. It is always in our interest to keep the senapati in our tent."

Kasyapa returned his attention to the senapati. "Your request is granted."

*****

WHEN AMIRA SAW KASYAPA NEXT, she found him pensive. To brighten his spirits, she started relating the story of her amusing adventure of pretending to be a princess. Kasyapa listened, but his mind was elsewhere.

"And then, they introduced me to this prince from the land of Sin-a-lad-vip-a."

"Simhaladvipa?" Kasyapa corrected, rolling over and looking at her wide-eyed.

"Yes, it sounded like that. Why?" She caressed his face with her hand.

"Simhaladvipa is another name for this kingdom," he said, curling his arm under his head and smiling at her with growing interest.

"What do you mean?"

"Some foreigners call our kingdom Simhaladvipa—the Island of the Lion People. You said you were in Desinganadu?"

"Yes. Why?"

Kasyapa propped himself up in bed and swept his tousled dark hair away from his face. "Moggallana is in Desinganadu."

"Moggallana, your brother?"

"You said you met a prince from Simhaladvipa there?"

"Yes. I think so," Amira replied somewhat tentatively.

"You met Moggallana?"

"I don't know. I met this man who they said was a prince. I assumed he was an actor like me."

"I know Moggallana has been making ends meet by masquerading as a royal prince from the Kingdom of Simhaladvipa. Of course, this is true. He is a prince of Lanka."

"Oh, how do you know this?"

"Migara told me some years ago, and the vizier confirmed it."

"But where does Migara get his information?"

"I don't know. You know, that's interesting. The queen asked me the same question when I told her."

Amira rested her head on the king's chest and ran her slender fingers over his stomach. She wondered about this man Migara. The more she learned about him, the more it reminded her of the mean-spirited palace folks back in Kapisa, conniving, scheming, and plotting. She was ill at ease. She sensed he would harm her king.

"You said he had a large red stone in his turban?" Kasyapa said, dragging Amira away from her thoughts.

"Yes."

"What did it look like?"

"I didn't look at it closely. It was red, oval-shaped, and quite large."

"I know that jewel! It belonged to the former queen. Moggallana absconded to Jambudvipa, taking his mother's jewelry with him."

"He stole them? From his mother?"

"I won't say that about my brother. Only that he took the jewelry with him when he fled to Jambudvipa."

"No!"

"Yes. Now describe him to me."

Amira hesitated. She didn't know what to say about his brother. "Oh, he is a man."

"Stop joking. Tell me the truth."

"Oh, Kasyapa, he is your brother. I can only say good things about a brother."

"So?"

"I can tell you he isn't as handsome as you, and he is shorter and thinner."

"Come on, tell me."

"No, Kasyapa. It is not right for me to talk about your brother."

"So, you weren't impressed with him?"

"I like you much better." She wrapped her hands around his head, trying to pull him toward her.

He resisted. "The reports I have received about him over the years have not been flattering. We used to play together as children. This kingdom is rightfully his."

Amira reflected on the dissimilarities between the two brothers. Besides the striking physical differences, Kasyapa was gracious, gentle, compassionate, and unpretentious. His brother, on the other hand, Amira had found callous and self-serving. The memory of him still sent shivers down her spine.

*****

A FEW DAYS LATER, THE VIZIER found Kasyapa pacing back and forth.

"Vizier, we often hear that my brother Moggallana lives in hard times across the sea."

"That is correct, my king," the vizier said, wondering where this conversation was going.

"Could we not assist him in some way?"

"My king? What do you mean?"

"Would we not be able to assist him? After all, I replaced my sister's dowry and protected the interests of the former queen. It seems so vile for me to enjoy such good fortune while my brother suffers from want."

"My king, your intentions are admirable; however, in this situation, it is unwise. Your brother plots against you even today. He harbors hopes of ousting you and claiming the throne."

"But Abaya, you and I both know the throne is rightfully his."

Abaya eyed his friend and responded calmly. "My king, no one today, questions your right to rule. The only way we can contain your brother—short of assassinating him—is to keep him destitute. Without money, he cannot arm himself against us. He pawned all his mother's jewelry. Only the Precious Red Ruby remains. He saves it to finance a mercenary army against you."

"I see."

"Fortunately, he has had little success so far. Even his kin do not support him. So why would you? And how would you help without making your hand known? What would be the implications if it became known you were aiding your avowed enemy?"

"My enemy. My brother, my enemy?" Kasyapa mumbled.

"I urge you against entertaining such a notion."

Kasyapa turned and walked out, reflecting on the realpolitik of kingship and the inequities of life. He had to be practical. Ethical and moral considerations were secondary in the pursuit of his interests and self-preservation. He had already forbidden any attempt to exterminate his brother, but it was clear he could do no more. He returned to his quarters, thinking; *does one attempt to aid a wounded cobra? Would it not strike with great malice at the first opportunity?*

51

It was a crisp April morning when the black eunuch from Arabia, knocked softly on the door.

"My king, the sthapati requests your attendance."

"It's early. Has some disaster struck? The scaffolding around the tapestry collapsed?"

"The sthapati did not say, my king. Only that I awake you urgently."

Amira rubbed the sleep from her eyes. "What is it, Kasyapa?"

"The sthapati wants to see me straight away." Kasyapa rolled out of bed. The black eunuch dressed him in the adjacent room, and Kasyapa shuffled sleepily downstairs.

THE STHAPATI WAS PACING in the garden, away from a view of the rock. The black eunuch ushered Kasyapa toward him.

"How did you get past the guards?" Kasyapa asked.

"I bribed them," was the sthapati's witty retort. "Come, come," he said, drawing Kasyapa toward him. Then he called out, "Chitrakar, come join us."

The chitrakar hurried up the palace stairs. He hadn't been to the Lake Palace since its completion, as it was the private residence of the king.

Seeing Amira, the sthapati called out. "Come, come Amira."

Amira smiled, flattered that he knew her name.

The chitrakar curtseyed to Amira as she approached. He had painted her portrait some months earlier when he had visited the harem.

"Now, look down and follow me. You don't want to step on any dog shit," the sthapati said, knowing all too well there would never be dog shit in the king's private compound. He lifted his dhoti and gingerly tip-toed across the dew-drenched grass, followed by Kasyapa, Amira, and the chitrakar, each doing the same. The black eunuch couldn't contain his curiosity and joined in too.

"Now, look up," the sthapati said.

The shroud and scaffolding that had hidden the tapestry for nearly ten months were gone.

"Oh my, oh my," Kasyapa said, clasping his head with both hands and clenched his hair in disbelief. He placed his hand on his hips and rocked back and forth. "It is incredible. Tell me about it, Chitrakar."

The chitrakar looked to the sthapati for guidance.

"Come, come Chitrakar, this is your creation. It is your masterpiece. I can't take credit for it, much as I would love to. Explain it to your king."

The chitrakar scratched his head, mustering his courage. He cleared his throat and began. "As you may recall, we agreed they would be apsaras throwing flowers. We all know apsaras are mystical flying beings. Flying and throwing flowers at the same time lacks grace, so our solution was to have them standing and looking down. Since they will be viewed from below, painting private parts, legs, feet, and toes of the ladies of the harem would have been inelegant. It would also have made them too human. So, this was my solution. Apsaras depicted from the hips up in the clouds in natural yet mystical poses, throwing flowers to mortals below."

"Brilliantly executed," Kasyapa's smile broadened into a grin. He walked over to the chitrakar, put his arm around his shoulders, and hugged him.

"Thank you, my king, for having faith in me." The chitrakar flushed, flashing his hallmark asymmetrical grin. "And of course, the sthapati, too, for giving me the freedom to do this."

The sthapati had been biding his time, allowing the chitrakar to bask in his moment of glory. But he couldn't restrain himself any longer. He burst forth in his oratorical voice to provide his summation, his critique of the tapestry, for the benefit of the assembled audience.

"Depicted as celestial beings showering flowers on those below, apsaras if you like, the women appear full-blooded and alive. They are not all young, lithesome, or waif-like. They are the ladies of the king's harem, dressed in their finest, to be admired but not touched. For this reason, they are depicted in true three-quarter form, voluptuous and desirable, but shorn of any worldly sexuality. They are not intended to be titillating. Instead, they are intended to be desirable but ethereal. To evoke a sense of wonderment, and to project the opulence and grandeur of the court of King Kasyapa the Magnificent, the all-powerful god-king." He paused for effect and added, "They are a celebration of beauty."

"Well said, Sthapati." The chitrakar beamed.

"Sthapati, you have such a penchant for poetry, with the flourish and timing of the finest orator. I think you rehearsed. Did you not?" Kasyapa joked.

"I never," the sthapati said with a loud chuckle. He wasn't going to admit it, but yes, it had sprung into his head when he had admired the tapestry in its full splendor earlier that morning.

"Now, Amira, walk to the edge of the garden and do what you did some ten months ago," Kasyapa said.

Amira walked toward the edge of the garden, disrupting a kaleidoscope of butterflies dancing and pirouetting ahead of her. Reaching the edge, she peered into the moat below. Where she had previously seen only the reflection of the massive rock, now it was ablaze with color. Reflected vividly on the surface of the water were the frescoes. She was sure no one had anticipated this.

"Come on, show us what you did."

Amira glanced at the king, bewildered. Then she remembered. She pretended to be throwing flowers.

Kasyapa was jubilant. "There. There was my muse—Amira. Gentleman, you have done my inspiration justice. It is breathtaking."

Amira blushed. She, too, was awestruck by the work of art and pleased her king had acknowledged her small contribution to this spectacular project. A warmness engulfed her.

Kasyapa grinned with a mischievous glint in his eye. He knew he had inspired the most exquisite work of art and architecture ever seen in the kingdom. It was indeed the creation of collective genius.

*****

THE GREAT FESTIVAL THAT YEAR, the sixteenth year of Kasyapa's rule, was an especially grand affair. The royal procession began from a large plaza about half a mile from the royal citadel and traveled down a broad boulevard toward the ceremonial western entrance.

Leading the procession was a contingent of lively musicians, dancers, and fire-eating jugglers. Following them were the royal banner bearers heralding the arrival of the king. The citizens lining the streets and craned their necks to see their monarch. They called out, "Long live our king, Kasyapa Alakamanda."

In keeping with his preferred dress code, Kasyapa wore a plain white knee-length dhoti and white blouse. Simply dressed and mounted on the royal elephant, Kasyapa was an imposing figure indeed. His long black hair was set in a conical bun atop his head and fixed in place with a single jeweled clasp. Around his neck was the *Ekavali*, the pearl chain of one string. On the little finger of his left hand was the simple copper ring. Seated behind him on the elephant was the royal parasol-bearer holding aloft the white *Senachatra*, legitimizing Kasyapa's right to kingship.

The mighty royal elephant bedecked in jewel-encrusted headbands, belts, and sashes, and its massive crescent-shaped tusks capped with gem-studded golden sheaths lumbered slowly down the boulevard. The bells and trinkets hung from its sides made a pleasant jangling sound as it walked.

The queen followed in a brightly lacquered palanquin carried by four footmen. She wore the most exquisite muslin cotton and silk textiles and was heavily jeweled to reflect the wealth of the kingdom. Her ladies-in-waiting accompanied her on foot.

Following her was a small carriage with the heir apparent accompanied by a bevy of attendants.

Then came the senior members of the king's court, including the vizier, chamberlain, senapati, sthapati, and chitrakar.

The ladies of the harem, who numbered in the hundreds, followed. Dressed in brightly colored, hip-hugging dhotis with fan-tail ruffles fashioned like the tail plumage of a peacock, they were the epitome of high fashion. They wore heavy gold ear ornaments and multicolored, gem-encrusted necklaces and bracelets that clinked and chimed to amplify their merriment. Amira was among them, the tallest and fairest of them all. Next to her was Siripali, who had been smuggled in at the last minute.

Happy, carefree, whimsical, and barefoot, the younger ladies of the royal harem danced. Twisting their lithesome bodies and rippling their arms blissfully, they tossed flowers at the enthusiastic crowd. Amira danced. She danced like she had never danced before. To many in the crowd, she was the true embodiment of a cosmic apsara, a celestial dancer to the gods.

During these festivities, Siripali remained discreetly hidden behind a cordon of harem girls arranged around her by the harem-keeper. Siripali's attendance was highly irregular as only current occupants of the harem were allowed to participate in the celebrations. But the harem-keeper had made an exception for Siripali. When Amira caught the harem-keeper's eye, a mischievous smile broke across her face. The old woman winked.

MIGARA ACCOSTED KASYAPA during the festivities. Kasyapa didn't see much of him these days, as he was often absent for long periods of time due to illness.

"Excellent festival, I must admit, oh King," Migara bowed, and without waiting for Kasyapa's response, he continued, "Did you hear about Moggallana?"

"What has happened this time? You always seem to have the most current news about our relative across the sea."

Migara leaned into Kasyapa's ear. "They almost killed the pissant—ah, Prince Moggallana, I mean," he corrected himself, realizing his name-calling was unmeritorious.

Migara's faux pas didn't go unnoticed. Kasyapa smiled to himself, thinking, *Old habits die hard.*

"They almost killed him, his debtors. He is up to his neck in debt."

Kasyapa turned to the vizier, who was standing next to him, and asked, "Vizier, did you know of this?"

"Yes, my king, news has reached my ears as well."

Migara continued, deriving great pleasure in his vivid commentary, "He was forced to sell the Precious Red Ruby. The one he stuck up his... to pay off his creditors."

Kasyapa remained silent.

AT THE END OF THE FESTIVITIES, the royal family and the ladies of the harem crossed the inner moat—the one stocked with man-eating crocodiles—and entered the inner citadel. Kasyapa and the royal family walked ahead.

As they walked past the Pavilion of Four Ponds, Sobhana touched Kasyapa's arm and whispered, "Now that the festivities are over, I must visit my grandmother. She is frail. I will take the children. You know how the old lady dotes on her great-grandson, the heir apparent."

"Yes, of course, Sobhana."

*****

THE HAREM-KEEPER ESCORTED HER GIRLS to view the frescoes first-hand. Standing in the Garden of Octagonal Pool, they happily jostled with each other to find their portraits in the gallery.

"At least he didn't paint me with a jackal's head," Siripali giggled, poking Amira in the ribs. "I look so serene. I think the chitrakar did that on purpose because I was boisterous during the sketching. And look at you, Amira, so radiant and beautiful with your red hair and blue eyes—like a goddess."

Amira blushed.

52

It was a balmy starless night later that year when the vizier and chamberlain climbed up to the Sky Palace for an urgent audience with the king.

"Why wake me at this late hour, Vizier?"

The vizier stood with his head bowed, staring at the floor. The chamberlain stood next to him, his arms limply by his side, his eyes bloodshot, and his face damp from hastily rubbed off tears.

"What is it, Vizier?

"It is my sad duty to inform you..." The vizier stopped mid-sentence, his usually unflappable face flushed, and his eyes swam with tears. He steadied himself and continued. "My king—the queen—is no more." The vizier's voice broke as he spoke.

"What? The queen is no more? What do you mean, Abaya?"

"News has just reached me that the queen and the crown prince died of the voiding disease two days ago."

"What?"

"It is true, my king." The chamberlain sniffled, rubbing his clammy hands on his dhoti.

"I must go to her immediately."

"No, my king. You cannot go," the vizier and chamberlain replied in unison.

"What?"

"I must advise you. You cannot go," the vizier reaffirmed.

"But I am king."

"That is exactly why you cannot go. Sadly, we have lost a queen. We have lost the heir apparent. We cannot afford to lose our king to this disease. You must stay here, Kasyapa," his friend pleaded, placing his hand on Kasyapa's arm. "Your royal duty must take precedence over your personal grief."

"But I must be with her. I must be with them."

"It is too late for them. We must safeguard the kingdom."

Kasyapa searched their grim faces in dismay. "What of my daughters and the queen's family?"

"Many have perished, my king. The princesses Bodhi and Uppala-vanna have not been affected."

"What can we do, Abaya? What can I do?"

"There is nothing we can do for them, my king. We have quarantined the entire town. We must wait out the disease. As a precaution, we have locked down this citadel too. No one is allowed in or out of the royal compound until further notice."

"I see. Thank you, Vizier, for your swift response." Kasyapa paced back and forth, twirling the little copper ring on his finger. An indifferent moon hung in eerie silence in the sky overhead. The air was still.

A polite cough returned Kasyapa from his thoughts. He turned, and there was the sthapati. He came toward Kasyapa with outstretched arms and hugged his friend.

"Why this misery, Sthapati? Why this pain?"

The sthapati had no answer. All he could do to console his friend was to be there for him.

Migara also called at the citadel to offer his condolences. The vizier, well aware Migara would only arouse more angst in Kasyapa, refused the senapati entry into the citadel, on the pretext that it was under lockdown.

*****

The ladies of the harem had also heard the awful news. There was lamenting by everyone. Many huddled together and mourned their loss.

"What can we do, Harem-Keeper?" Amira asked her guardian.

"Nothing, my child. We can do nothing unless asked."

Amira walked around the compound in a daze, her face flushed cherry-pink from her tears. She had loved her queen. The one who had been so kind to her and called her Nilupulesi—one with eyes like blue water lilies. Now she was gone. The emptiness within her was profound; it was as if something had been wrenched out of her body.

Her thoughts drifted to the king. What of his grief? If her sorrow was so acute, his would surely be a thousand times worse. She knew he loved his queen very much. He often told her so. Amira wished she could comfort him, but she had to remain in the harem, she could not go to him. She could only suffer for him and wait.

*****

KASYAPA RETIRED TO HIS QUARTERS IN THE SKY PALACE and headed straight for the bathing pavilion. Using a bucket, he dowsed himself with the cold freshwater over and over again, dressed himself, and climbed into bed.

It was then, in the inky darkness of the night, the black jackals came once more. In their cruel multitude, they circled around him. They taunted him, they snapped at his heels, they blathered over his head and demanded his soul.

Slowly, slowly, his world started spinning, spinning round and round. Now he was sinking, sinking. He couldn't stop the sinking. Down, down into darkness, cold, uncaring darkness, unending darkness, he fell. When he opened his eyes, he saw faces—thousands of them poking through the darkness, berating him.

When he closed his eyes, he was alone, suffering in his living hell.

*****

THE ROYAL PHYSICIAN VISITED the following morning. He determined there was nothing amiss with the king's body, but his mind was in a perilous state. The vizier and chamberlain remembered seeing their king in a similar state many years earlier. This time, he didn't have the queen to comfort him. On the third day, they called in the sthapati.

The sthapati visited the king in his chambers and emerged ashen-faced. The vizier and chamberlain cast anxious glances at each other, hoping he had an answer.

"Call in that harem girl, the king's favorite," the sthapati ordered.

The vizier and the chamberlain wavered.

"Look here. The king needs someone he loves to nurse him through these times. Can you nurse him, Vizier? Or you, Chamberlain? No. There is only one person who can. Send for the harem girl, Amira. I pray she will restore him to good health. Let her spend time with our king."

****

THE HAREM-KEEPER RUSHED INTO Amira's cubicle and grabbed her by the arm.

"Get dressed quickly!"

"Why, Harem-Keeper?"

"We are going to see the king. Hurry girl. Don't worry about the jewelry and makeup. Come, we must hurry." The urgency in her voice was intense.

Lifting her dhoti to her knees, the harem-keeper rushed to the Sky Palace. She waddled her ample body up each step, huffing and puffing, and gasping for breath.

"We must help our king," she panted. "It is not the time to grumble about our petty ailments."

Amira was bathed in sweat when they reached the Sky Palace on top of the rock. Under normal circumstances, the harem-keeper would never have let Amira near the king in this condition. But these weren't normal times. This time, it was urgent.

"Go in, Amira. Do whatever you must to help our king. I will be outside. Call me if you need anything."

The black eunuch, his eyes glossy with tears, pushed open the door and let Amira in. It was nearly midday. The room was dark.

The color drained from her face at the sight of Kasyapa curled up into a little ball. She held her breath to steady her nerves and approached him. She placed her hand on his forehead. He opened his eyes and stared at her with empty, desolate eyes. It frightened her. But this wasn't a time to be afraid. She had to help him.

She sat on the edge of the bed, kissed his forehead, and whispered. "I am here for you, Kasyapa. Please come back to me."

She lay behind his curled-up frame and pressed her body against his. For hours, she held him. She wanted him to know she was there for him. He fell asleep.

A few hours later, he moved. She repositioned herself and persuaded him to rest his head against her. He stared at her and opened his mouth to speak but said nothing. She held him close. She cradled his head against her chest and sang to him, songs she had learned in the harem and lullabies she had picked up as a singer in Kapisa.

"Is everything all right?" the harem-keeper hollered every once in a while, from the outside.

Not wanting to disturb him, Amira did not respond.

Hours later, the harem-keeper called out through the heavy timber door, "Amira, I have brought you food."

"Come in, Harem-Keeper."

"No, I cannot come into the king's chamber. It is forbidden."

"Come in, Harem-Keeper. I cannot come to you."

"This is no time for protocol," the black eunuch murmured, pushed open the door, and ushered the harem-keeper in. She took three tentative steps toward Amira and the king and gasped, nearly dropped her tray of food.

"Oh, what has become of our king?" A great sob escaped the older woman's lips, her face puffed up, and her plump body trembled.

"*Shh*, Harem-Keeper. He will be all right. I know he will. Let us trust in the gods for his deliverance."

"Yes, my child, you are right," she murmured, snorted, wiped her cheeks with the back of her hand, and withdrew.

Amira coaxed him to get up, drink some water, and take a bite of food. She repeated this many times throughout the day and into the night. While he rested, she related Jataka stories she had read in books in the harem library.

Two days later, the king's sister, Sakula, came to see him. She was just as Kasyapa had described her: elegant, unpretentious, and likable. He had told her much about Sakula and of her miserable marriage to the senapati.

Sakula looked at her brother, touched him, and glanced at Amira.

"What's your name?"

"Amira, Your Highness."

She flashed a sad, thin smile. "You look exhausted. How long have you been here with my brother?"

"Three days and nights, Your Highness. I am frightened to leave my king alone."

"I can see. Why don't you go and freshen up and get something to eat? I will watch over him for you."

Amira hesitated. She didn't want to leave him, but she did as she was told.

The harem-keeper was waiting outside and rushed her away to be fed, bathed, and dressed in fresh clothes.

"How is our king?" the harem-keeper asked, wringing her hands.

"I am doing my best, Harem-Keeper."

"I know, my child. I know. Just be with him. Show him that you love him. That's all you can do in circumstances like these. I know your inner goodness will bring him back. Don't give up. Bring our king back, my child," she pleaded with tears streaming down her cheeks.

Amira had never seen the harem-keeper cry. But she understood her distress. No doubt, the harem-keeper was very fond of her king.

****

SAKULA WATCHED HER OLDER BROTHER lying helpless in the darkness. She touched his arm and his cheek. She brushed the hair away from his face.

"Do you remember our childhood, Kasyapa? Your grand oratories in the King's Park?" She spoke softly, tears shimmering in her eyes. "They were such carefree days, weren't they? So much has happened since then." She sniffed and wiped her tears with the back of her hand.

She took his hand in hers. The hand with the little copper ring—the story of which she knew nothing. "I need to tell you something, Kasyapa. I know you had nothing to do with our father's death. My mother, the queen, knows that too. You did what was best for us all. Come back to us, my dearest brother."

She cried and prayed in silence.

****

SAKULA WAS SEATED NEXT TO HIM when Amira returned. She beckoned Amira to sit by her. The princess and the harem girl sat together in silence as time slowly passed by.

"My lady, it is late, and you must be tired," Amira finally said. "I will look after our king."

Sakula smiled weakly. "I haven't been a part of my brother's life for many years. Circumstances don't permit me to be. He is a good man. Look after him, Amira." Tears raced down her cheeks as she patted Amira's arm, and left.

That evening, after the king's ablution and bath, Amira persuaded him to walk outside. She steadied him as he ventured outdoors into the beautiful gardens just below the royal quarters. The king sat on a bench there. Amira sat on the ground at his feet. He said nothing for a long while and then slid to the ground beside her. She took his hand in hers. They watched the sun slowly abandon the day and slide beneath the horizon. She took him back to his quarters, fed him, put him to bed, and cradled him once more. He slept well that night.

WHEN SHE AWOKE THE FOLLOWING MORNING, he was gone. She jumped out of bed and rushed outside. She found him standing alone, gazing into the distance. On hearing her, he turned to her.

"Thank you, Amira," he said in a hoarse whisper. "I heard you sing. It was akin to that of the sweetest songbird in a wilderness. I also heard your stories. Especially the one about the monkey king—a lesson in self-denial, duty, kindness, and leadership—an excellent choice. Thank you for reminding me. My life is not about me. It is about my duty to my people."

"Oh, my king, my master," she whimpered and wept. He had heard her. She had helped him overcome his demons.

"Come, Amira, I must resume my work."

*****

THE VIZIER PAID A VISIT LATER that morning.

"My king." The excitement in his voice conveyed his relief. After a few moments, he shuffled his feet and coughed delicately.

"Let her stay, Vizier," Kasyapa said. "Whatever you wish to say to me, you may say in Amira's presence."

The vizier nodded, pulled himself up, and brought him up to date on the state of affairs.

Kasyapa nodded and dismissed him. The vizier bowed to his king and hesitated. Then the proud aristocrat bowed to the slave-girl concubine and left.

53

Once the epidemic that had consumed the queen had passed, Kasyapa visited the place where she had left him. There, he built a fitting tribute to her and his son.

Set in the center of a large rice field and visible from all around, the memorial shone like a treasured white pearl in a field of emerald green. Sakula and her mother, Dhatusena's queen, attended its consecration. Since the king and the vizier could not be out of the capital at the same time, the sthapati, chitrakar, and Buddha-datta accompanied the king on this sad occasion. Migara too attended.

Returning to his palace, the king resumed his regular duties. He walked alone in the Boulder Gardens after his meals, taking the same paths he had followed with the queen for so many years.

It was about this time that Kasyapa stopped smiling.

THE LADIES OF THE HAREM no longer visited the king. Amira was the only exception. She joined him each evening and spent the night with him. This arrangement was put in place by the vizier, chamberlain, sthapati, and the harem-keeper. They agreed that the king was not to be left alone at night. They put their faith in Amira.

Kasyapa spent much of his time alone. He meditated often. And he found comfort in the company of Buddha-datta, the sthapati and, of course, in Amira.

The Queen's quarters in the Western Gardens and harem were closed and sealed.

*****

SIRIPALI CAME TO VISIT soon after hearing of the queen's death. It was her fourth visit since her wedding. This time, she came with her husband and newborn baby. Siripali was allowed to visit because she was now part of Amira's family, her sister. Also, everyone understood Amira's unique position.

"Aren't you going to ask me what her name is?"

"Oh, yes, I forgot. What's the baby's name, Siripali?"

"Amira."

"Yes?"

Siripali giggled. "No. I mean, her name is Amira."

"Oh."

"And you are her guardian aunty."

"Oh, Siripali," Amira cried, tears rolling down her cheeks. Siripali cried with her.

"I have a present for her," Amira said, pulling out a little pouch she had tucked into her dhoti. Siripali was excited. She fumbled to open it. Inside was a beautiful set of earrings set with star-sapphires. Amira had spent a large part of her allowance, collected since she had joined the harem, to get the harem-keeper to buy them for her. Siripali was ecstatic.

The two friends talked for the entire afternoon. Most of the conversation was about the events that had recently taken place. For once, Siripali was serious. She listened without interruptions.

"You have done the right thing, my sister, and shown great courage and kindness. Stay loyal to your king and be virtuous and kind. We don't know where things will lead but be one with your king."

Amira was sad to see her friend go, but she understood that her place was here, with one man. She wasn't going to let him down.

Later that evening, she told Kasyapa about Siripali's visit. "And Siripali's baby girl is named after me."

"Does she have beautiful blue eyes like you?" he half-teased with a wistful glance.

"No."

"Only the name then?"

"Yes."

She wished she could have his baby. But how could she tell him that? She sighed.

54

After an adequate period of grieving, the vizier and chamberlain appeared before the king.

The vizier cleared his throat, a signal that he wished to discuss a topic he knew would be fraught with difficulties. The chamberlain stood close by, clasping his hands against his chest, happy that it wasn't him who had to discuss the urgent matter at hand.

"Greetings, my king. I hope you are well?"

"As well as can be expected, Vizier," Kasyapa said, casting them a joyless glance before staring out into the gardens.

"My king, it has been nearly six months since our dear queen's passing, and that of the heir apparent."

"Yes, Vizier?"

"It is most urgent we consider the future of the realm and your dynasty."

Kasyapa raised his eyes and forced himself to pay attention.

"We need to consider a new queen."

"A new queen?"

"Yes, my king. If your dynasty is to continue, we need an heir. If there is no heir upon your demise, the crown will pass to your brother Moggallana or Senapati Migara."

An audible gasp escaped the chamberlain's lips, "Migara!" The chamberlain had never hidden his loathing for the senapati.

"Does she have to be a noblewoman?"

"Yes, my king. Never in the history of this kingdom has there been a king who was not born of a noblewoman. To be frank, you are the only exception, the only king who has not been a full-blooded Kshatriya. It's a question of legitimacy."

Kasyapa did not respond.

KASYAPA WAS WALKING in the Boulder Gardens a few days later when the sthapati joined him.

"Sthapati, it's nice of you to come to see an old friend."

"My king, you know visiting you is such a chore," he joked.

Reaching a pavilion set on top of the massive boulder overlooking the Octagonal Pond, they leaned against the railing and admired the view together. A light breeze rustled the leaves of the nearby tree, disrupting the beams of sunlight dappling through its foliage.

"Sthapati, I am troubled."

"Why, my king?"

"I have been asked to remarry—to take a new queen—to procreate. To sire an heir."

"And why does this trouble you? It is not an unreasonable suggestion."

"Sobhana was an exemplary wife and queen. I have no desire for another queen."

"Yes, she was exemplary, Kasyapa. We all miss her."

"They want me to marry a noblewoman."

"That too is a reasonable request. However, I sense your issue is not so much with matrimony. But instead, with the choice of marriage partner.

"What do you mean, Sthapati?"

"Let me get right to the point, Kasyapa. Your mind is clouded. I sense it is more than just grief?"

"As usual, Sthapati, you put me on the spot. I will answer your question directly. Specifically, I have no desire in me for a new queen. I am so melancholy, Sthapati, I have no desire left. Life, queen, dynasty, legacy...none of these things appeal to me anymore."

A squirrel with three white stripes down its back, scampered up a tree shading the pavilion. It stopped to glance sideways at the king and his friend, bobbed its head up and down as though he understood the conversation, and scurried off.

"You know, my father gave up the woman he loved for the sake of this kingdom."

"Kasyapa, I have suspected for a while that you have feelings for that harem girl. Am I correct?"

Kasyapa blanched. "I am fond of her, indeed. That is true."

"In your circumstances, you don't have to give up such a person. It is perfectly acceptable to have a queen and one or more concubines."

"True, but I feel it unfair to both women. To marry one for convenience while loving another."

The sthapati studied his friend's tired gaze. "Are you seriously entertaining the idea of making a harem girl—a slave girl, a foreign slave—your queen, or even a royal consort?"

Kasyapa crossed his arms and stared into the distance. An unflappable beetle buzzed past in front of them, disturbing the stillness of the moment.

"You know that would be untenable. Don't get me wrong, Kasyapa. I too am fond of the girl, Amira. She would make an admirable companion. I am confident she would also make an excellent queen. However, she cannot be queen, not even a royal consort. Opposition from all quarters would be strident. The religious fraternities would be up in arms. The nobility would oppose it too. You would not be able to ride this out, my friend. As you are no doubt aware, the reign of any monarch depends on the support of his army. All you would need is for the army to defect, and you are finished."

"Migara has remained loyal all these years. Why would I doubt his loyalty now?"

"Kasyapa, you have never tested his trustworthiness. He is an opportunist, an unscrupulous man with no convictions. Given his new-found religiosity, in a situation like this, he may throw his lot with the fraternities to curry favor and win merit in the afterlife. You know, as of late, he is obsessed with what will happen to him in the afterlife."

"Yes. I am aware."

"Even if you were to survive, there is little guarantee that your progeny by a slave girl would ever be allowed to rule. It has never happened in over a thousand years of this kingdom's existence. Never."

"Sthapati, neither was there a half-caste king like me before."

"That is true. Your circumstances were fortuitous."

"Yes. Very fortuitous."

IT WASN'T LONG AFTER THAT Buddha-datta came to visit. They walked in the citadel gardens.

"You know Buddha-datta, as a young man, I often questioned the injustice of being deprived of the right to kingship. But in my heart, I never yearned to be king. It was thrust upon me. In the ensuing years, I have tried to do my duty."

"It is laudable you didn't covet the throne, which by custom was not rightfully yours. It is also meritorious you have done your duty."

"The vizier and chamberlain advise me I ought to take a new queen and sire an heir."

"Their advice is sound, oh King. There needs to be a legitimate line of succession."

"Legitimate? Throughout my reign, I have been reminded of my illegitimacy."

"My king, unkind men say foolish things. They do not weigh their words. Circumstances today are different. No one questions your legitimacy any longer. You have proven to your people that you are a righteous monarch."

"Buddha-datta, I have no desire to create a dynasty. I have no desire to pass on this responsibility to an heir. I have no desire to wed a new queen."

"I understand."

"Am I selfish not to think of my people? But who am I to presume my progeny are the rightful heirs to this kingdom? By right, it is still Moggallana's." Kasyapa did not wait for an answer. "Oh, Buddha-datta, I grow so weary."

TIME DRAGGED ON. Kasyapa frequently invited Amira to join him on his afternoon walks. She also joined him at public events, where she remained discreetly in the background. Amira was happy in his company and never sought to advance her station.

THE GREAT FESTIVAL THAT YEAR WAS A SUBDUED AFFAIR. There was no grand procession. The king and his daughters visited the temple named after them at the Niyyanti Park. Amira, chaperoned by the harem-keeper, followed at a discreet distance. Among the luminaries present were the king's closest advisors and friends, the vizier, chamberlain, sthapati, and chitrakar. Migara attended too.

Amira and the harem-keeper had been standing away from the crowd when Migara approached them.

She had heard much of this man, Migara, from the king and others. She watched as he approached, upright but with stooping shoulders, his military regalia hanging baggily on his wasting frame. He walked past them, stopped, retraced his steps, and stood in front of Amira.

"So, you are the girl who saved our king? Good work."

"Thank you, Senapati." Amira curtseyed.

"You are indeed attractive. As pretty as I have heard."

Amira blushed and bowed her head.

"So where are you from?"

Amira glanced at the harem-keeper and back at Migara, "Kapisa, sir. That is where I am from."

"Slave girl?"

"She was a gift from the King of Kapisa." The harem-keeper butted in and huffed.

"I see," he said and walked away with his hands behind his back.

"Brr," the harem-keeper shivered.

A brittle smile crossed Amira's pursed lips. The tiny hairs on the back of her neck stood on end.

55

In the seventeenth year of Kasyapa's reign, Migara visited the audience hall once again.

"What brings you here, Senapati? I notice you spend most of your days in the fair city of Anuradhapura."

"Yes, my king. It is on account of my poor health. My doctor is in that city."

"I see. The air here is much purer. More suitable for a speedy recovery. Did you not like the royal surgeon I sent to you?"

"Yes, the weather is better here. As for the doctor, thank you for making him available to me. However, I am set in my ways. I prefer my personal physician. I have known him most of my life."

"I understand. I hear your new image house for the Abhiseka Buddha is a sight to behold."

Migara's face brightened up. "Yes, it is. This is what brings me here."

"I see."

"I wish to hold a consecration ceremony for it."

"Another consecration ceremony? Was it not consecrated by my father?"

"Yes, but I wish to have an even grander one."

Kasyapa gazed over to the vizier, who took two steps closer to his king.

Kasyapa watched the man, his cousin, his senapati. Gone was the swagger and bravado of his youth. Instead, he was a stick of a man, frail, stooped, wizened, balding, and sullen. He coughed and cleared his phlegmy throat often.

"Is it prudent, Senapati, to outshine the works of a great king only recently deceased?"

"What? Are you refusing my request?" There was venom in Migara's voice as he sputtered, squinting his eyes.

Kasyapa leveled his eyes at the Senapati. "I think it imprudent."

Migara straightened himself up. "Very well, I will say no more about it for the moment." He turned around, and as he made his way out of the Audience Hall, he muttered, "I shall seek permission again under more favorable circumstances." The maliciousness in his voice did not go unnoticed.

Kasyapa tapped the ring on his little finger against the arm of his throne. It made a slight ticking sound.

56

Later that year, a Nigantha, an ascetic monk of the Jain sect, arrived at Moggallana's doorstep.

"Sire, I bring you news."

"Who are you? Moggallana eyed the man suspiciously, fearing him to be another debt collector.

"I sire, am from your native land. An influential friend there has asked me to convey an urgent message to you."

"What is it?" Moggallana responded in a high-pitched yip.

"Sire, your powerful friend wishes to offer you his support to regain the throne, which is rightfully yours."

"How do I know this is not a hoax, a plot to lure me back and murder me?"

"I was warned you might doubt the sincerity of your benefactor. As proof, I present you with this?"

The monk pulled out a linen pouch and handed it to Moggallana. Moggallana stretched open its mouth and peered inside. He didn't need to take the object out to know who it belonged to. With trembling hands, he closed the pouch.

"Your powerful friend told me you would recognize it as proof of his genuineness."

Moggallana braced himself and sucked in his breath. Having pawned the Precious Red Ruby, he had no means of getting anywhere, let alone his homeland across the sea.

He sent out an urgent message to a group of his friends, mostly scalawags, rogues, and petty criminals he euphemistically referred to his twelve distinguished friends. When they arrived, he gathered them together.

"Now, Nigantha, tell these gentlemen what you told me."

"A powerful benefactor in Lanka have expressed their willingness to help Prince Moggallana regain his throne."

The local moneylender was a large blob of a man, rather tall, with a prominent belly, slicked, black hair, and untidy mustache. He sat across from Moggallana with his legs splayed. "So, what you were babbling on about all these years is true? You are a prince, then?"

"Yes."

"So, you want us to help you? You are already up to your eyeballs in debt. How do we know you won't vanish from here without repaying what you owe us already? What's in for us?"

"My friends, my true and loyal friends, I tell you this. If you help me regain the throne of Lanka, I will shower you with wealth. More riches than you can imagine."

The moneylender who had dark, shadowy circles around his sunken eyes glared and spoke with a booming voice.

"Don't trifle with me, Moggallana. Many widows and countless limbless men walk the streets of this city on account of me."

"It is true. I have waited all these years. Good fortune has finally befallen me. Help me, and I will reward you generously. Not once, not twice, but a hundred-fold times my indebtedness."

The moneylender rubbed his hands together, undulated in his seat, and belched loudly. "I warn you, Moggallana."

"I will reward you handsomely. I promise."

"But there may be little treasure for us, young man. Not worthy of our effort." The moneylender scratching his ample belly.

"Trust me, my friends. For your assistance, I will shower you with unimaginable wealth. I will bestow on you all the treasures of the Palace of Alakamanda."

"Alakamanda?"

"Oh yes." The nigantha stepped forward and interjected emphatically. "I have heard with my own ears, from good authority, it is the most opulent palace in the world, with precious jewels and gold everywhere."

"Yes. I will reward you all with the wealth inside my brother's palace—the one he had the temerity to name after himself. You may take whatever you wish from there. You will be wealthy men, my friends, all of you, I assure you."

The moneylender scratched his crotch. "Good. It's agreed, then. I will fund the expedition. Let's get this man home, gentlemen, and accompany him ourselves to collect our booty."

57

About a month later Migara requested an urgent meeting with the king.

"My intelligence sources tell me Moggallana has returned," Migara announced as he entered the audience hall. "Did you know Moggallana has returned?"

"I know."

"You know?"

"Yes, Senapati, I know. I heard some two weeks ago that he was making plans to leave Jambudvipa."

"Well, he has landed already. Near Mahatittha on the west coast and disappeared. Do you know where he is now?"

Kasyapa did not respond.

Migara had visibly aged since Kasyapa had seen him last. He stooped more. His voice was lower, his speech slower, and his words slurred. His bug eyes still darted from side to side, but they were glazed and watery now. Kasyapa wondered whether it was his illness or his addiction that had brought him to this state.

"Aren't you concerned?"

Kasyapa thought long and hard. "My question to you is this. How did he arrive here, on our shores, and disappear without a trace? Would your spies not have known of this?"

Migara sidestepped Kasyapa's questions. "Did you know he intends to assemble an army against you?"

"Yes, I have heard."

"What are you going to do about it?" Migara said, peeved that Kasyapa didn't seem to be listening.

"Nothing at the moment."

Migara's posture stiffened. He thrust his furrowed neck forward. "Nothing?"

"Yes. Nothing."

"Why?" Migara's voice grew shrill and reedy like a note from an out-of-tune flute.

"At this stage, we can only speculate. Don't you agree, Vizier?"

"Yes, my king. Conjecture would achieve nothing. Better to first establish the facts and draw the appropriate conclusions before we act."

"You can't do that. Your brother grows stronger by the day," Migara said, brushing aside the vizier's comments.

"How do you know that, Senapati?" Kasyapa said.

"It's common sense. You don't think he has come back to hunt jungle fowl in the forest, do you?"

"What am I afraid of, Senapati? Do you not command the finest fighting force in the land? Have you not assured me of that many times?"

"Yes, they are the best."

"Then why do we fret?"

"Because, because we must crush our foes before they gather strength."

"I see. What do you propose, Senapati?"

"I propose we attack, attack, attack. Destroy the pissant—ahh Prince Moggallana—before he causes trouble." Migara coughed, causing his whole frame to shudder.

"I ask you this, Senapati," Kasyapa said slowly. "Where is Moggallana deriving his support?"

"It is not my business to speculate."

"Clearly, someone of influence is supporting him, don't you think?"

"I do not know," he snapped. Kasyapa's questioning irritated him.

"It has been over seventeen years since my brother fled to Jambud-vipa. By all reports, he was unsuccessful in rousing support before. So why now? Who is helping him?"

"It is not my duty to know everything. My duty is to defend the realm."

"I remind you, Senapati, your duty is to defend the kingdom, my king-dom." Kasyapa raised his hand, bringing the interview to a close.

A crooked countenance crossed Migara's face. He turned and departed without further comment. Kasyapa watched him leave, a shell of a man with a lopsided swagger.

"What do you think, Vizier?"

"The senapati is right. We must quash the insurrection swiftly."

"But Abaya, I don't want to fight my brother."

"I understand."

"What am I to do?"

Abaya remained silent. After all, Moggallana was his cousin. Like Kasyapa, he too detested violence. Together, they had governed in peace and prosperity. Now they were confronted with a stark choice.

"Am I to kill my brother? They have already accused me of murdering my father. Surely, I will be damned and rot in hell."

Abaya said nothing. He didn't know what to say.

KASYAPA WALKED ALONE in the Boulder Gardens. The wind rustled through the jade-green leaves of the trees lining the footpath. Two large branches, rubbing together, produced an eerie monotonous creaking sound. He sat on a bench in one of the many idyllic caves dotting the landscape.

On the ground, a few feet away, an army of brown ants had ensnared a grasshopper. It was a beautiful grasshopper. Unlike any, he had seen before—truly one of a kind. Its underbody, now turned upside down, was a pale green. Its thread-like antennae were orange, onyx blue and tipped with yellow. Two black eyes sat like large orbs on top of its head. Its upper body had a luminescent green strip down its center, flanked by two burnt orange stripes on either side. Below these, from its thorax to its tail, was onyx blue. It was such a splendid creature.

But these stilted assassins, they did not appreciate beauty. They were bent on murder and mayhem. They fell upon their ill-fated victim, burying their jagged, dagger-like pincers into their hapless prey, puncturing its abdomen and tearing at its limbs. How could a gentle creature such as this fend off this frenzied mob?

They were ruthless and single-minded. One nipped at a hind leg, dismembering it at a joint, and jubilantly rushed away with its cruel trophy held high above its head. Another gnawed at its throat. While still in its agonizing death throes, the murderers lifted their prey, mounted it on their collective backs, and triumphantly hauled it away. Such a beautiful creature slain.

Kasyapa stood up, dusted himself, and wondered if he too would suffer a similar fate. He returned to his palace in the sky.

THAT EVENING, Kasyapa sat alone at the edge of his private garden in the Sky Palace.

"Good evening, my king," Amira purred in her melodic singsong voice as she approached him.

He looked up, moved over on the bench, and beckoned her to sit with him. This was highly irregular for a concubine to sit at the same level as the king. Only a queen did.

She blinked, color rising in her cheeks, and attempted to sit at his feet.

"No. No. You will dirty your beautiful dhoti. Sit here with me."

"If it is your command, my king." Amira bowed her head and obeyed her king.

"Look, Amira. Isn't it beautiful?"

"Yes, Kasyapa."

The world lay before them in ghostly silence. Not a sound reached their ears. A tranquil breeze wafted across them, fluttering wisps of Amira's red hair into the air. Below them lay the city, radiating in all directions from the citadel. In the distance, just past the city limits, tiny ant-sized figures tilled their fields set amongst a network of silvery irrigation canals connected to two vast reservoirs near the horizon.

Closer to home, near the eastern gates, a trio of elephants lumbered homeward, fodder neatly tucked beneath their trunks. A hawk circled overhead.

"My brother has returned from across the sea. He is assembling an army against me."

"Oh, Kasyapa." Amira gasped and touched his hand, grazing over that little copper ring he always wore.

"I am advised from all sides that it is my duty to confront him. Migara wants me to launch an attack immediately and destroy him. The vizier also supports this view."

"Then, why does their advice trouble you, Kasyapa?"

"I don't want to fight my brother. We were so close when we were young. I have no animosity towards him."

"But isn't it him who wishes to fight you?"

"Yes. But does that change anything?"

"Shouldn't you defend your kingdom?"

Kasyapa rested his elbows on his knees, cradled his head in his hands, and gazed out over the paradise he had created.

"I do not want to kill, to maim, to destroy." His eyes remained fixed on the distant horizon. "I have seen the carnage of war firsthand. Many will die. If I am victorious, I will have to put my brother to death. If he is victorious, it will be the end of me. This is the Kshatriya code. I do not want to kill my brother. I do not want to have anything to do with violence. I am forced to take a path I do not wish to travel."

The sadness in his voice stabbed into Amira's heart like a thousand daggers. She wished she knew of a way to wave his ache away, but she didn't. Tears welled in her eyes.

"Do you smell it? The sweet smell of burning sandalwood. I smell it. The smell of death."

She leaned over and kissed his head, slid her arms around his shoulders, and held him close to her.

"I have diligently followed the Ten Precepts. I have harmed no one, not even those who have caused me angst. Why do I suffer such torment and doubt?"

"Because only a good man aches at the thought of inflicting suffering, Kasyapa."

He shuddered. "Sometimes, life gives us no choices. What can I do besides confront my adversaries? I didn't ask for this. Will my brother be a better king than I? Will he be compassionate to the people? Am I to forfeit it all for peace? Will there be peace? Or will he rain vengeance on those who supported me?"

Amira leaned her head against his.

"I don't know who is stirring this discontent. Moggallana has not been able to do so before. Abaya tells me it is not from the fraternities, nor the nobles."

Amira's mind drifted to her chance meeting with Moggallana some six years earlier. She had been an ignorant slave girl then. But even then, even though she knew little of men, and even less about the ways of the world, that man had made her skin crawl. She could think of only one other person who had a similar impact on her. But it wasn't her place to postulate on her hunches. So she would hold her tongue.

Nearing the horizon, the sun burned brazen, casting a surreal orange haze over the landscape. There they sat, two inconsequential spectators— silhouettes against the dying rays of the sun on a gigantic monolith traveling through the vastness of space and time. They watched in silence as the world drained of color, to be replaced with the mediocre monochrome of a mute moon.

58

A week later, while the vizier was away in Anuradhapura, Migara approached Kasyapa once more. "Moggallana is on the move. He has a militia of at least a thousand. He grows stronger by the day."

"A thousand?"

Migara wagged his gnarled index finger. "I warned you. Moggallana is inciting the population. He is holed up at the Kuthari Vihara with a band of the most unsavory characters from Jambudvipa.

"I see."

"He has promised to restore the supremacy of the fraternities. The abbot at the Kuthari Vihara is actively supporting him."

"Anyone else supporting him?"

"What do you mean?"

"Is it only Moggallana, a renegade monk, and a handful of unsavory foreigners?"

Migara brushed aside Kasyapa's question, "The monk at this temple goes by the name of Dama-rakita. You may remember him."

"Yes, I remember. The monk who humiliated my father. The bhik-khu who humiliated me also. This man crosses me once again."

The news submersed Kasyapa in gloom. *Who is undermining me? Surely not a single disgruntled clergyman and my brother with a handful of scruffy foreign mercenaries?*

"I know you detest bloodshed," Migara continued in a condescending tone. "That's why you have people like me to do your dirty work. To keep your hands clean. Let me attack him." Migara paused, touched his chin as though he was thinking and added, "But according to the Kshatriya code, he is of equal rank to you, so shouldn't it be you who leads the attack?"

Kasyapa remained reflective. *What choice do I have? It is an all-or-nothing end game.*

Migara paced about stiffly. "What do you wish to do?" he said over his shoulder with an impatient snort.

Kasyapa gently twirled the little copper ring on his finger. *I cannot allow zealots to return our kingdom to the stultified past. I must confront my brother.*

Kasyapa slowly lifted his heavy glance from the floor. "Is it not foolish for a jackal to antagonize an elephant? The gentle beast may be slow to anger, but once provoked, its wrath is boundless."

"Yes, we must seize the jackal and devour him."

Kasyapa, drew his lower lip between his teeth, released a burdened sighed, and said. "Then, I have no choice. I will seize and devour him."

Yes. Seize and devour him." Migara slapped his boney fist into his palm. His voice rose to a shrill. "We will strike at once." Losing his breath, he coughed up phlegm into his handkerchief and strolled out of the audience hall.

Kasyapa sat alone, tapping his little copper ring on the arm of his throne. The omens were not good—his soothsayers had already warned him so.

AMIRA VISITED HIM THAT EVENING AT THE SKY PALACE. They sat on the bench at the very edge of the garden. Below them lay the city transitioning to the night with tiny pinpricks of flickering household light. Above them hung the moon, especially large and eerily silent. It appeared so close they only needed to stretch out their hands to reach it. But no, it was an illusion. They could not touch the moon.

"My brother promises to restore the religion to its former preeminence. He is gaining support among the masses. A single rogue priest, by the name of Dama-rakita, the antagonist of my father and my opponent also, is fanning the flames of religious fanaticism."

Amira stroked his hand.

"You know Amira; religion can be such a virtuous conviction, bringing out the best in us all. But it can also be destructive. Commandeered by zealots fanning intolerance and hatred, it can incite people to unimaginable cruelty. Little do they understand what destruction and misery they may unleash upon themselves."

Amira had never shared her misgivings with her king. It was not her place to do so. But she couldn't restrain herself any longer. An inner voice inside her screamed out to be heard. She had to warn him.

"Kasyapa, could it be Migara?"

He sat motionless for a long time, turned to her, and searched her face with his piercing brown eyes.

A melancholy countenance washed across his face. "What would he gain from it? He has been loyal for nearly eighteen years. Why would he betray me now?" He spoke in a distant, detached voice, almost floating above the precipice of this mighty rock. It was a voice she could not decipher.

As they sat in silence, Amira watched the moon overheard. She wished the moon would speak and comfort her aching heart. Amira was certain the moon knew but it would not speak.

There they sat, two silhouettes against a moonlit sky, gliding towards their fated destiny. She dreaded the future. She held him close to her that night.

When she awoke, he was gone.

59

Dismissing the dire warning of his soothsayers, Kasyapa abandoned the safety of his citadel early that morning and set out to annihilate Moggallana.

As he headed south, he gazed back at nature's mighty monolith, gleaming majestically in the morning sun, a pristine beacon to all goodly men, radiant with such promise. He looked away in sadness.

By the time they encountered Moggallana's forces halfway between Kasyabgiri and Moggallana's basecamp, the incendiary heat of the midday sun bore down on them like a breath out of hell. Beads of sweat dripped from Kasyapa's forehead, nose, and cheeks and ran in small rivulets down his face.

Mounted on his mighty war elephant, the white Senachatra held aloft over his head, Kasyapa led the charge. Migara, astride his stallion, followed a short distance away, at the head of his army.

Their mounts struggled over the sodden ground, muddy from an overnight downpour. Seeing a swamp ahead, Kasyapa maneuvered his elephant to the left in search of an alternate route. Then, from the corner of his eye, he glimpsed Migara turn his horse sharply, and raise his arm, signaling the army to retreat.

The shout went out, "Our commander flees!"

The grand army broke and fled.

Migara had entrapped his king and executed his defection. He was exacting his revenge. This was his payback for Kasyapa's refusal to grant him permission for the Abhiseka ceremony, which, he believed, was his path to salvation in his afterlife.

Bodur looked at his king and master in disbelief. They had been together since that fateful night of the long knives.

"Go, Bodur. Save yourself," Kasyapa ordered.

"Master, I will stay and die with you."

"No, Bodur, no. Go. I command you. I have been betrayed. All is lost," Kasyapa replied in a tired voice.

"Oh, Master," Bodur croaked as tears gushed down his cheeks. He knew Kasyapa was right. There was nothing more he could do. He kissed his king's foot and fled into the forest.

KASYAPA REMAINED ALONE AND FORSAKEN. He had been warned of this betrayal. Was this the consequence of his desire not to harm others? Was this the price he would pay for his righteousness? He didn't know the answer.

He had to leave. His fate was now inescapable. It was his time to go to another world. Whilst he was a half-caste, he would die a true and honorable Kshatriya king.

He drew out his jewel-encrusted dagger and placed its cold metal blade against his jugular. He drew the unforgiving blade sharply across his neck and slashed his throat.

A sad tear welled up in the corner of his eye. He recollected the little stream, his mother, Nalu, and the bubble man. He felt guilty for erasing them from his memory. He remembered Abaya. He remembered Sobhana and her dedication to him. He remembered splendid Alakamanda and radiant Amira with her flaming red hair and blue star-sapphire eyes.

His eyes rolled lazily in their sockets, but chivalrous to the very end, Kasyapa raised the bloodied blade high into the air and sheathed it.

As his life ebbed away, the words of the Ten Precepts played out in his ever extinguishing mind.

> *Let your conduct be for the good of your people.*
> *Let the love of your people exceed the love of yourself.*
> *Favor no one to the injury of another.*
> *Injure no one to benefit another.*
> *Be upright and let no fear prevent you from doing justice.*

Heed good counsel and avoid doing evil through ignorance.
Be charitable...
Be patient, and mild of speech...
Be merciful and without malice...
Inflict no torture...

And he fell dead.

THE ROYAL ELEPHANT STOOD SILENTLY, swaying to and fro, its fine livery tainted crimson with the fallen king's blood. The white Senachatra, the parasol of sovereignty legitimizing Kasyapa's kingship, fluttered gently over his limp body. All was quiet now. An indifferent breeze wafted across the rustling swamp grass.

MOGGALLANA APPROACHED WITH TREPIDATION, wary that this was a ruse, but soon lost all compunction and rushed to his brother's side. He sucked in his breath and gnashed his teeth as he surveyed the bloodied corpse. Overcome by guilt, he shuddered, hobbled away, and vomited on an aide standing close by.

His brother was dead.

Trembling, he approached once more. He reached for his brother's lifeless hand, dangling over the royal elephant's side, and slipped off the little copper ring. His mind wandered back to happier times with his older brother—the ring—the park. *"One day, Moggallana, you may gain this from your older brother."*

It was prophecy fulfilled.

*****

WITH HIS HANDS ON HIS HIPS, Migara paced impatiently back and forth. Stopping by Moggallana, he sneered, "Throw him in the swamp for the crocodiles and wild jackals to eat."

"No!" Moggallana snorted in a whining, nasal voice.

"Why bother with him? He was only a lowly usurper. Surely, he would have gone to the lowest hell by now."

"Shut up! We will give my brother a memorial worthy of a chivalrous warrior. Let us build him a funeral pyre."

Migara walked away, wondering if he had made the right decision. This man was a dwarf with a whiny voice. A midget of a man, not merely physically, but mentally also. He was ugly, with a gaunt face and small eyes. His teeth protruded out of his mouth like a devil. Most of all, he had the uncouth characteristic of grabbing his posterior and pulling away his clothing. That, Migara found loathsome.

Ever since their school days, he had regarded Moggallana as a weakling, a pissant. Looking at him now, he was convinced Moggallana was piss turd—birdshit. Kasyapa, at least, he had grudgingly respected. But Migara had little choice now. For better or for worse, he had cast his lot with this man. And through this midget of a man, he, Migara, intended to earn his merits for the afterlife.

*****

KASYAPA WAS PLACED ON THE FUNERAL PYRE and covered with a white linen shroud. Moggallana walked to it, took the little copper ring he had collected earlier, and placed it on his brother's chest. Then he made a slow circuit around the funeral pyre, setting it ablaze. That night, flames licked high into the sky and consumed Kasyapa.

All that remained the following morning was a small pile of smoldering ash occasionally picked up by a wayward gust of wind and whiffed away to eternity.

Buried within this pile of ash lay a tiny lump of metal—the remnant of the little copper ring, given to a village girl by a warrior-king so many years ago, and inherited by their illegitimate son who became a great and righteous monarch.

60

It was mid-afternoon. The air was still and sultry. The ladies of the harem were resting in their communal sleeping quarters. Amira awoke with a jolt and sat bolt upright. Panic flared in her eyes, widening her pupils with terror and hopelessness. She turned a frightful shade of white as a terrible dread filled her bit by bit. She jumped up, looked about her, and ran out into the courtyard. She spun around hysterically, tearing off her heavy jewel-encrusted earrings.

"My king, my master—my master, my king—is dead!" she screamed.

"What are you doing? What are you saying, you crazy child?" the harem-keeper shrieked, beating her chest and gasping in horror as her most prized possession disfigured herself. Tears streamed down the older woman's face as she watched Amira writhing in pain and anguish, screaming and sobbing, only pausing to catch her breath.

Blood dripped from her ripped earlobes, splattering on her shoulders and staining her beautiful blouse. Droplets tumbled to the ground as she shook herself like a palm tree in a storm, spraying crimson beads of blood intermixed with precious gems on the recently swept courtyard.

"What is it, girl?" the harem-keeper pleaded.

"The king is dead. My master is dead," Amira wailed.

"Stop it, you silly girl. How do you know that?"

"I know. I know. I feel an unbearable aching in my heart. He is dead."

A chilling silence descended over the compound. The ladies of the harem whispered among each other and shook their heads. Amira had gone mad.

"Oh, what will become of this place, Harem-keeper? What will become of this beautiful, beautiful place?"

The harem-keeper grabbed Amira by her shoulders, wrapped her flabby arms around her, and hugged her until she stopped shaking. Then she escorted Amira to the infirmary.

IT WASN'T LONG BEFORE NEWS of the king's death reached the city. Many of its inhabitants packed their belongings and fled.

This time, Migara had a well-orchestrated plan. His spies had previously determined the hiding place of the Ekavali, and he already had the Senachatra. A special contingent of his troops charged the citadel and went straight for the hiding place of Ekavali. Having secured this prize, they raided the royal treasury and loaded fifty-seven cartloads of booty, which they spirited away.

The sentries guarding the palace, who hadn't put up any resistance to Migara's advance guard, melted away, taking with them whatever loot they could carry. They left the citadel unprotected, and the harem unguarded.

*****

THE VIZIER HAD BEEN IN ANURADHAPURA at the time. On getting word that Kasyapa intended to confront Moggallana, he rushed back to Kasyabgiri. He feared the worst. He didn't trust Migara. He never liked the man. Migara was Kasyapa's poison. Ever since their childhood, Abaya had tried to protect his friend. He loved Kasyapa. He was a good and decent man who strove to rise above his station in life and serve his people righteously.

On reaching the outskirts of the city, he received word. The king was dead. In the privacy of his carriage, he broke down and wept. It was too late to help the king, but he had to save the royal family. He rushed to the citadel, and into the House of the Royal Ladies.

"We have no time. We must flee," he said, rounding up the royal family. As he exited the harem gates, he glanced over his shoulder at the beautiful ladies of the king's harem. Pangs of guilt tore at his heart, but he couldn't save them. He steadied himself against a wall, gathered the royal family, and whisked them away.

The woman of the harem, sequestered behind their harem walls, they had no one to protect them, they had nowhere to flee.

THAT EVENING, THE HAREM-KEEPER BOLTED THE GATES TIGHT as the harem guards had fled.

"They will not harm the harem. They have never harmed the harem," she muttered to herself as she battened down the gates. She collected all the jewelry, dug a large pit at the back of the compound near the kitchen, and buried it. The ladies of the harem slept fitfully.

Close upon midnight, a raucous mob gathered outside the harem gates. Their leader was a large toad of a man with a prominent belly, slicked-back hair, and an untidy mustache who barked orders with a heavy foreign accent. Imbued with alcohol and hashish, this band of men was hell-bent on mayhem. Had they not already looted the palace? What more did they hanker for?

"Come out, you king's whores," they shouted. "Let us enjoy the dead king's favorites," they bleated.

Failing to break down the harem gates, they requisitioned an elephant. Just two mighty shoves by the commandeered elephant brought the harem gates tumbling down. The ladies of the harem were defenseless.

Torches ablaze, a raging multitude streamed in. The harem-keeper grabbed Amira, dragged her to the rear of the compound, and hid her in the latrines. With her feet squishing in the slime and her dhoti dragging in the muck, Amira clung desperately to a beam above her head. She felt the putrid dampness of the place seeping into her clothing and rising around her ankles. The stench was overpowering. It made her queasy. She wasn't sure if it was because she had missed her menstrual period or because of the smell of the place. She squeezed her eyes shut and waited.

Outside in the courtyard, a girl was seized, roughly stroked, and cruelly teased. They laughed at her tears. They stripped off her clothes and spun her like a top from one grubby hand to the next.

The fat ugly man with the foreign accent grabbed her by her hair and took her to the veranda. He raped her and passed her on to another, who did the same, and then another. She screamed and screamed as they defiled her. Oozing blood, she groaned feebly and lost consciousness. Then the fat ugly man with the foreign accent grabbed two of the youngest, still virgins, and left. Their screams filled the air throughout the night.

Mitiya's former handmaiden, hoping to avoid a similar fate, revealed the location of the hidden jewelry, but they raped and murdered her too.

Then a group among this seething horde cornered the harem-keeper. "Where is the king's white slut?" one shouted.

"I don't know," she replied.

They beat the old woman, punched her ample belly, and dragged her around the courtyard by her thinning hair. They threw her to the ground and kicked her, picked her up again, and repeated their cruel torture.

"I do not know. I do not know," the harem-keeper cried out as they beat her mercilessly.

Unable to bear the harem-keeper's heart-rending screams, Amira came out of her hiding place.

Seeing their frightened quarry present herself, they dragged the harem-keeper to the middle of the courtyard, forced her to kneel, and lopped off her head.

It rolled to the ground, a blood-splattered mess covered with sand.

A terrifying blood-curdling scream burst from Amira's beautiful mouth, and she vomited uncontrollably. They grabbed her, dragged her to another part of the courtyard, and surrounded her. At close quarters, they hounded her. She tried to cover her breasts and face from their fury. One man, rather tall, with a prominent mustache and a large nose with tufts of hair bristling from his nostrils, stuck his face close to hers as betel juice the color of blood frothed from the sides of his mouth.

"There you are, my pretty flower." He leered at her, licking his lips. "The king's favorite whore, were you?"

They tugged at her red hair, now matted with grime. They tore off her clothes. They squeezed her breasts. One scrawny onlooker with a crooked nose and a bent ear, and much smaller than herself, tried to finger her between her legs and gyrated obscenely at her. Memories of the women in that caravan many years ago flashed before her eyes. She quivered.

Then a solid, broad-shouldered man, middle-aged and balding, barged his way through the melee.

"This wretch is mine." He declared in a commanding voice.

"Why take our whore? Let us sully her," the man with the crooked nose and a bent ear grumbled.

"She is mine, you imbecile," the broad-shouldered, middle-aged, and balding man said, slapping the man with the crooked nose and a bent ear across his face.

Grabbing Amira by her arm, he pushed his way through the throng and dragged her to an adjacent room. She was too weak to resist and stumbled after him. There, she stood in front of him naked, her ear-lobes torn, still oozing and encrusted with blood, her beautiful red hair matted against her head, her lightly tanned translucent skin blemished, bruised, and covered in excrement and grime. He grabbed some clothing and handed it to her.

Casting his eyes upon her, he shook his head. "So radiant you were that day, dancing at the Great Festival. A beautiful apsara—a celestial dancer to the gods," he said with a quivering voice heavy with shame. "Now, look what they have done to you." He shuffled his feet and walked out.

She wrapped herself tightly in the clothes he had given her, slid down against a wall, and curled herself into a tight ball. She sat alone, shivering, listening to screams reverberating through the night. Not a single woman was spared, except her. They were all pillaged.

HE SAT OUTSIDE THE CUBICLE and stood vigil over her. But he knew it was only temporary. He could not stop the gathering storm. As morning broke, he nudged her awake.

"Come, it is time to go." He looked at this beautiful woman's face, rigid with tension. She had aged a decade in just a few short hours. "Be brave," he whispered. "Overcome this madness with dignity."

LATER THAT MORNING, THE WOMEN of the harem were rounded up. Those that could not move as a result of the previous night's debauchery were speared or hacked to death.

They were marched up the Zig-Zag Staircase, along the Mirror Wall Passage, up through the Lion Staircase and to the Sky Palace on the summit of the rock. There, they walked along the main walkway, with its beautiful translucent paving and sparkling white terraced walls.

This paradise in the sky once so radiant had, in an instant, become a dark and miserable place. Priceless gems had been gouged out of the wall decorations, frescoes disfigured, statues overturned, sculptures carved out, furniture destroyed, precious metals and jewels stolen, and buildings set alight. If only Amira could weep. But she had no more tears to shed. She was too hollow to cry.

"Oh, Alakamanda, what has become of you," she screamed out in her head, over and over again.

But no one heard her. Her lament went unnoticed.

They were escorted single file to the utility quarters near the latrines. There, these wicked, wicked men hurling abuse at their hapless victims, goading them with their spears, swords, and pointed sticks. Caught up in a circle of violence they did not comprehend, these bewildered young women whimpered and bemoaning their fate. The rabble militia, their eyes burning with fanatical hate, prodded them onward to the brink.

The first in the line slipped and fell. Her shrill scream pierced the air as she tumbled to her death six hundred and fifty feet below. Others followed one by one. Without a sound, they stepped out to their doom.

NOW IT WAS AMIRA'S TURN. She didn't resist her fate. To her, it was inevitable. To her, it was release. To her, it was to be with him once more. A serene tranquility swept over her, like the soft, caressing breeze that often kissed her face when she visited this once-beautiful place. She remembered happier times here. When she first cast her eyes on him. When he had held her in his arms. She remembered how she had shared his bed. His tenderness. And how she had witnessed this glorious palace as it shone in the sky the beacon of civility, art, and culture. Now it lay a smoldering ruin.

Amira didn't wait to be pushed. She was happy to leave. She willingly stepped out into the abyss.

As the Earth hurtled toward her, she whispered, "My king, my love."

And she was extinguished. Just a crumpled corpse among many at the bottom of a precipice.

SUDDENLY, A SQUALLING WIND picked up and howled low over the treetops and slammed against this mighty monolith.

The mountain wailed.

The golden-colored ones on the mountainside
have the appearance of those hurling themselves
down from the summit of the rock,
their hearts unable to bear their grief
—the king indeed is dead.

6th-century graffiti - Mirror Wall, Sigiriya

EPILOGUE

Alas, so it came to pass,
that beautiful Alakamanda turned to dust
and floated away on gossamer winds.

And this rock,
it has stood in majestic silence
clutching its untold secrets
for over a thousand five hundred years.
And still wails today.

Author's Note

I first visited *Sigiriya* as a child. My earliest recollection of that time was the eerie stillness of the place. Over the years, this 1500-year-old ruin kept luring me back, each time filling me with a renewed sense of wonderment.

In 2013, I published my non-fiction historical account of Sigiriya and its king, Kasyapa. In doing so, I was constrained by the dictum of verifiable accuracy. I had to stick to the available evidence. However, I often felt history had done a great disservice to this great king. There was more, much, much more to this man and his story.

This novel weaves known historical facts into a tale about a man who rose from humble origins to become a great king. It is also the story of the women he loved.

Historical Characters

DHATUSENA (ruled AD 460–478) was the father of Kasyapa and Moggallana. He had trained to be a monk, but took up arms and expelled foreign invaders. His greatest contributions to posterity were the construction of numerous irrigation reservoirs, including the Ma-Eliya and Kala Wewa tanks, and being the instigator of the compilation of the *Mahavamsa*.

DAUGHTER (Sakula) was the daughter of Dhatusena, the step-sister of Kasyapa and the sister Moggallana. Dhatusena gave her in marriage to Migara to cement an alliance with him. She was beaten by Migara which was the cause of Dhatusena's rage. The Culavamsa is silent as to her whereabouts during the reign of Kasyapa. Once Moggallana became king, in a moment of exuberance, betrothed her to Shalika, who had returned home with the supposed hair relic of the Buddha. We do not know if she consented to this marriage.

MAHANAMA was the uncle of Dhatusena and the grand-uncle of Kasyapa, Moggallana, and Migara. A scholar-monk of the Thera School (monks who followed the more orthodox Theravada doctrine of Buddhism) and credited with writing the first thirty-eight chapters of the Mahavamsa. While there is no historical record of Mahanama during the reign of Kasyapa, we hear of him once during the reign of Moggallana. We can deduce, therefore, that he lived to a ripe old age and died sometime during Moggallana's reign.

THE MAHAVAMSA (CULAVAMSA) is the oldest authenticated chronicle of any country's history. It was commenced in about 475 AD by the monk Mahanama, the uncle of Dhatusena and the grand-uncle of Kasyapa, Moggallana, and Migara, all key players in our story of Sigiriya. Later chapters, referred to as the CULAVAMSA, were added by other monks commencing in the thirteenth century and do not have finesse or accuracy as works of Mahanama. The Culavamsa sums up the story of Kasyapa and Sigiriya in a few terse paragraphs. In the eyes of these Buddhist scribes of the Thera School who wrote the Culavamsa, the construction of Sigiriya was the gross secular extravagance of a deluded low-caste usurper not worthy of mention. Consequently, their coverage of Kasyapa and his huge accomplishment is biased and limited.

KASYAPA (ruled AD 478–496) was the eldest son of Dhatusena, born of a woman of a lower caste and, as a consequence, not eligible to inherit the throne. History accuses him of murdering his father and seizing the throne. However, there is no compelling evidence to prove this. He may have instead been a pawn in a larger power play by his cousin Migara. While he is vilified in the Culavamsa, written six hundred years after his death by the monks of the Thera School, it is more likely that he was a benevolent and secular leader who was highly regarded for generations after his death. The kingly name "Kasyapa' was used by four unrelated monarchs after him. This suggests that many subsequent rulers wanted to be identified with Kasyapa and the glory of his reign. (The name Moggallana was used only once more. The name Dhatusena was used none at all.)

MIGARA was the nephew and son-in-law of Dhatusena. He was also the cousin of Kasyapa and Moggallana. Migara mother was executed by Dhatusena and was the impetus for the tragic event of this story. He is the real villain of this whole sorry saga. With Machiavellian skill, he brought about the demise of his own mother and two kings but cleverly evaded earthly retribution himself. If not for Migara's callousness, duplicitousness, and deception, Sigiriya may never have been built. Why Dhatusena, Kasyapa, and Moggallana were all beholden to Migara is hard to fathom. None removed him from his post as Senapathi. It is also hard to understand why Migara chose not to seize power himself. Migara remained the senapathi under Moggallana and was given permission to have the consecration ceremony denied him by Kasyapa. Soon after, he disappears from history.

MOGGALLANA (ruled AD 496–513) was the son of Dahtusena, born of a queen. He was the younger half-brother of Kasyapa. Moggallana ruled for eighteen years and reversed Kasyapa's secular rule. His first act on acquiring the throne was to visit the monks of the Thera School at the Mahavihara. He ingratiated himself with the clergy by building and renovating religious monuments and undertaking other acts of piety. The Culavamsa notes that 'the mighty' Moggallana put to death more than a thousand of Kasyapa supporters and cut off the ears and noses of many others before sending them into banishment. He striped Sigiriya of its treasures and handed over the site to be used as a monastery. He never visited Sigiriya.

SIGIRIYA then known as *Alamanakanda* or *Kasyabgiri*, was the largest and most sophisticated construction project ever undertaken in ancient Sri Lanka. Built around 485AD, by King Kasyapa, its centerpiece was a vast 4-acre Sky-Palace built on top of a gigantic 600-foot high rock and its surrounding parks and gardens. Upon Kasyapa's death, the site was stripped of its treasure and handed over to the clergy. Over the years, it was gradually abandoned and finally forgotten and relegated to a dusty footnote in history. The palace in the sky crumbled and was carried away by wind and rain. The forests and wild animals reclaimed its parks and gardens. The local inhabitants feared this looming monolith. They believed it was haunted by devils and demons. Few dared venture near it. For over a thousand years, no human set foot on its summit.

IISURAMENU & VESSAGIRI These are two of the oldest temples in Sri Lanka. For many centuries after the death of Kasyapa, they retained the name he gave them, namely *Isuramenu-Bo-Upulvan-Kasub*. The complex, or what remained of it, was later known merely as *Kassap-agiri* Vihara. They reverted to their original names, which we know them by today, with the resurgence of the Thera School sometime in the 13th century.

ISURUMUNIYA LOVERS, ROYAL FAMILY AND OTHER SCULP-TURES There is much conjecture about how these sculptures found their way to Vessagiriya and subsequently to Isurumuniya. Since it is unusual to find secular art in a religious establishment, one may surmise that they were brought here from somewhere else. The jagged edges of blocks on which these sculptures are carved suggest that they were hastily removed from a larger setting. Their present sizes are about that which would fit in a bullock cart. Maybe the abbot of Isuramenu-Bo-Upulvan-Kasub, witnessing the wanton destruction of Sigiriya and its beautiful artworks, rescued these sculptures of the benefactor of his vihara and secreted them away for safekeeping. There they lay in safety to be unearthed over a thousand years later.

THE FRESCOES are the most exquisite example of ancient Sri Lankan art and show the opulence and beauty of the court of King Kasyapa. They were part of a vast tapestry that extended in a gigantic band around the waist of the Sigiriya rock. This immense picture gallery of over five hundred semi-naked females covered an area of approximately 5600 sq. meters. Unfortunately, only nineteen paintings survive today. Over the years, the rest were lost to environmental factors such as wind and rain and being intentionally removed by humans. Many female characters in this novel are based on the frescoes still present at Sigiriya today. See if you can identify them —Amira, Siripali, the Harem-Keeper, the Queen, Mitiya, etc.

www.ingramcontent.com/pod-product-compliance
Lightning Source LLC
Chambersburg PA
CBHW030623110726
47901CB00002B/296